Late Driver

ALSO BY JOHN MUCKLE

It Is Now As It Was Then (with Ian Davidson)
The Cresta Run
Bikers (with Bill Griffiths)
Cyclomotors
Firewriting and Other Poems
London Brakes
My Pale Tulip
Falling Through
Mirrorball

CRITICISM
Little White Bull: British Fiction in the 50s and 60s

GENERAL EDITOR
The New British Poetry 1968-88
        (with Allnutt, D'Aguiar, Edwards, Mottram)

Late Driver

John Muckle

Shearsman Books

First published in the United Kingdom in 2020 by
Shearsman Books Ltd
PO Box 4239
Swindon
SN3 9FN

Shearsman Books Ltd Registered Office
30–31 St. James Place, Mangotsfield, Bristol BS16 9JB
(this address not for correspondence)

ISBN 978-1-84861-730-8

ACKNOWLEDGEMENTS
'Toy Town' and 'Late Driver' previously
appeared in *Golden Handcuffs Review*.

CONTENTS

Snowballs in June

The Highfields Estate was a sprawling congeries of small, sand-coloured bungalows and houses ranged along curving tongue roads that were laced up by narrow alleys, sheltered and shaded by dark shrubs and trees and at night dappled by the light of low street lamps and pale-yellow windows, all of which lent it a feeling of justified warmth and safety. Louis Way, Kennedy Way, Walden Road; Tower Way, Platt Drive, Simcoe Road, Whitebeam Road, Liberator Way, Catalina Close, and Mitch's Stile. The names seemed to tell a story that would be known one day.

Pauline and Bill's bungalow was small; it had a conservatory built onto the back, and a short windowless corridor that had once been a box room led down to it. And once the conservatory had been built, creating another large room filled with light from all angles, a burning glass in summer, a resonator for rain, Pauline perched in a big brown swivelling armchair and watched the birds at the bird feeder and critically contemplated the garden, and began to notice the darkness of the resultant corridor, which had a narrow divan bed in it, and to want a window put in the box room.

There was a lot of underused skill on the estate. People who knew how to do things but were no longer needed, and the damp Devon air revived them sufficiently so they wanted to exercise these skills, just to make sure they still had them. Alf, a retired builder who lived a few doors down, said: "I'll do that for you, Bill," and he knocked a sizeable hole in the ticky-tack wall and stuck in a window in a single afternoon, perfectly, and he wouldn't take any money for it apart from materials. Bill serviced his car in part-exchange.

Old habits of thought kept their attitudes where they'd always been: stoked, seething, even anguished at times, and all about things that didn't really concern them in the slightest. This was caused by frequent appeals to another kind of feeling they had, ideas which seemed to spring up in them like the airborne manned kites spiralling up and down from the airfield; from a distance reassuring, like beautiful flowers, but dangerous, and all too fragile as the ground rushed up to meet them.

A small miracle of community had occurred, at least amongst some like-minded elderly folks, chilled transplants from everywhere, and, like all the best miracles, it was self-replenishing. The few immigrants who lived there turned out to be good neighbours, religious many of them, competent women from Malaysia and Indonesia, a South African guy into model aeroplanes, helpful and kind, gift-bearers of trinkets and inedible foodstuffs, and so they overcame the prejudices of the old people, who nevertheless continued to complain and to vote, some of them, if they bothered, for parties who wanted to expel their neighbours from these shores.

Pauline was wool-gathering, all the snagged black sheep wool in the world. She was throwing snowballs in June. She was cycling on a clear summer's morning to her job at the Milk Marketing Board in Thames Ditton, 1947. Wearing comfortable sandals and a flowery blue cotton dress. Came flouncing in. Except she didn't. Very meek and mild, she had been. Enjoyed being told what to do and getting on with it until lunchtime. Looking in shops. Going into a clean café. Walking down to the riverside to sit on a bench to watch arrowing swans and circling ducks. Admiring the lines of Hampton Court Palace on the opposite bank, still standing, its long water, criss-crossed by the wakes of moorhens, stretching off through a colonnade of tall trees.

She couldn't remember now what she had got up to at work, perhaps just sat at her desk and chatted to one of the older women. Her job was to type up the daily submissions of milk yields into neat columns. Buttercup, Daisy and Bluebell in multiple incarnations, each animal inundating the nation's cornflakes to the tune of something like fifteen pints a day. Highly necessary, she supposed, to make sure the farmers weren't diddling the government by selling their milk on the side. If yields were consistently lower than what they should have been, this aroused suspicions. It was a responsible job and important not to make any mistakes, because the farmers would bounce them right back at you.

It had been a boring job, but there you are. She told one of her carers about it, Margot she thought it was, and she agreed. But she looked it up on her phone – on which she logged every lot of tablets Pauline swallowed – and said milk yield had quadrupled since then. Genetic engineering. Poor cows. It was something nobody thought about in those days. Probably gone on for centuries. Another Daisy and Buttercup and Bluebell. On and on and on. The cattle were lowing.

Margot had something to do with farms, she thought, but was more interested in talking about her daughter – a real bookworm, and a horse rider. Unlike Margo. Margo liked nothing better than to get into a nice hot bath with her battered copy of *Fifty Shades of Grey*. Reading for her was an immersive experience. Pauline told her she couldn't concentrate on books any longer. She read a page, turned over, and lost her place immediately. Margo joked that with the kind of books she read that didn't matter.

Margot completed the rolling record of her visit on her phone outside in her hatchback and called up a fresh blank field for the next of her three remaining twenty-minute slots. Bill emerged from the bedroom once he was sure she was gone, cautiously peeping around the corner on his walking frame.

"You're a cowardly man," Pauline greeted him. "I know what you're trying to do to me, DON'T worry, I know alright. I KNOW WHAT YOU'RE DOING." She glared at him with the sense of triumphant certainty she had always enjoyed about his motives.

He lurched towards her, grinned at her savagely.

"Stop that! Stop that!!" She reached for a fresh cigarette. After all these years she was still burning money like water.

Her husband fell back into his own chair, pulled a strange, mad face, and clamped his right hand over his eyes like a small child blotting out the world. But he knew enough still to know that the world could not so easily be blotted.

Not so long ago things had been livelier. He'd been sitting next to the radio, angrily chewing a sandwich as he listened. Pikeys were everywhere. He knew that alright. He'd even had few of them round to chop down the branches of an overhanging tree, not realizing until it was too late that they were Irish travellers from around the corner. He was also convinced the Indian workers in the new restaurant on the parade were slave labour, and to his delight a dawn police raid netted some of them, actual illegal immigrants, living in another house on the Highfield estate.

He'd puttered about in the garage, not just idly puttering, but purposefully working on his bikes, and as usual, slowly, surely getting somewhere, moving from one to another, bringing them to states of near completion. He'd bought himself a new ramp to jack them up to a comfortable height, set up his little compressor and his spraying equipment. Sifting through boxes, cleaning off corroded old parts from the forties and fifties in petrol baths, searching for carburettors at autojumbles in Taunton and Exmouth, and three boxes of bits from his second cousin's stash of bit-boxes stuffed with encrusted dark jewelled residues of other machines. Three Ariels had begun to materialize, taking shape with newly chromed details and downpipes, new rims, re-laced wheels.

Puttering along until all the puttering was done, well aware it soon would be, but the last days had seemed to go on so long; perhaps he'd been lulled by them, unprepared for the hammer blow of Pauline's, and his own, final, definitive crash landings. Bill didn't miss the garage. He hadn't been out there in months and months, or it was years? He didn't know or care.

Pauline heard a quiet tap-tapping at the door. It was Jessie from next door, the adjacent bungalow. Bill was locked into some inner muttered dialogue, he was cowering behind his frame in terror. He hadn't heard the knocking. Pauline lurched to her feet and shambled out to open up to her. "Bill! Bill!" she shouted in passing. Jessie was a small Malaysian woman in her thirties. She stood below the step, smiling, with a miniature basket in her hands. "Hello Pauline," she said. "I've brought you a present."

"Ooh, lovely. Come in then." Pauline stood back, started trembling from head to foot in confusion, overwhelmed by emotion as Jessie stepped in for a moment and tried to give her the basket of small foil-covered Easter eggs nestling in green paper. "You are good to me, you are a lovely girl." Pauline put her arm up and tried to hug her. Thank you, thank you very much."

Jessie followed her through to the living room, where Bill had managed to pull himself together for a moment. "Are you alright, Bill?" she asked.

"We can't complain," he said.

"Bill, look what Jessie has brought us," Pauline said. "For Easter." She looked around vaguely as if expecting to find or see something she could give in return. She showed the basket to Bill.

"Lovely Jessie." Bill peered down at the small eggs, some blue, some wrapped in silver and gold foil, and saw the trouble she had taken. "Did you make these yourself?"

"I always do, Bill," Jessie laughed.

Jessie was a hesitant and briefly alighting visitor. She was not the type to impose herself or to pry. She soon left, backed out chattering and smiling amiably. Mission accomplished. A believing Christian, she thought that the efficacy of her visits was contained in the nature of gifts themselves, the sacred gifts she had borne, which would go on working their goodness after she had left. They were symbols of Jesus's redeeming love; therefore they were real. Job done, she trotted cheerfully back to her husband. Giving healed her.

"Isn't she a lovely person?" Pauline said. She dropped the basket on the footstool, herself back onto the brown leather sofa where she lit up another Superking Blue.

"Good as gold," said Bill. His head once again descended into the cradling cage of his hands.

"What did you say?" Pauline shouted. "I can't hear you when you mutter and moan like that."

"Good as gold. I said she's as good as gold. Jessie is."

Pauline grunted. He would soon wake up again and get all busy when it was time for them to have their soup and to give Pauline her insulin injection, before the next carer came in at six o'clock.

Bill gave her her injection and the district nurse came and went; Pauline sat on the settee in her usual place. They watched some things that happened to be on, the usual ones, and each night he remembered to pull the curtain across the front window, which offered a panorama of the whole empty street. Louis Way. Shadows passed over their faces, the big bright shadows from the wide flat screen, and despite the kitchen light throwing a patch across them, there they were; two small, shriven beings being bathed in all-blotting bright shadows, occluded, hidden from each other. This was their last pleasure, their rest, as after nightly agonies they finally succumbed to sleep.

Pauline found herself in Bushey Park looking up at the Diana. It had been covered over completely in the war, shrouded in nettings and camouflage because it was too easy to spot from the air, a glowing blob of a white marble fountain surrounded by a low circular pool to act as a reflector said come and get me, this way London to attacking German aircraft. It was as if one of the most beautiful things in the world had been re-revealed to her. Diana herself stood atop the high rectangular fountain, the filament of the bulb, an imposing blackened figure with green shoulders, a little like Queen Victoria. As a child, she had thought it was Victoria, but then she had been told she was not really Diana the goddess of the moon but another wicked woman who had drowned all her children in the lake, which was a lake of tears.

The cherubic boys with instruments cavorted around at a lower level, grasping fishes with gaping mouths and young girls with uncovered breasts were perhaps her daughters. She remembered it had been lovely once with all the crisscrossing water jets spouting – she could not remember where they had all been spouting from – Diana and her pissing sons – but they weren't spouting today.

The American base was tucked away, big when you found it. Or perhaps she had hopped off the bus that ran through the park, she remembered, and walked through the sparse silver birch woods where groups of deer scarcely stirred at her tread, suckling, scraping themselves, moulting, steadily staring towards her with melting eyes to show off their great mossy antlers, rutting in season. There were still a lot of vegetables planted back there, she remembered, seedling trees planted out, and flowers being brought on. Inside the base was a different story. A parade ground where they all marched up and down to comical music, wearing ridiculous chrome helmets. They took it all seriously, but they were just like a load of kids playing soldiers.

She'd worked in the *Stars and Stripes* office, the English headquarters of a worldwide US Army glossy magazine. She was a shorthand typist – she knew Pitman's, she had to learn American spelling, and they'd treated her well. But she did remember looking out of the office window at the parade ground, and them all marching by with their silly chrome hats shining in the sunshine. There had been coloured soldiers on the base, she did remember, but they weren't allowed to mix and had to be kept separate, have their lunch at different times and live on their own. They'd said to the girls who thought it wrong that they didn't understand, and when one of the English girls went out with a coloured soldier they got rid of her.

She only had one photo of herself on the base, so thin, from when she had meningitis and had to leave. They thought she was going to die, people did die of it. In the photo, she was like a stick, but she liked to remember it, how she was smiling out of her skull with lipstick on, and other people in the office she could no longer put a name to were there beside her, supporting her, loving her. They were very caring people, the Americans. At first, she had thought it was fake, but then she realized they were sincere, they really did care about people and what they thought of them. Except some of them really hated one another in the office. They used to tell her all their secrets, about what a bastard this or that one was, and they were always trying to do one another down. They were nice to her. But they had some funny ideas.

"And what do you think, Pauline? What's your opinion?" they would ask her about this and that going on in the world, as though what she thought mattered to anyone, as if she had an opinion. What did she know? She was only a young girl who didn't know anything.

Bill always made a lot of his memories, as if they were possessions he could put on display, events which had made him who he was, but now they didn't seem to matter so much, and he was baffled as to how he'd thought the things he'd spent his life on were anything. They seemed like nothing. And yet, at moments of recovery, there was nothing to do but remember, nothing to return to but those things which had defined him, made him get up in the morning and carry on.

Del Withers was the first of the Molesey mob to rub out, lung cancer. Bill was choked. He couldn't believe there was no more Del. They hadn't been close for years, but he'd still lived around the corner with his wife (who wore a bright red wig), their two kids, Steve and Candy. Bill had sometimes popped in there for a cup of tea.

Charlie disappeared somewhere off the map, he was the son of a builder's merchant, an heir, but he drank all the money, ended up going inside for something. Derek Bowers turned out to be shifty – he stole a box of lead soldiers what Charlie had bought for the boy. Brum went back to Brum, and that was that, apart from the time they all rode up there to see him.

And Ray, his brother, he taught him to ride a bike. Holding the saddle, watching his little brother wobble away like yesterday.

There were stories never told again, stories of friendships that had broken and never mended … put aside, forgotten. I was glad to see the back of him … he did that because he could do it, he knew he could get away with it … smiling about the dog, as if he'd accomplished something … sided with the others at the end of the day … never stuck up for me as I did for him … she was strange, too friendly … I didn't really like her, did you? No, I didn't like him either. Amongst them were many stories he'd simply told too often. Dice-ups with the Kingston law along the Fairmile, who'd had the new Triumph 110s, didn't matter who it was, Pete, Ray, Charlie, on Bonneville, Ariel, Vincent – but his Black Shadow had left them well back. The law nodded admiringly. "Catch you next-time, lads."

Jessie listened to them, shouting, and fighting, day after day, through the shared wall. Joe would be watching television, or sitting at his computer working or sticking together one of his model aeroplanes at the dining room table. She would be lying on the bed, reading her bible. She heard them. And she heard them every night in the middle of the night when they were quarrelling, Pauline was telling Bill he was a monster, and Bill would be telling her to get back into bed. Sometimes she heard one of them falling over, groaning. And she heard a high keening, moaning sound, which she had at first thought was Pauline, and then she had realized it was Bill.

She felt so sorry for them. She wanted to help. She knocked on the door, but they took so long to answer. She persisted, but finally she realized they no longer wanted to see her. It was when Bill had told everyone who knocked that he and Pauline didn't want them to come. They were doing fine on their own and just couldn't cope with visitors. They didn't want anyone to see them the way they were. Bill felt ashamed, ashamed to be saying this, but he felt he had no choice. Somehow, he had to stop everyone from coming to the house. It was the same with the carers, but eventually he had been forced to get used to their visits three times a day.

"They break the china – they leave the pieces on the draining board. Now they've broken the drawer in the bedroom by putting too many clothes in it."

"Don't worry about it mum," Mikey said. "I'll have a look at it."

"Don't worry! Don't worry, he says!" She tottered angrily, nearly tripping on a clothes hanger, steadying herself on the edge of the stuffed washing basket. "Your father's had a look at it. What good is a look?"

The top drawer had been wrenched off its runners by the carers, stuffing too many socks and knickers into it. Of course, they'd tried to jam it back in. Mikey took it out and emptied it, saw that in fact the left runner had come off completely and was now mysteriously lying in the drawer, minus any of the screws that had formerly held it in place. He found a screwdriver in a kitchen drawer, a few screws in a jar at the back of Bill's garage. A brief glance around reminded him of the man his father had been until lately. Mikey went indoors, carefully refitted it – the drawer ran in and out smoothly now, and he replaced the bits and pieces of worn under clothing. Amongst them was a brown velvet bow-tie with broken elastic which he remembered his brother had used to wear as a teenager.

"Don't leave me here with him," his mother said. "Your father – he's completely lost it. You're not going to leave me in here with him, are you?"

"No," he said.

He pulled the drawer in and out a few times, admiring the smoothness of its run, then putting the screwdriver and a few remaining screws back in the kitchen drawer. But he did leave her. Every day. He hung up the phone on her. And he had been the one to take her out for a drive, and she was so grateful to get away from Bill for a couple of hours. So Pathetically grateful.

Looking past the stained, wrinkled rug out into the garden, Mikey surveyed its half-submerged pig, its papery dead plants, its carpet of dead leaves covering a deeper layer of black leaf residue, a rotting decorative wheelbarrow, toppled flower pots, and an empty cottage birdfeeder swaying like the leaning tower of Pisa. Behind the back fence some of the trees had been chopped down, and through the bare branches of those that remained, the criss-cross dark red roof tiles and gable ends of further, newer bungalows were shouldering for attention. They didn't get it from Pauline or Bill anymore, not very often.

Margot had forgotten to empty the clothes drier, a note from one of the other carers reminded her to do it please. Hung on its wire from the curtain rail, a smiling tin sun, punched and twisted out of a single sheet, continued to revolve in the breeze, winking in and out as light passed through it from outside. The short, steeply sloping rail leading down the steps from the conservatory was no longer enough to steady anyone who'd wanted to go down there, which they no longer did.

Another of their carers, Beth, often brought her dog around, a big Irish setter. Pauline loved the dog, but Beth's boss said she wasn't to take the dog in to see the clients in case it jumped up and knocked someone over, which it sometimes did. It was an old dog, anyway didn't have any teeth left. Beth kept bringing her around. She brought the dog in to see Bill when Pauline was in the hospital.

Pauline talked to them a lot, about her jobs, like managing a string of clothes shops, Antoinette, and how she drove around from branch to branch to sort out the women's problems. Her boss used to phone her at night to ask her for her marital advice. Things were never running smoothly with Monique. He idolized her, behaved like a little boy, threatened to throw himself off Marlow bridge when they had an argument. Listening to his problems was part of the job, but overall he treated her well. She'd started as a part-timer, had an eye for what older women wanted, what suited them, and soon she was a buyer for him, going up to Oxford Street to see fashion shows. Once she was attacked by a slasher on the escalator, not realizing until she felt the breeze that the back of her dress had been hacked to ribbons with a razor blade.

At Alderton's she was a wages clerk, she worked on a computer and did double-entry bookkeeping, and all the men came and tried to quarrel with her about their overtime, but she never made a single mistake. They loved her there, the bosses who'd built up the small printing firm, and the other women who worked in the office often looked to her for support, and the complaining printers asked her advice about their girlfriends.

Jessie's boss at the airfield was a young woman. The units in the industrial park next to the airfield had been designed and reserved by the county council at reasonable rents for start-up businesses, especially those run by young people and women. She wasn't too bad of a boss. The job didn't pay very well, but that didn't matter very much with Joe's wages from Exeter University. She liked working with the other women. They'd quickly become friends. Assembly work was boring for some people but Jessie liked it and had come to see it as a form of meditation.

Every weekday she left their bungalow at 7 o'clock and strode down to the airfield with her knapsack on her back, down into the dip and up again on the other side, rounding the corner at the Royal Oak – now a pricy gated housing development – onwards to the airfield, scarcely feeling the effort in her short, powerful legs. She burst into the assembly shed, full of life and energy, and everyone was always pleased to see her, which is how she thought it should be? Why wouldn't they be pleased to see her? God lightened her steps through this world. Her strength was that of an army on the march. She liked that idea although not really armies as such.

Pauline went first. Just turned that corner one day from her usual outbursts and sullen recriminations, into an ever-replenishing volcano, a magma of molten hatred splashing over them; Bill especially. It never cooled off, not even with a fresh packet of fags. But was it just tobacco withdrawal as he always thought and said? Those bloody fags? It wasn't of course, but he had no other explanation, nothing else to pin it on. She was demented alright; then again, she always had been. And there it was in the letter from the hospital to the doctor. Written plain. Dementia. Alongside cancer. Far too plain. Did they really know? That last after she'd coughed up a bucket of blood. Two or three Christmases ago and yet she was still here, she still had them – or him – in her grip.

But there were still those times when she broke and sobbed and said she was so sorry. "I've lived too long," she said.

"We both have, Pauline."

And then one day he had been working on one of the bikes on his new ramp. He passed clean out and smacked the back of his head on one of its sharp edges, and lay there unconscious, his life's blood spreading in a red tide across the floor. Pauline had run out in her flapping nightdress, calling his name. She'd known something was wrong. She'd known somehow. Stood there shouting down at him to wake up, ran out into the road shouting, and someone had been passing by, and had come and called an ambulance, which came and took him away to the hospital in Exeter.

That day she had actually saved his life one last time. Things like that happen, quite regularly – something cuts through everything, a shaft of light, and makes the rest of life seem like play-acting – but there's no explanation, no accounting, and so it's not remembered except by those who were involved, if even them. Two days later Bill was sitting up in bed in Exeter and demanding to be let home, and Mikey was taking her over there twice a day with fresh pyjamas and all the rest of it. In a few days he'd been home again, but he no longer had any interest in finishing the bikes, even though they were nearly done, not the resuscitated North African desert thumper, nor the two red Ariel Hunters.

Some things actually were unforgettable, just as Nat Cole had sung in what had once been one of her favourite songs. Even if they were forgotten. Some things actually were incredible, *Beautiful Dreamer*. She remembered her brother John whistling that to her mother as he arrived home on leave from the air force, a weekend's respite from the missions over Germany in his Lancaster bomber. Flight engineer out of Lincoln He had sat next to the pilot, ready to take over. She still had his letters to her mother in the wardrobe, faint blue handwriting that had barely touched the surface of the air ministry forms on which they were written by a boy on his bunk in 1943.

Compelled to hoover up the last of the ghost dust, Pauline puffed and coughed, coughed and puffed her way through yet another packet of king-size cigarettes. A framed photograph of a middle-aged looking nineteen-year-old boy hung on the wall just above her head. Smiling in his RAF uniform, a cap on the side of his head, he was surmounted by a spray of red paper poppies. Reframed across from grandfather Leslie, her father, a tall survivor who had graduated from railway clerk to army lecturer on how tanks had stood up to battle. Drove his eldest daughter away, and his sons. Burned her mother's clothes, buried her things in the garden.

Mad about flying, John always had his nose pressed against the fence of the local airfield. Flight Engineer on a Lancaster bomber. He sat next to the pilot. Johnnie to them. Johnnie head-in-air in that wartime poem. Bill and she had driven up to the airfield in Lincoln where he'd been stationed. They talked to a few old soaks in the pub. John didn't drink, which was unusual with that lot, they pretended to remember. John to her. John and Joan, her runaway sister, who during the war had been an ack-ack gunner in Hampton before she was sent off with the women's land army, cut herself off from the family after the war, ran off with an Arab, then a married man, a disgrace to her father and mother.

Her brother looked old in the photograph, as though every sortie over Germany had burned off a year of his life. But he hadn't really looked old, just like her big brother. John never lived to become an estate agent or a draughtsman, like her other brothers, swap his Brough Superior for a Standard Eight like Bill's first car. "No," Bill said from behind his walking frame, "it was that little Hillman, remember?" Behind his wall frame, John would always be proudly smiling, sacrificed.

"No," she spat. "My brother served his country, not like your family. He was a brave man, not a filthy coward like your horrible family." From cigarette cards – bang – straight up into the blue order books, named in the exhibition of great marble refrigerators at Runnymede. At Lincoln too. Sometimes she had used to get his letters out and just look at them, letters to their mother she had kept all her life.

Faint handwriting specimens traced onto a pale form supplied by the air ministry. Is it normal to be in love like this? he asked their mother. People's feelings were very intense during the war. He'd found a girlfriend. Her parents came around to Hampton when he was shot down. They asked her mother not to write to the girl again. In the letters, he expressed his doubts, misgivings about dropping high explosives on civilians. People like him. The enemy, the Hun, was always some mother's son. They had all been taught that at school, and by their parents. Pauline won a prize for her poem on the subject, and for her recitation of Shakespeare's sonnets with cut-glass vowels, just the way they were supposed to sound.

Back on home leave, he lay on her bed, beautiful dreamer, with a tube of Rolos and a bottle of Tizer she'd bought for him with her sweet ration. Propped on his elbows, looking out of the window at Priory Road, Hampton. He couldn't tell them about what he was doing, or how it really was. They were told not to worry their families unnecessarily. Careless talk cost lives. But he liked being there. Or just sleeping. He'd slept a lot when he was at home. Pauline slept a lot now, slept as much as she could. She needed a hundred pounds from the cashpoint. The Nazis had stolen the black patent shoes she was wearing when she came in. They were living in Windrush, weren't they?

They'd listened to Nat King Cole and all things like that on gang nights in a hut they did out and met in to dance and mess about. They were songs with a meaning of some sort, a story. She had only owned one or two records, same as Bill, but that was one. Nat King Cole in his trilby, his welcoming smile, a coloured man, a sports jacket over his shoulder. It wasn't that she'd liked him in that way. She'd never seen what they saw in Frank Sinatra. There was someone she never told about who was unforgettable. That was later. Someone who had given her a record of Astrud Gilberto singing *Only Trust Your Heart*.

Jessie and Joe were walking back and forth in front of Pauline and Bill's sitting room window, unloading their jeep. They seemed to have been away somewhere, Pauline wasn't sure where. Suddenly, unexpectedly, the doorbell rang. Spotting Mikey inside, seeing he was there to open it for her, Jessie had grabbed an opportunity to bring them presents. A nice bunch of yellow flowers for Pauline. A Tesco's carrot cake for Bill. She tried to hand them to him, but he stepped back and beckoned her indoors. She dashed into the sitting room in a semi-crouch, almost bowing but insistent after all. Sort of apologetic for intruding, her long black hair swayed from side to side as she waved, blew kisses, handed over her gifts, and exited. Joe paused halfway across the window, a box in his arms, smiling in at his wonderful wife and her amazing behaviour.

The cards carried on tumbling through the letterbox at Christmas, but she could no longer remember exactly who had sent them. After years of dutifully keeping in touch with the women she used to work with at Alderton's – women whom she used to miss so bitterly, who respected her, knew her in a different sense – even their names had fallen away, along with relatives of Bill's and everyone else she'd ever known. Many departed, others indifferently recalled shadows for a time, then no longer worth a stamp, an act of faith she had performed by rote for years, but no longer did.

But she hadn't forgotten to feel afraid, that was the most terrible thing, her naked fear of dying, and with it her failure to believe she would ever see John again, her father, her sister Joan, who she had traced to Birmingham through the Salvation Army but never seen again, or anyone else she had used to care about.

Windrush – named not after the famous immigrant ship but for the Blackdown winds rushing up the wide-open slope of the field which fell away behind the property and howled around the large wooden bungalow as if it might blow it over one of these nights. Bill sometimes looked back at their days at Windrush.

They'd ended up where he wanted to be. They'd followed his plan and it had come to fruition. Pete would call round, and John Wasley, his cousin, full of advice about how to fireproof the place, his old charm gone. Bill and Pauline were retired, but she was still a fierce, proud woman, who had organized them, chivvied them, always insisting things must be done properly, her way.

Bill remembered when she'd come with him round to Wasley's place. She was disgusted by the half-filled coupons and medicines strewn over the floor, John talking on and on about nothing. The parrot had got out of its cage and was shitting everywhere. The situation was immediately clear. The parrot was quite likely to jump off its perch but would soon settle down in much the same position, its green wings ruffed up huffily around its scraggy neck as if to say, "Fuck off." Precisely as Wasley had taught it, now busy filling in coupons in respect of some fictitious special offer, with mixed results to judge by the opened cartons.

How green was my parrot? It had taken wing again, swooping, hopping, one eye beadily judging from the highest point it had discovered, near the ceiling, on the flex hanging down from a light fitting, defying electrocution. Here the parrot was king. Below it, John was blinking behind his strong bifocals, the large black Zapata moustache still etched where it had been on his long dramatic face. He was a good builder at one time, an expert bloke. Now nothing was going anywhere. His family had left him on his own for Christmas, social services couldn't be contacted. Pauline had tried to tidy up but he wouldn't let her. She gave him a piece of her mind and went out to wait in the car.

After all, it's where any of us might finish up. Some more than others as it happened, if it mattered. Nothing more to be said about it. Goodbye Ray, see you soon, he had sent on his wreath to Ray's funeral. John Wasley, it was hard to credit: the big man. If Bill was being honest he didn't like him anymore. How could anyone let himself get into that state? It frightened him. As it often did, his fear turned into a kind of furious disgust. He preferred to remember the birds' nester.

He preferred to remember nothing, nothing at all, not even Guernsey, not even the fox cub Nobby and Floss had raised on a baby's bottle, kept in the coal bunker, became a family pet. His son used to take it for walks on a lead in Bushey Park, a picture of him doing so had appeared in the *Surrey Comet*.

"Alright, Pauline?" Bill called to her from the side of his mouth. It was as though they had been strapped down in their places, a yard or more apart, as a storm broke over them.

She didn't answer him.

"I said, are you alright?"

"I'm alright!" she said. "It's you who isn't alright!"

Pauline owned so little, apart from a few racks of clothes she never wore; the ruined garden was overtaken, choked, uncleared. She put all her energy into temporary things, into people as fragile and passing as flowers and shrubs. Kit, Dorrie. Tish. Kit grew up in a Dr. Barnardos home, had a cleft palate. Wondered if eggs could be unscrambled by whisking them in the opposite direction. Did a plant thank you for watering it? Did a bird? A cat? Dorrie in her mini-skirt and white thigh-length boots, sprawled on the bonnet of her red Alpine sports car, laughing. Tish Styles: a nice girl, that's all.

These were things she'd tried to control: herself, the weather, her husband, her two sons. Their demands had been continuing, they nagged at her mind, but she was past all that now. She didn't recall, forgot to hoover. She owned so little, held on to few interests apart from how somebody might be doing, a place they used to go. She had once, not so long ago, enjoyed telling the stories of books to her sister on the phone.

Now she was lying alone in a public ward. Mikey was there to hold her hand – no private room available, impossible to move her anywhere, but the nurses were kind. It was like being at a last party, with the hollow-cheeked reaper, their consultant, as a somewhat jaded, still smiling guest. She thought she had been a terrible mother. One side of her brain blamed herself for everything wrong that had ever happened in her family, but the other side was completely defiant, self-righteous, patrolling still on its relentless fault-finding mission. Why hadn't anything gone well for her children? What was wrong with them? Why didn't they seem to care about her, look after her like her sister's son and daughter did for Carolyn?

All she could manage was recriminations, which rose gradually into a torrent of abuse, then subsided into endless, useless regrets. It was all her fault, and now too late to do anything about. She collapsed into sobs that were wrenched up from her depths, punished herself with ghoulish nightmares too horrible even admit to – evil dreams which sent her scurrying from her bed, teetering into the kitchen to drink something and shake herself awake, smoke a cigarette or two on the settee, crawl under a coat to try and sleep there. What brought those dreams? Where did they come from? Because she thought they came from outside her experience, her waking sense of anything she'd known, sent by a God, or a Devil she believed in even less, deliberately to torment her.

Why did she have to feel so bad? The answer had to be that others had made her feel that way – it was cruel and senseless, proof of her wrongdoing, but all she could do anymore was spit out the poison at her poisoners – the useless men who had consumed her life. Men who admitted nothing, dodged responsibility and carried on the same as they always had. She knew alright. She knew what they were doing to her, and why they had done it. Because she was too much trouble, that was why. They were selfish to the bone, to the marrow.

She hadn't always been good, she admitted. At school, they had had to make lunch for their teacher. They all hated this teacher; she was cruel and always criticizing them. Pauline and the other girls spat into her lunch, right into the salad and tossed it over so it didn't show so much. Over and over again. Afterwards they asked her if she enjoyed her lunch and she said thank you, it was delicious, she'd especially enjoyed the salad. And she tried to sell her sister to a passer-by from her cot when their mother left her to look after her outside. She didn't like Carolyn all that much in the beginning.

She drifted in and out of consciousness, one day trying to tell the nurse about her grandmother's family, then just a tiny hump in the bed, mouth wide open, murmuring something, she didn't know what, amounting perhaps to the word home. A woman was shouting and screaming her abuse in a bed across the ward, singing Land of Hope and Glory. Pauline beckoned an ear towards her moving mouth. "She's a silly bugger, isn't she?"

Bill was stuck at home, uselessly trying to watch *American Pickers* when Mikey finally walked in. No-one to talk to about her, the nurses knew nothing; maybe they were on holiday – no, Mikey, on another shift – and his mother's eyes would flick open, barely able to recognize him, and she would close them again, plunge back into her own mind, in fragmented darkness, her blurred ending.

The Irons

The photograph, blown up and framed from a tiny original, showed three young men in an alley bestriding their motorcycles, two Triumph Tiger 110s, and a Sunbeam S7. Bill's hair was combed over to one side, his jacket collar up, and he looked at the camera in a would-be dangerous pose, almost side-saddle on the Sunbeam, a shaft-driven flat twin whose pea-green paintwork had been reduced to mid-grey screened dots by the enlargement process.

Ray, tallest of the three, was in the middle, just out of the Army, with an intense, impassive expression. Peter May, his hands thrust deep in the pockets of his baggy trousers, a small, bespectacled man with a serious set to his jaw, wearing a long, stylish motorcycling coat, sat in the saddle of his Triumph, identical to Ray's machine. They were parked somewhere in Molesey, at the back of some garages, and the likely photographer was Ray and Bill's mother, Alice. But where in Molesey had it been taken exactly? Try as they might none of them had ever been able to place it in a particular alley they remembered. Pete had no recollection of the occasion. Neither did Bill. Ray was dead, but it had been his youngest boy who'd come up with it, got it done.

A moment snatched out of time, but their inability to recall exactly-where-that-was lent it a further air of mystery, and made it dismissible, as though holding it up to the template of memory and discovering a gap there made it less real; a message from the realm of non-existence, something you didn't have to believe in. But there they were and there it was, incontrovertible evidence of those young men, boys really, fresh out of the crucible of their making, on irons they were each of them buying on hire purchase from Comerfords.

The blown-up picture resided in the conservatory of Pauline and Bill's bungalow, in a cheap wooden frame, between a painted Mosquito fighter-bomber and a seventies colour photo of Bill and Ray, sitting on the ground beside the open sliding door of a red camper van. They were at a roadside somewhere sunny and hot. This time the snap had been taken by Pete himself, later enlarged and passed on as a gift to Bill when Ray was no longer alive. Bill was a smaller man than his younger brother had been, his bony shoulders shadowed sharply by the sun, and he was smiling.

Pete was in his bungalow, thawing out a kangaroo steak. It lay on the draining board, thawing and slowly dripping, a process which was going to take some time as he didn't believe in running good food under the hot tap and spoiling it. At first, he had been reluctant about buying and selling his council maisonette, but once the old lady had gone there wasn't anything to hold him back. He'd seen that he had a limited time window to jump through. He wanted to take advantage of right to buy and leave himself with a lump sum to help his pension, along with his modest portfolio of investments: a couple of thousand here and there in various accounts yielding reasonable interest.

He relaxed in the sitting room while he was waiting. He'd done it out himself with brown floral medieval-pattern tiles, which lent the room (and every other room: he was a fanatical tiler) an autumnal glow and a feeling of varnished antiquity, the atmosphere of a well-tended municipal toilet. They were easy to wipe a rag over, always newly done. He tended to think they were good insulation, and worth every penny for something he was never going to have to think about again.

He squinted intently at the computer screen. Something was blocking it, causing it to stall there wherever it was and getting him nowhere nearer to where he was trying to get – to check some bed and breakfast prices in Norway – so that he wanted to chuck the whole piece of modern junk out the window. But he wouldn't do that, he'd have to wait for Mikey to come around and have a look at it, which he'd said he would do after they'd had dinner, so he'd just have to wait for him.

You'd think that working to high tolerances on a capstan lathe for half a century might have prepared him for the pointless fiddliness of the computer age, but it hadn't, not at all. His skills, like tiling or rigging something up with household electrics, were flexible to some degree, but when you came right down to it they were specific and manual. The operating system of a modern-day laptop might as well have consisted of a team of herberts passing messages up and down the wires for all he would ever understand of how it worked, or more accurately, how to make it function properly, like it was supposed to go.

A small man with neatly clipped white hair, heavy glasses, and a hearing aid, Pete sat looking blankly at the error message on his computer screen. It had seemed amazing at first to be in direct contact with Sweden, Germany, and God-knew-where-else from his dining table, but you soon grew used to it, you took it for granted, even though he found it fucking annoying when this sort of thing often happened.

On many an occasion Mikey had had to come around and patiently explain – it was a matter of the order in which you had to do things, sticking to one menu at a time and not accidentally clicking on some other so-called icon next to it. And never closing your window when you were in the middle of a transaction.

All he wanted was to pay for his travel online and read a few emails. It was the kind of situation he found funny on television, old man comedy, would laugh silently with the volume as high as it would go, sitting at the other end of the room listening with both hearing aids turned up high (the only way he could hear a programme properly while keeping it in focus, so not as eccentric as all that) at the antics of some angry codger. He didn't always manage to see the funny side of it in real life but he knew you were supposed to and he laughed at himself quite often.

Peter had always been a traveller, bringing back a cactus for the old lady or a black Canadian duck carved out of obsidian tree wood and scribed with duck feathers by Native peoples on the shores of Lake Ontario. A person of inventories and itineraries, he'd documented everything, originally in small black notebooks, later on loose sheets of paper arranged in neat folders. His bungalow was arranged, by reflex and habit, with the same sense of meticulous ordering; although some of his ways had somewhat frayed around the edges, his housekeeping standards remained high, and the house – which he'd rechristened 'The Irons' – in truth resembled nothing more risqué than a carefully unpacked inventory.

The largest set of shelves, deep and towering, held his more recent purchases. These were from a book club, came by post, and had soon filled up the pale wooden shelving unit he'd assembled himself from Lidl. It would be exaggerating to say he'd read all these books, although he knew roughly what was in them. Many were glossily illustrated volumes dealing with various aspects of motoring history. He preferred the more encyclopaedically arranged of these. Cars of the twenties. Cars of the forties. All over the world like. Good for browsing, on the lavvy. Photo-essays on the Le Mans 24 hours he took or left. Not much in them really once you'd flicked through all the pictures, spreads with hardly any words, surprising angles on barely recognizable cars – nothing like cars he remembered, but still they were cars, as always bent around a corner of the future.

Books about porcelain, faïence, plastic arts, and tomes on various different countries he'd visited, had taken his own photos of, drawn up his own accounts; but these books were full of pictures he could never take, things he hadn't got around to seeing. They were generally informative and good, printed like all these books on fresh shiny paper so sharp it might slice your hand open. Military history, mainly second world war stuff: places he'd been stationed on National Service; the Desert Rats and the Fall of the Reich; Monty and Rommel. Not so much the bombing of London. His interest was still a boy's interest, in machines and leaders. Unlike Bill and Ray, he hadn't been evacuated but stayed behind to look after the old lady. Art books of this and that. Pre-Raphaelites, Art Deco figurines of busty women, his guardian spirits, also deployed in every room of the house. Tucked in somewhere, next to *Aircraft of the Fighting Powers*, was one book he'd never read at all: *Art, War and Revolution in France 1870-71*. For some reason, he'd just ordered it and when it came he had put it away for a rainy day.

Two squat bookcases at either end of the sitting room were older, and these contained the older, stockier books. Here were to be found old guides to Morocco and the Netherlands, Austria and Finland, novels by Alastair Maclean, Nicholas Monserrat, H.G. Wells' *The Island of Dr Moreau* and James Hilton's *Lost Horizon*, the latter both favourites of his mother, stories as familiar to him as the scarred wooden chair she had occupied for most of her life, propped up on stacked cushions, leaning back on worn embroideries: a box chair which had built-in side compartments with retaining slats for her big-print library books and boxes of Kleenex.

He'd burned her chair in the garden of Winston Drive, but he kept a couple of her smaller bits of furniture in the back room leading to the conservatory. Perched on a sideboard was a photograph of her in a long nurses' uniform at Putney Hospital; a beautiful eighteen-year-old girl in 1910, with fond memories of playing English and Boers in the school playground. Pete's memories of her weren't all that fond. Looking after his mother had taken up too much of his life. But he'd shown the tiny, torn print to Mikey, who had repaired it carefully and blown it up for him. Mikey had bought a frame for it. Pete propped it up out there to survey the prickly succulents she had loved.

He got up from the table and wandered out to calm himself down. Only in the conservatory things had started to go a bit haywire. Stacked plastic seed-trays, each recess neatly labelled, were sprouted, but he hadn't yet got around to taking them out to the greenhouse. Nor to planting out those that had come on out there in the neat rows gridding his back

garden, guarded by a wooden-winged pterodactyl in flight beside the
bean-poles and straggling tomato plants. It was far too cold to go outside
and tidy up. Everything grew too quickly in the Devon rain and you had
to wait patiently for the frost to come and kill most of it off.

Nobody would ever know his opinions about nasturtiums, the
nose-twisters his mother introduced him to; so many varieties could
be brought on from seed: they grew easily in any soil, grew like weeds.
They twined around other plants, strangled them, but the flowers were
quite pretty if you could get it to produce any blooms. He had pots
of bushy ones around the house, more on the way in the greenhouse.
Their brightness – glaring, poisonous-looking buttercups – reminded
him of the hot places he had travelled to. He'd never sprinkled them
on his food, but he understood some people did in those countries. He
liked most succulents and grew glads for sport. Even the dwarves were
gigantic. Who would take care of his things when he was gone?

Back in the kitchen, he decided to get his kangaroo steak underway.
He lit a ring on the stove, added oil and flopped the meat into a small
frying pan. He had decided to have butter beans with the steak and
emptied half a tin into a small saucepan to heat through. Outside a boy
was running backwards in the snow, hood up to shield himself from the
small whirling flakes, driving in quite heavily now as the light fell away
and everything took on a grey cast under early evening's shifting spell.
Pete looked out at him through his kitchen window.

He'll fall over in a minute, he thought, if he doesn't look out where
he's going. But the boy didn't take a tumble, just kept hopping backward,
with an occasional glance behind him where parked cars along the road
were being rapidly shrouded in a white protective dusting of snow. Pete
turned his steak over with a wooden spatula and reduced the heat under
the butter beans to let them simmer for a few more minutes and to kill
any germs that might have found their way into the tin.

Finally, he levered the kangaroo steak carefully onto a plate, drained
butter beans through a battered colander, watching the thick milky fluid
they came in run away into the sink. He poured the soggy remnant onto
the plate and took his meal through to the sitting room. He pushed back
the computer, which had turned itself off, sat down on the chair and ate
his food. Kangaroo steak, venison. He liked those gamey exotic meats
and the bland chewy butter beans complemented them to perfection.

He never thought on the old lady now, back there under her tartan blanket in her chair in Winston Drive. She'd lived in that front room with a budgerigar and a windowsill full of small labelled cacti brought back from his travels. Crippled with arthritis, very frail, she seemed such a sweet old woman to outsiders. *Fly away Peter, fly away Paul.* Bill's oldest used to come around. He'd liked drawing her. She always had a story to tell him: playing English and Boers in the school playground, Queen Victoria's death, or something from the novel she was reading, perhaps a bit of description that had caught her fancy, and he would listen to her for hours on end.

When Pete's father died, they lived on her widow's pension. They were poor during the war. He was sent out to work in a fish and chip shop at twelve years old to help make ends meet, and when he left school won a scholarship to Kingston Technical College. He was so happy to get out of the house. He felt his life was going to change. He found work in a little engineering shop, rode motorbikes. When it became obvious his life wasn't going to change much, he started riding around Britain, and then out onto the continent, where his real life of adventures began.

When he was away on one of his trips, as soon as he reached Calais, or wherever it was, he became a different person, especially if he was with others; but more generally, even in the old days when he went off on the scooter on his own, it had been a jaunty, curious, inquisitive man who stepped from his waterproof coat, and a wild, impervious type who rode forth encased in its armour. He'd willingly argue the toss with a French *douanier*, deploying his phrase-book vocabulary with aplomb, refusing to budge until he got his way. "Monsieur," the official would say. "You are right. I must apologize."

In Austria he once smashed open the door of a bed and breakfast joint whose landlady had locked him out. He quibbled over the last pfennig of a bar bill. He mocked the French and the food they were so laughably proud of – it was just a place you had to go through to get to the other side. The Turks he liked, their towns were neat, their food reasonable, their hotels welcoming to the motorcyclist and reasonably good value. Travelling with others, his suggestion was always to do some crazy thing, to climb up through the woods in the dark to drink a bottle of beer in the ruins of the old castle, walk into Rommel's old pub and order his favourite drink, and scorn the fare they put before him if it was worthy of scorn. He neglected to swim naked in the fjords, dropped a sharpened penny off the leaning tower of Pizza, refused to leave a tip if it said *tout compris*, carefully scanned everything, cursed foreigners or what they didn't know, and was loved by the proprietors of small hotels around the globe for his old-world courtesy.

Did Heidi conceal herself in his room? Did the friendly goats yield cheese? Did Etna shower him with gold? Did he reap the harvest from the fields he sowed with dragon's teeth? Did the Bosphorus light-up at the sight of him? I've been everywhere! he could boast with the song. Awaiting his return, his mother was still trying to knit with her crooked fingers, holding on, holding off her suitors, home help and district nurse.

Abroad he could be as fierce as he liked and nobody really cared. He could laugh at people. He could ride forever, the ribbon of road turning under his front wheel as onto a bobbin, stretching away behind him, laid back precisely in its place, so that the countries travelled through became irrelevant, in a way: a blur of Swiss chalets, Turkish minarets. It was the distances between them that counted: miles covered, punctuation of stops, commas, and roadside brew-ups. Pete's stopping! And then *everyone* would stop to pump their primus stove, set up their Camping Gaz in its blue metal box-shield, and drink strong tea made with a glorious British tea-bag.

Night-riding across Romania, the Maicoletta's steady headlight had attracted a storm-cloud of pipistrelles, which hurled themselves upon the machine, clung to his Stormguard, and some had even managed to get their fangs into his neck. Brushed away, blood on his hands wiped away with a petrol rag kept in the scooter's glove compartment alongside a bottle of two-stroke oil, and a pair of gauntlets he donned immediately.

These far-off lands were best seen in the early morning light, or at dusk, as the heat rose from the fields and shadows fell from the leafy trees, and a barely perceptible mist rolled off the still lakes like profound thoughts taking form in the mind of a traveller. It was a better experience to cut through, buffeted by wind and rain, better by far than to be cocooned behind glass in a boring car or a caravan.

Once, cruising the fjords on a Finnish ship, he had found himself sharing a dining table with a convicted murderer who had told him the strange, convoluted story of his crime, trial, and eventual incarceration. He admitted he'd been guilty and held up both sets of fingers twice to convey the length of his sentence. But apart from this Pete had learned nothing of the detail of his crime. The man possessed but a few words of English, and his listener the bare rudiments of Portuguese.

In Russia, the roads were washed out, and he had been forced to ride for two-hundred miles along a railway line, bumping over sleepers, a branch line in the Urals abandoned for some reason at the time of the Russian revolution. In Italy, Lake Como, full of surfers, and boys surfed their mopeds along the pavements, robbing pedestrians, dodging past in their tight Italian shirts and immaculate shoes and gold jewellery. Pete had managed to knock one of them off his bike, and of course, he hadn't been wearing a helmet. The Italian police were armed to the teeth but had been most understanding once he explained the position with his phrase book. Peru – he had ridden a Maicoletta up beyond the end of the mountain road to a tiny village where they wove quilts of white alpaca and had bought one of them for his mother, although she'd refused to use the disgusting thing as a leg warmer.

Pete moved down here in the wake of Bill and Pauline. He'd liked their large wooden bungalow on the Honiton Road and saw that house prices on the nearby estate were very reasonable. A year or two later he'd arrived, finding himself in a bigger place than he left behind, with a large garden in which he could grow whatever he liked, renting a nearby lock-up for his remaining bikes: a new Honda scooter, a Triumph Trident he could no longer hold up, and a Maicoletta whose engine had been extracted and sold to another fan of these 250cc German irons on which he had criss-crossed worlds once unknown but by now perfectly familiar.

He used to write articles for the club magazine once upon a time, but he had never bothered sending in his poems. Now he pulled them out, flipped through a spiral-bound reporter's notebook from which most pages had been torn, and read them over.

> We came from a far, far country
> On bikes to the number of four,
> And we crossed the Arctic circle
> At absolute full bore.
>
> We descended down from Saltfjell,
> The ride it was a pain.
> So cold and wet – a freezing hell.
> It would not cease to rain.

In the hytta it was a thaw job
All gathered round the cooker's hob,
And soon we were all a-dozin'
Spite of toes and cobblers frozen.

South, it can rain as much as it likes
For the Hurtigrute carries all our bikes;
And we are safe and warm on board
With toes and cobblers nicely thawed.

Well, he didn't tear it out anyway, but looking back now it seemed he'd meant to say something more expansive about his feelings for Norway and the Norwegians. He'd tried next a mock-auction of the country's attractions, a Scandinavian Katmandu or Shangri-La – a hymn to fjords and tumbling crevasses.

What am I bid for the mountains high?
What am I bid for the clear blue sky
            in Norway.

What am I bid for the fjords deep?
And a nice warm hytta for a cozy sleep
            in Norway.

How can I tell of the waterfalls high,
The lakes and the forests as we ride by
            in Norway.

September's the month when the countryside's best
With the trees in their autumn colours dressed
            in Norway.

Our last day's run was Route 57,
Scenically a piece of heaven
            in Norway.

The blazing sun did not cease,
We could quite easily have been in Greece
            'stead of Norway.

Will we not promise again to return,
The mountain hairpins to re-learn
    in Norway?

Yes, we'll come once more from G.B.
These wondrous sights again to see
    in Norway.

This satisfied him a bit more. And as if in celebration, he struck in his final poem a playfully historic note, as he compared himself and his companions to the Viking adventurer and his crew setting off in their longships to discover and conquer the Americas.

When Eric the Red for the New World sailed
The storms split the canvas and the seamen bailed.
They made light of these snags as best they were able
'least they weren't plagued with a duff speedo cable.

Continuous rain lashed down on their route
And not a soul amongst them had a Barbour suit!
Tho' the wind and the cold were a terrible bane
'least they weren't plagued with a duff rear chain.

As they made their way down the Labrador coast
Eric the Red made this timely boast;
"This good ship I have truly trusted
for never did the head-bearings get adjusted."

He was hardly going to dare call himself a poet on the strength of this. Nevertheless, he fiddled with a couple of lines before closing the spiral pad and replacing it at the far end of the top shelf of the bookcase nearest his dining table.

Out in his lock-up, he was looking at his remaining irons. There were only three left. Two and a half to be more accurate. The Honda Goldwing, low and comfortable-looking, as immaculate and beautiful and golden as it had been on the day he had brought it home fifteen years earlier. He'd ridden it around the lakes of Norway, looked up at fairytale castles on the Rhine from its saddle, those beautiful old places that had been playgrounds at one time for the Nazi high command.

The Goldwing had to go. He liked it. It was a good bike, but he'd had his use out of it. He could no longer hold it up, couldn't even pull it back on its stand. The newer iron he'd bought to replace it, on which he'd made his last few trips, was a large three-wheeled Honda scooter, which was even more like riding along in an armchair. Pete found that he could still handle that one quite comfortably.

Number two and a half was an elderly German scooter, minus its powerplant: a bloke who was restoring one had obtained his email address through a contact, and had come round and bought it. Pete kept its shell in his empty museum, as a reminder of the original scooter, on which he'd first discovered the actual vast extent of the world, autobahns and *routes nationales*, cities of the plains and the backs of beyond, steep mountains and friendly goats: noted, photographed, conquered.

The Goldwing would be next. He wasn't sentimental. He'd didn't have anything to be sentimental about except his friends. He took pleasure in the final paying out of these possessions. It would help pay for his next trips, however many he had left to him. But he hadn't been tempted to let the bloke take the whole bike away. He had hung on to the shell, with the semi-excuse that another motor for it might come along some day. Well, you never knew.

But he did know where his money was going. It was going to Guide Dogs for the Blind and the British Legion. They were the two things he most believed in at the end of the day. He had no-one else to leave anything to, except for a niece, his cousin's girl. Perhaps he should leave her a pound or two, a surprise birthday present from someone she barely knew. Perhaps Mikey might like his books.

He pulled down the garage door and locked up. Only as he was walking away did he realize he'd completely forgotten what he had come out for. But what was it? Oh yeah. An oilcan. But what for? To oil his hearing aid. To oil his mother's cacti. To oil the earth between the rows of plants. To make a row of valves spring up. To oil a door hinge he couldn't hear creaking.

Bill – he'd let that go too. After all, he had other friends, he had friends all over the world. They didn't seem to realize that he had a life of his own. Fact was though, he'd moved down here because of Pauline and Bill. He'd followed them, mainly because he liked their old wooden bungalow, Windrush, and seeing that place he thought this would be a good joint to spend his last years in, which it had been.

All the same, he had found it disturbing when Bill came around at the beginning of Pauline's illness and told him not to come anymore. Pauline found it difficult. She couldn't cope, didn't like to be seen. Couldn't cope with making him a cup of tea and giving him a biscuit? Pete was baffled, but he saw from the way Bill was talking, sort of rehearsed, that he was having his own mental problems. He was going too.

And now he found it difficult to look after Pauline. But blow me down if Pete hadn't spent most of his life looking after his mother. It was just one of those things, and Bill had got it at the end instead of all his life. Pete could see where it was going to end up. Bill had cut off all his escape routes, one by one, but the fact of the matter was there weren't any ways out and there wasn't anything whatsoever either of them could do about any of this.

After all, they'd never lived in each other pockets. What did they find to talk about at the end of the day? Just a load of stuff about Molesey, relations remembered but never known that well. But for people who had nothing to say to one another, there was a hell of a lot of it. Bill was still the absorbed boy thinking through his latest job, Pete the boy who'd just returned from his travels. Bill had come along at one time, quite often. Remember that Zündapp we saw in Marrakesh? Ray and Viv were both gone now. Ray and Bill were the nearest he'd had to brothers, except he never managed to fall out with them.

But the old lady – his mother – well all that was gone now. Scenes that were the brightest. A chocolate Mallard locomotive at Christmas time. All he could remember was he ate it in one go and had a diarrhoea all over the holidays. Nineteen thirty-eight. The old lady was gone now, years ago. Truth be told he'd tried to forget about her as much as possible when she was alive. But what else was he supposed to do? He had a strong sense of what was and wasn't his business. Looking after the old lady, year in year out, had been his business. And so was how he chose to spend his own time and money.

Pete had acquired a tendency to float above things, an instinct for disappearances. He didn't really miss Christmas dinner round at Pauline and Bill's, and he was buggered if he was going to lash out fifty quid on a pub carvery. He didn't like those things. There was always too much to eat and he didn't find it very good. Besides, nowadays he couldn't hear what anyone was saying half the time. It didn't matter so much with Bill – he knew what he was saying – and usually what he was going to say before it came out of his mouth.

They'd separated gradually, then completely. Pete heard of their disasters, their one thing after another, through Mikey. He wondered how long they'd last, and who'd go first, but not much really. Maybe he'd be the one to go but it didn't matter. They were gone already. Not really the people he used to know. Pauline getting on the bus in her long summer dress that day. Bill, who couldn't believe his luck, and the way he changed so quickly after he met her. Pete had always known he'd never have any such luck himself if that's what it should be called. He remembered that day on the bus – Greenline, via Addlestone – he hadn't spoken to Pauline, just turned away and looked out of the window.

She thought it was because he was too shy to speak to her, but it wasn't. It was because he wasn't sure she'd remember who he was let alone want to speak to him. Then he'd got confused and it was too late. Two years later, at his funeral, Pauline would pull herself together, perk up, as she still could in public, and tell stories about him to friends of his she'd never met before. They were stories about Pete and his mother, Mrs. May, and how they'd taken her on the river. They carried her onto the boat and she'd waved like the queen mother. And how when Pauline first knew Pete he had been so shy he wouldn't even speak to her one day when she got on the same bus.

He floated, planned trips, unencumbered by responsibility. Doing the same things he'd always done because there was nobody to stop him. All he needed to know from the doctor was that he was given the all-clear for the moment. That was all he could say anyway. Who would have known that the girl to whom he had been unable to speak would turn out to be somebody he had known all his life? Nobody. He offered her bird identification books and gardening tips for as long as she would accept them.

One day he just felt ill, went to the doctor and was given a week or so to live. He waved to them from his hospital bed, a final wave, refused the procedure which might have given him a few months but probably wouldn't, and left the world with an air of modest resignation, a small white hump under the covers. Pete slipped out of their lives quickly and easily. He finally rubbed out overnight, a few hours after they'd gathered to say goodbye to him.

An old friend of his, Pedro, had turned up, appearing out of nowhere: a mild, intelligent old man from Argentina. He'd been heir to a printing works but had come to England in the fifties to study and married an Englishwoman he met at technical college. He had shared many of Pete's adventures, ridden beside him on high mountain passes across the roof of the world, and now slept in a hospital bed they had kindly found so that he could be there when his friend passed him for the last time. The scope of motorcycling was limitless, after all, *sans frontières*, and Pedro's attendance at his bedside sprang from a deep belief in friendship, a final loyalty. There was something special about him, this friend who meant every word he said and was so reluctant to let go. And although Pete had been left little choice, he refused the offered treatment that had not a cat in hell's chance of prolonging him, and faced death with calm resignation, as if it was his own decision.

He had put almost everything in order, including a will in which Mikey was named as sole executor. Mikey was left his books and his large silver scooter. On the day he died, Mikey and his brother went into his house to look for documents, and his nosy brother soon found his poems neatly written out in pencil in a small spiral bound notebook. Pete had left them there to be found, it seemed to him. Mikey managed to sell the whole lot of books to a bloke up at the airfield.

The funeral itself was well-attended, mainly by his motorcycling friends. At the mention of the word 'bikers' the minister had expected Hell's Angels, not the fairly affluent and well-behaved crowd whose machines filled the crematorium's car park. She delivered an effective eulogy based on some funny stories Mikey and his mother had told her. Mikey's brother came down from London and read out something he'd written: memories of Pete, his mother, and what he had meant to their family. Pete had asked for his Stormguard overcoat to be placed in the coffin with him, smiling, "in case of any turbulence, like." Bill would not attend, absolutely refused to leave the house.

Afterwards, in the Throgmorton Hall, the mourners had been invited to help themselves to photographs, drink up his assortment of wine and beer and nibble at the community nibbles. Nobody wanted to drink – they were all driving – but a few did choose photographs to remember him. Mikey had got talking to an American lady from New Jersey who was married to one of Pete's friends. She explained to him how she'd first got interested in motorcycling. A Christian by upbringing, when she was a young girl her favourite book had been *The*

Cross and the Switchblade, which was the memoir of a courageous priest who had worked with delinquent gang members. So it was that she had first been attracted to her English husband by his Triumph motorcycle, on which she'd loved to ride pillion.

The Good Son

The contract workers were in self-organized gangs. There was a Kosovan gang, a Russian gang, a Polish gang, and a Jamaican gang who came down to Avonmouth every day from Bedminster in a white Transit with a couple of mattresses thrown in the back: a mobile den of iniquity. The gangs all hated one another. They rode around the warehouse hanging off of the electric picking trolleys, hurling violent abuse at the Ukrainians. It was the Ukrainians they really hated, the Kosovans and the Poles, but they didn't like each other much either – simmering tight-lipped contempt, silence – and the Ukrainians were ready to take on anyone at a moment's notice. They were toughies. Used to it. Proud to be hated. The Jamaicans loved everyone equally, although this love of theirs wasn't returned, so they moved together and refused to be pushed around.

Mikey was the ganger of the Honiton contingent. He had a love-hate relationship with being in charge but the contractor had groomed him for leadership. An ancient species of West Country reptile, the old boy had seen him coming and screwed every last ounce of work out of him. Playing on his fragile sense of self-worth, showing him respect. Mikey could work. He could work hard. In the chill for ten hours at a stretch until his back was well and truly buggered and fucked up for good. What a fucking idiot. Shouting at the others, chasing them around like a mother hen, teaching them patiently the correct way of doing everything.

He was good at it, that was the funny thing. He liked how everyone came to him, he liked showing them how it was done. "Take it easy, man," said one of the Jamaicans, but he wasn't going to take it easy. No. Somebody was going to do some fucking work in this place, be a worker. This was it. Here you were alive and this is where you were. You had to do the robot thing. So you did it.

The full-timers, the union workers, hated them all equally; were, in fact, more likely to direct their hatred of ethnics at the Honiton crew, who might understand them and were far less likely to physically retaliate. They were a bunch of misfits, led by a man looking for some sort of pride. They were a crew desperate enough to sign on for an early morning pick-up and a hammering, bickering journey down the motorway, crap music blasting out all the way down there through the van's distorting speakers, down to the gigantic Sainsbury's warehouse in Avonmouth.

Mikey had been to a union meeting, held in the big canteen because contract workers were officially encouraged to join. But it was like a Nuremberg rally, only without a Führer to whip them up. They didn't need one: hatred welled up from the floor, spat out in ridicule and anger. All contract workers were their enemies, the ethnics double negatives. Grabbers of overtime, greedy little fuckers. "What's my old woman gonna say when I tell her no more overtime? I'll never get another shag out of her again. What about my kiddies?" They were all pretending to be scared of their wives, Mikey noticed, or just using them as an excuse for this filth. And the union officials, although they tried, it was obvious they were well used to working with these speakers from the floor, who leaned back on their chairs, shouting the odds, laughing savagely in the long echoing space of the canteen.

Back in the chill for four hours, basting in cold sweat that had nowhere to go but deep down into your bones, where it melted and rotted your spine. Turkeys, legs of lamb, chickens by the brace, sides of a pig, sawn off slabs of beef. Bits of every edible animal, all of it frozen solid, assembled from a printed-out chit and stacked high on the trolleys in one long, crouched bending motion. It was disgusting, but somehow you didn't connect it with eating. The Jamaicans did, they claimed to be vegetarians and melted away, melted away for a spliff in the back of their Transit whenever they felt like it, which was often, coming back only to laugh at the foolish white man breaking his back because that was what he had been taught to do. A crazy man. No. No. No wonder, he'd thought. No fucking wonder. It was as though a cloud had descended over his thoughts and they were his no longer.

A black man was running along behind the dust cart, clumsy-looking in his loose over-trousers, fluorescent vest, big boots. Young and light on his feet as he picked up every plastic waste bag and bundle of cardboard on the pavement in front of the shops, sprinted forward, tossed them in the back, hit the big green button on the side of the waggon to trigger the relentless circular crumpling of the grinder, fell back to pick up the pile of cardboard stacked at the next lamppost. A seemingly tireless performance, although when you looked at his face he was glazed with sweat under the pale blue sky above a circular moated island of prosperous Victorian shops.

He knew his brother was thinking about him, up there in the smoke where you could think what you liked. Down here he was facing pure hatred every day of his life. People who would spit at you and kill you at the drop of a hat. If you spoke to them they showed you their knife. OK, so no-one had shown him their knife, but he knew they carried them. It was obvious. They would be stupid not to. For Mikey, this was reality not the dream-world of fairy tales his brother still believed in. What the fuck did he know about anything? But it wasn't hard to wall him out. It wasn't difficult.

He signed himself in at the door of the Highfields social club and moseyed up to the long empty bar with its full ice buckets and its fresh beer mats ready for Friday night. He bought himself a pint and went over to the Quiz machine with a fistful of pound coins and prepared to do battle with the riffling, lit-up categories. Unable to put his glass down on the sloping roof of the apparatus he kept hold of it, feeding in five quid, pausing to deposit another two in the wall-mounted jukebox beside him and punch in a few old tunes. It was still cycling through stuff from the night before he didn't like.

Mikey stabbed at the quiz machine's start button and began to answer a few multiple-choice questions on general knowledge, feeling the tension slip out of his shoulders as he sipped his refreshing beer. The place filled up a little, and by the time he had sacrificed thirty quid to the cause of proving he was no fool, Friday night was heaving. It was like going to sleep in an empty bedroom and waking up to find a crowded party in full swing.

Good Golly, Miss Molly came on and he was ensconced in a corner with Jackie and Judy and Bobby and Tommy and several other people he didn't know all that well, and they were all yakking and drinking away under the overhead strip-lights. Bobby was from Liverpool and, like a lot of them, he never stopped talking about the place. Mikey didn't mind, he liked it. Bobby gave him permission to loosen up himself and to tell him exactly how his six months in Avonmouth had been, disgorging repetitive strain injuries. Bob didn't blame him, he knew how he felt, but all the same, he said a few wise words.

"Yeah, yeah, Bobby, you're right," was all Mikey could muster by way of a reply.

Bobby stood beside his wife Judy's motorized chariot, plastered with faded stickers from their cruise holiday to the Soviet Union, and after asking what they were all having he threw himself into gear to lurch to the bar, a fragile man in his wide-swinging gait. Mikey looked down at Judy, raised his eyebrows. She flickered, almost immobile, looked up, floating like a giant amoeba in the middle of the padded seat of her contraption, exactly where Bobby had carefully placed her before they came out.

Mikey thought they were the most amazing people he had ever met, this thought recurred again and again. He couldn't believe what they were like. But, Judy confided one day, her parents had been dead against it. They didn't believe people like her should experience happiness or sexual fulfilment. He couldn't believe the cruelty they'd survived, Bob and his missus. They were immensely strong people, people such as he couldn't imagine himself being.

Mikey looked across the crowded room; the band was just about to start up, the jukebox turned off. He liked this lot, had looked forward to seeing them. The younger people positioned at tables around the social club bar were suddenly audible, crying out, shouting, laughing abuse, bouncing in their seats, and hugging each other in bursts of affection enhanced by rapid alcohol intake. You had to hand it to the youth of Dunkeswell, they knew how to let go. Mikey knew better than to speak to any of them. They grew up on this estate and they had nothing to say anyway.

Judy moved her head slightly, hooked her long, sensuous mouth around the straw protecting from her drink and drained it for refilling. She couldn't drink much because of the drugs, but it didn't take much to get her completely off her face. She was a thalidomide victim, her tiny body with its vestigial limbs surrounded neatly by a child's frilly dress. She was difficult to love since she found overtures of sympathy patronizing. She was unable to adjust to the presence of others. There was no need for that: the world had always been brought before her.

"You all right, Judy?"

"I'm right, Mikey."

"Been up to anything today?"

"Babs gave us a lift down the garden centre, so that was nice of her. Bobby bought me a nice shrub, a red one, to go on the back windowsill." Having bluntly informed him of this, she picked up the straw again with her agile lips and sucked out the very last drops of her drink.

"She's in a world of her own, that one." Bobby's eyes were floating behind his thick-lensed glasses. There was a tray in his hands, with five drinks on it, which he'd carried from the crowded bar, swinging his braced legs from the hip, without spilling a drop. He handed them around, removed his wife's dead lager glass and replaced it with another: a fresh plastic straw, ice bobbing in the turquoise alcopop. "She'll soon be singing, Mikey," he shouted.

The band started playing Eagles covers, things of that ilk. The middle-aged guy in a cowboy shirt played reasonably good guitar to a backing track and a drummer with a small, toy-like kit; a young woman, possibly his daughter, stood behind a keyboard ironing the keys. The man began to sing lightly, about California and Tulsa and Texas, and the young lady supplied backing vocals, stepping forward sometimes to take the lead on a Carpenters number.

At the tables, girls were getting rowdier. One of them eventually took the mike for a rendition of an Adele song, which sounded like she'd been rehearsing it in her bedroom with her phone. Everyone gave her a good hand, her could sing, although Amy Winehouse didn't happen. But it was her song, wasn't it, the song of her life, or so she believed at that precise moment.. The band's backing machine didn't know the chords and so she decided to quit while she was ahead.

Some of the younger people got up to move around, a few lurching men angling themselves towards nimble, twirling females, and a small whirling dervish of a woman in her forties who only got up for the fast ones. Mikey knew her and her husband, a slender, balding guy, an ex-stock car driver at the Smeatharpe circuit. Any excuse and he would whip out photos from his wallet of his long-bodied seventies car. The kids knew the estate, that was all, maybe they had a few mates in Honiton, but even on their home ground they were unreliable on any subject under the sun. That was his opinion.

The younger dancing girls were surrounded, first by their mates, then by a circle of boys with their trousers hanging down, and, orbiting these in concentric circles: pocked, deeply-banded outer planets. They knew something his smart-arse brother didn't – this was their only way to be themselves, their own place. If you wanted to know if a thing was good or bad you had to look at it through your own eyes from where you stood. It was what they had, what they were, and what made you think you were any better.

Mikey was up at the crack of dawn. He got ready, warmed up the minibus and crept through the silent estate to pick up the first of his crew. Most of the labyrinth of small pathways that run around Highfields were lit by mid-height staves planted in the ground and topped by tapering cylindrical lamps which emitted a soft unearthly glow. They were like light wands. Even as he moved along they clicked off an alley at a time, and behind the windows of the bungalows and two-storey houses the odd light was on, sometimes upstairs, sometimes in the kitchen.

He nosed out of the estate and turned left onto the Honiton Road. His first couple of pick-ups were a few hundred yards along, young people done up in fleeces under semi-waterproof jackets, who'd crawled out of bed on a farm back there, in a cottage, and managed to make it up to the end of the track to stand on the verge at five o clock in the morning. The two boys looked as if they'd just been born and weren't too happy about it; their faces were almost bloodless, raw-looking, pinched and inflamed, sunk into undisguised misery. Mikey said hello but they barely replied, just shuffled to separate seats at the back and looked out of opposite windows. One of them was shaking like a leaf. He took a gulp from a bottle of water he pulled from his duffel bag and lit a Superking.

A couple of hundred yards further on, up by Wolford Chapel, a slightly older woman, around thirty, got aboard without fuss. Somebody else who never said nothing, never tried to make conversation. Past the chapel they turned left and swooped down the long bumpy narrow lane down, down through the dense woods, all of them enjoying the van's flying roll and jounce as they plunged over crackling branches under creaking boughs. At a row of cottages near the bottom, they turned off and picked up Jim. Mikey had to hoot the horn to rouse him, but he hurried out and got in behind the driver's seat. Jim was working to send money to his bitch of a wife and his daughter, in Poland, but he managed to drink most of it. He would be cracking open his first bottle of beer once they got out on the motorway, down under the seat where he thought Mikey couldn't see him.

The girls were waiting at the top of the high street, outside what passed for a nightclub where many of their more violent traumas had been acted out over the months he had known them. They slid back the door and climbed up behind Mikey, opposite Jim. Julie, a bullet-cropped young woman, stocky and fierce-looking, got in ahead. Her friend flounced up afterwards and immediately seemed to become, in her own eyes anyway, the centre of attention. "I can't do this," she said. "I just can't fucking do this, alright?"

She did indeed look desperate and incapable of doing anything at all. She was disorganized and gabbling about something that had been done to her and in tears. Her eyes were smudged and puffy. Mikey didn't look at her. He didn't want to be drawn in, to have to look at her while she tried to wind him up about some crap that had nothing whatever to do with him. Why were women such useless pieces of shit? Why were you supposed to be so nice to them all the time? He was fucked if he knew, but he also knew that eventually, probably when they were approaching Avonmouth, things would get to the stage where only a display of anger on his part would settle them down.

Down in Honiton, a right past the deserted carpark – where a UKIP double-decker was the only resident vehicle – Mikey made his last pick-up. Barry, a skeletal bloke who seemed to be permanently foaming at the mouth. A heroin addict, so they said. Mikey believed it without trouble. He wondered if he was going to kick off again this morning. The gang's all here, he thought. Dolebusters Massive. They'd been written up in the local paper as that name, photographed beside the van as shining examples of getting on your bike, proud space fillers to inspire Honiton's youth to pick up their beds and walk. Great photo.

Out on the motorway, Mikey put a CD in the van's player, turned it up and tried to blot them from his consciousness. The music helped. His own music, but he didn't mind if they brought something to listen to, and when they complained about T-Rex he put on a CD which Holly fished out of her bag, of missed tunes, mixed tunes, and after that he had to switch off altogether as the woozy, floating kitchen music matched the drone of the minibus and matched the beat of the motorway to its tinny hammering metronome. There was nothing to it really but it seemed to pacify the crew. It made them comfortable, settled them down. Except little by little, much as Mikey didn't want to do anything but watch the road ahead, he noticed the noise-level in the back of the minibus rising above that of the sounds on the CD. He reached forward and turned it down.

Holly was doing most of the shrieking and crying. She'd got into some sort of fight with Barry, who was matching her, telling her to shut the fuck up, she was doing his fucking bonce in. The stupid little bitch deserved all she got anyway. Holly was going to hit him now any second. He couldn't talk to her like that. "Don't touch me, babe," said Barry. "That's all I'm asking you, girl." He was off his medication, apparently. He didn't want to go on. He was off his trolley. He wanted to get out of the van right this instant and hitch a ride back home.

Mikey could see he was semi-delirious, but he wasn't going to let him do that. He twisted in his seat, feeling a slight twinge in his back. "Look," he said. "I'm driving this fucking van, alright, and I do not want to hear you lot shouting behind me. Music, okay. Have what music you like on. But do not distract me when I'm driving at seventy-five miles per fucking hour down the fucking motorway to get you to work on time." He looked at Barry. "If you're unwell you'd better come all the way in, see somebody about it there. They've got a doctor. I can't let you get out here – what if you was hit by a car or something? I can't take that responsibility."

Barry quietened down. "Oh man," he put his bony head in his bony hands. "You just don't know, man."

"I'm not proper well neither," Holly burst in. "Honest, Mikey, I just can't do this, I don't deserve it, do I? I've done nothing wrong. And this little druggie shithead has got no right, no right at all to talk to me like I'm nothing." She was snuffling but really shaking as if she too had some drug coursing through her fragile, trembling frame. She wasn't even dressed properly for work; looked like she'd just got out of bed and pulled a pair of jeans and a cardigan on over her nightgown. Mikey wished she'd made the decision to stay there and be somebody else's problem.

"Don't fuck with her," said Julie. "Or you'll be the one that's fucking limping home. You listening to me? Cunts!"

Mikey ignored her. Ignored all of them. He started the engine and inched out again between a couple of cars into the flow of early morning traffic. Twenty minutes later they were flying over the Avonmouth bridge and into the carpark of the giant Sainsbury's warehouse. He pulled up between a couple of other vans. The Jamaicans from Bedminster were stretching their long legs around their van, the only exercise they were going to get all day. The Honiton crew struggled out into the daylight, a sorry bedraggled bunch. One of the friendlier members of the So Solid Crew looked across and laughed. A gang of ethnics – Mikey didn't know what they were exactly – was already gathered outside the warehouse doors, hanging back before the shift started at 7.30. They were rangy, poisonous, intense; one of them spat heavily on the ground as the Honiton workers straggled past and squeezed in through the crack of the sliding doors. The others laughed, ignoring them.

Mikey took pride in the fact that he had taught his gang how to do their jobs. He was a brilliant teacher. Patient and thorough. He showed them everything, made them go through it until they were confident. Making up the orders from the table and the racks in the chill, reading them off the chit when they were printed out. Stacking them on the pallets so they didn't slide off and strapping them over with bubble wrap and a tape gun. Above all, keeping it going, because by the end of the shift the floor would be swimming with melted ice and glutted semi-thawed carcasses and their collective fingers would be too numb to grasp anything as it should be grasped.

It wasn't a job anyone would be making exaggerated claims for in the annals of the dignity of labour. Julie squinted angrily at a docket; Holly snivelled, intermittently peered at, and slapped, a very dead item of indeterminate poultry; the two pale boys from Dunkeswell were side by side, operating in unison like clockwork automata, and the lady from opposite Wolford chapel, name Penny, worked methodically, mechanically, self-contained. Barry couldn't settle. Mikey was uncomfortable about him handling knives and scissors but what could you do? He was slashing and stabbing at the meat soon enough. "Control that fucker! Keep that fucker away from me!" cried one of the Jamaicans.

Barry took care of himself in the end. He flung down the knives and charged out in search of the doctor, because he needed to know what shit was going on here, and the supervisors stood back to let him pass them by.

Mikey let him go, ploughed on regardless. At the mid-shift mark, they were given a twenty-minute break to munch their sandwiches. Nobody came anywhere near them, and they were glad of that, queuing for the toilets, huddling along the metal wall outside the chill, well back from the high-stacked gulleys where Kosovans and Ukrainians faced it out, hanging off electric trolleys, sparking like trams in their own cities, spitting on each other and on English shit, because in these circumstances you were part of whatever gang you had been born into.

Much later they found Barry huddled beside the minivan's rear wheels, waiting for the ride home. Mikey tried to ask what happened with the doctor – did he find him? who else had he seen? Barry's lips were sealed, he wouldn't say a word to any of them. They flew back to Honiton in top gear, in rankling silence.

Mikey was crawling along a long dark tunnel, an unlit damp conduit to nowhere whose close walls dripped with freezing, slippery black ice. It was fucking terrible, the worst experience of his entire life, but fortunately he was incapable of exaggerating or lying. He was also dragging a wooden sled stacked with frozen chickens and turkeys and legs of lamb and sides of beef, and the smaller rock-solid chickens were always rolling off, clogging the path behind him for next time. But he couldn't give a fuck about that right now. His fingers frozen to the cutting nylon rope, he felt panic rising. He wanted desperately to get down to the end, out into the bright white light of the stacking room where they were waiting for him.

He woke up with a start, sweating like a pig, suddenly not cold at all but boiling hot, wringing wet. He tried to sit up, but his spine was in some sort of agonizing stiff spasm. Instead, he wallowed to one side and switched on the bedside light. It was half-past four. He was in a lot of back pain, a lot. He popped a couple of co-dydramol out of the foil strip on the bedside table, gulped them down with the remains of the water glass and carefully eased himself down to stare at the ceiling, not daring to move an inch, waiting for the worst of the pain to subside, slowly, slowly, until he managed to drift off again.

When he finally came to it was midday – this was Sunday – and his mobile phone was ringing beside his bed. He picked up. It was his mother on the line from around the corner, asking if he was coming round to go up the airfield for lunch. Mikey explained he'd put his back out and wouldn't be able to make it after all. He could hear she was put out. As if his absence was some sort of problem for his parents. They could go on their own, perfectly well, but it didn't seem worth it going on their own up to the carvery without him. Mikey just said flat out that he couldn't go, he was in pain. He managed to get her off the line before she started asking him questions about what he was going to eat.

He eased himself around to do his ablutions, went downstairs, filled up the glass with Sprite from the fridge and dutifully munched his way through a bag of crisps. The Sprite cleansed his mouth with its sharp citrus tang, then he went back to bed and booted up the laptop to see what they were doing at the space station, how the experiments were progressing – and all the latest from the mechanical crawlers that were finding what looked like traces of prehistoric life on the plains and in the foothills of the carved red mountains of Mars.

Mikey loved the NASA website. He spent a lot of his free time listening to the live webcasts from the station, the astronauts standing there formally, shyly lined up to tell the watching millions how the hydroponics were shaping up, only it wasn't millions now, more like thousands. Still, if no-one else was interested in what was going on, he still was, even though a lot of it was obviously routine. It calmed him. He felt reassured, absorbed in a way he always had been by actual space, real astronauts. He liked the Hubble telescope too. The whole amazingness of the cosmos, photographed in such incredible colour and detail.

All the same, he liked to see what could be seen from Earth, if not with the naked eye then by means of the electronically assisted refracting telescope in his garden shed. The rings of Saturn never bored him. The Constellations. The pictures he himself could take of them. Stargazing. It was something he'd discovered when he was thirteen years old and nobody was going to take it away from him. He lay back and tried to remain motionless, his back-ache settling to a steady low throb.

Judy was surfacing from her recurrent power dream. She was a mermaid, a siren trying to lure sailors onto the beach. They thought they were too clever for her. They clung to their pathetic land-borne lovers, but still they tried to empty their harmful desires into her, to trap her and use her with their rough hands. She would float away and drown them. She woke up, still floating in the calm sea. Bobby was leaning over her; his legs were strapped on but his trousers still at half-mast, looking down at his malevolent little mermaid. "Time to get up, sweetheart," he said. "Hospital today."

"Pull your kecks up, you filthy man." Judy glanced up at him from the centre of her crooked little body. Bobby gave her a lopsided smile back, hoisted his trousers – and, bracing himself against the edge of the bed, lifted her up and swung her around like a doll, deposited her in her light-weight house chair and wheeled her through to the bathroom.

Ablutions completed, he wheeled her through to the kitchen and fed her a bowl of cornflakes and a cup of tea. A few minutes later Mikey knocked on the door. Good. Judy was ready. She dragged a comb through her hair and applied a circle of pink lipstick to her wide mouth. Wide and dropped it into the handbag on her lap.

"Alright, Mikey?" Bobby said.

"Yep," said Mikey. "What time's your appointment?"

"Ten-thirty."

"We'd better get going then."

They manoeuvred Judy into the back seat of Mikey's car, stowed her chair in the boot and were soon heading towards Exeter on the dual carriageway, its pale ridged surface drumming monotonously under the wheels of the car.

"This is good of you, Mikey," said Bobby in his clicky-spitty accent. Judy concurred from the backseat. She couldn't see much from where she was, just the back of the passenger seat and the roof trim. She closed her eyes, floated. A whole day of treatment to come. It was routine but she was resigned. They'd pop her in that oven-thing, scan her, prod her, weigh her, take her blood and everything else.

"How's your back, Mikey?" Bobby asked.

"Not too bad. A bit better thanks." Mikey sat bolt upright in the driver's seat, his hands resting lightly on the wheel. He'd swallowed a couple of co-dydramol before coming out. Of course he didn't mind at all helping Bobby and Judy. He'd said anytime, and he meant anytime.

Judy lay back in her semi-supine position and closed her eyes. There was nothing much else she could do. Now she was being towed behind a speedboat on a pair of water-skis. The sailors were floating up, being cut aside by waves of desire, their own wants, spread out bobbing in her wake. It started raining on the way down, lashing across the windscreen and the dual carriageway.

It was still raining when he pulled up outside the main door and helped her and Bobby into the building. He left them to it, was thanked; they'd find their own way back, maybe one of those pricy mini-cabs from the Blackdown surgery; but now they trundled down long crooked corridors, passing franchises against the slow tide of people being wheeled about on their backs or surfacing for a few yards of tottering ambulance with worried relatives past hurrying doctors and nurses with pagers and clipboards, chatting orderlies, cleaners

They moved on down a long white corridor decorated with a series of stencilled illustrations of important events of the twentieth century: the Austin Mini Moke, the ascent of Everest and the Sputnik, the moon hopper, the moon landing, film stars and pop singers and miniskirts. A trip down memory lane, one last look at the ducks. Things you needed to be reminded of in hospital. Things everybody knew. That nobody looked at. It wasn't so bad. At least they tried. Bobby and Judy turned a corner and waited by a lift to take them up to the clinic where they too were awaited.

The two nurses soon had her settled in bed and hooked up to the dialysis machine, which would slowly suck out her blood, clean it and pump it back in, leaving her feeling fresh as a daisy.

Later on, after Judy had been unplugged from the dialysis machine and was resting in a recovery ward until the ambulance was ready to take her home. The whole process of having what little blood her body could hold pumped out, cleaned, pumped in again left her feeling, well, drained. Rained on. But after a good night's sleep, she generally woke up feeling sharper, clearer, at least for the first week. After the first few times, she'd stopped noticing any difference. Bobby was lurching around outside by the nurses' station, cradling a half-drunk cup of coffee and replacing the lid, trying to make small-talk.

"Where you from? If you don't mind me asking. I'm from Liverpool. Me and the wife, like."

"Sri Lanka," said the nurse. "It is near India."

"I always wanted to travel," Bobby said. "At least I got down here, like."

"I like it too, Mr. Ruffolud. You can sit here or sit with your wife until the ambulance comes. I will get her ready soon."

"Rutherford," he said. "Bob Rutherford." He stuck out his free hand, grinned lopsidedly, and the small brown woman shook it. Abruptly, he swivelled off to sit in the chair next to Judy's bed. "How're you feeling?" he asked. "Like a brand-new person?"

"O shut up do," she said. "You're like an old woman. You're always trying to get yourself distracted. Try and sit still for five minutes."

"You can talk," he said. "I've seen that faraway look in your eyes."

"Come on, get me ready now," Judy said decisively. "I want to be ready when they come for me."

Mikey had signed him in at the door, bought him a drink and introduced him around they table as his cousin, but there was something about the big, friendly man that people just wouldn't take to. Richie couldn't settle in the Highfields Social Club. He couldn't sit still for one thing. In the usual corner with Bobby, Judy, and the others, he had perched on the edge, taking up far too much room, and had been unable to join a proper conversation with Bobby. Mikey quickly realized that he had to be the centre of attention, wanted to be telling people all about what he thought and what he'd done, but they didn't really like it. However friendly he was, and however friendly they tried to be, he was just too much, too insistent, too aggressive.

As for Judy, it was obvious he found her disgusting to look at and could barely stand to look down at her small, frog-like body. From Judy's perspective, he must have looked like he had climbed down from a beanstalk. *Fee Fie Foe Fum*. She looked at him once, grabbed her straw in the corner of her mouth, and went impolitely blank.

Richie stood up, walked across the bar, and started talking to someone he thought he recognized from the airfield. He'd bought a wheelbarrow from this guy (for no purpose whatsoever) but now he didn't seem to remember, or if he did remember didn't think it a sufficient basis for bonding with him in a lengthy conversation. Richie got annoyed quickly, he always did. "Alright buddy," he said. "Please yourself." And he walked right through him to the bar, waggling a twenty-pound note in the face of the barmaid, who was otherwise preoccupied.

Mikey watched it unfolding, asked everyone what they wanted to drink, stood up and walked towards him. He managed to wedge himself in beside his cousin, reaching for his wallet. "Alright Rich?" he asked. "What you having? I'll get these in."

"Yeah, see if you can get served," he shouted over the programmed music.

Mikey seemed to attract the young woman's attention more easily. He ordered a round of drinks. Three Otters, a Mule, a Bacardi Breezer, and, for Richie, a brimming pint of Stella. The barmaid produced a small metal tray, which she loaded up, and he left the Stella on the swimming surface for his cousin to retrieve. He did so. But he didn't rejoin them in the corner dog-leg. He was still trying to talk to other people at the bar. "Alright buddy?" he said to nobody in particular, a flushed young man with crudely sketched in features, who failed to respond.

There was no live band tonight, it was karaoke night. Mikey sat down next to Bobby and Judy and passed the Mule over to Fred's missus, who thanked him, and they all sat back, chatting comfortably, to listen to various punters as they got up to do their turns. Not one of them could sing but it didn't matter. A steady procession of performers, some rehearsed but baffled looking, others pushed by mates or alcohol, playing catch-up with a tune they'd requested but didn't know, plus a couple of young women who'd had the benefit of a lot of practice, rotating and emoting without apparent effort, generally able to hold a tune, doing their patented dance moves, centred in their ego-bubbles of supreme magnetism. Nobody cared, although it was fun to see how people would do in the transforming lights, in the treated-up echoing synth-pulse. Bobby loved it. Good natured. A steady lurch in and out of the makeshift dance area as beer-bellied lurkers attempted to match their moves to those of the twirling, elusive girls. No boos or catcalls, except from Cousin Richie, who staggered dangerously amongst them like an escaped giant polar bear menacing children, reared up on his hind legs and roaring. Nobody seemed to share his sense of fun.

Towards the end of the night, Russ got up to sing. He was a slim man in his early forties, dressed in a style calling to mind the disco era, or the late eighties; a smart, enduring short-haired style he still held in focus. Mikey knew him too. Everyone at the corner table knew him, as did most people in the club, although the volume level of laughter and conversation didn't go down significantly as he took the radio microphone. Mikey had chatted with him on his way in with Richie. He'd told them he was going to get up and sing tonight. One last time.

Russ was dying, in the final stages of cancer, Mikey could plainly see he was weakened, but determined to give something good to the people who had supported him. He was a loved man. He sang *Angels* by Robbie Williams, his voice soaring up and breaking open with passion, but still controlled, mastered, delivered from a place where he had left emotion behind, nailed it with humility and strength.

When he died a few weeks later, a lot of people turned out to pay their respects. There was a procession around the estate, at least from his house to the Honiton Road, and a lot of people walked behind the hearse before some of them got into their cars, but many were just people who'd known him socially and wanted to bid him farewell. Afterwards, there was a party in the Throgmorton Hall went on until all hours, everyone laughing and telling stories about him while his girlfriend sat there silently and his daughter cried quietly.

The next time Mikey went into the club the bar manager told Mikey that his cousin Richie had upset quite a few people. "It's no reflection on you, Mikey, but I've told him not to come in here again," he said. "I'm only telling you now in case he tries to use you to get back in."

Mikey had been just plain Mike until Bobby and Judy came into his life. Bobby had started calling him Micky first. Then it had changed to Mikey, and soon he had the bar staff, the old bar staff and everyone in the snooker room calling him by that name. Mikey it was. Bobby was good at snooker, far better than anyone in the club, a semi-pro, and they didn't like him much. He could be abrasive, aggressive; it was his Liverpool side made him that way, the hard knocks of his handicapped childhood, his criminal father, his thug of a brother who chucked him out in the street without a penny. "Hello, our kid," he'd said, years later, passing him in the street as if nothing had happened. "Still getting about then."

Some people hated it when he beat them at snooker, because he beat them by being a proper snooker player. Bobby always played for the snooker, right to the death, and they tried to tell him to get on with it, just try to sink the ball, in the pocket. But he wouldn't and he always won. He toured around, played top snooker in tournaments, but always argued the toss over every shot with the referee. It was how he was – totally competitive. A pain in the arse to everyone he met. Mikey had always liked him a lot. A totally straightforward person, a heart of gold.

Judy. Judy. Some of the things they'd experienced in their life! When Judy's best friend got married to an American she met when they were on holiday together on the Isle of Man, a wealthy oil magnate over for the TT, the man had moved over to Liverpool with her to start a new life. Judy used to go and visit them in their big house, but after a time her husband said. "Can you please ask your friend not to come round anymore, just looking at her makes me feel sick." And her friend had told her this and gone along with it. And that was the last she'd seen of her so-called best friend. Judy was quite old now, in her seventies, older than Bobby, but she'd wasted no time in telling Mikey this story, and many others he didn't remember so well. They were his best friends, but they had issues. And, he now realized, he had his own issues. Always had had but they were getting worse, not better.

Mikey had driven into town to pick up some toiletries at the pound shop. A few Honiton hoodies were hanging around at the entrance to Lace Walk, gooning about in their skinny, would-be cool fashion. "Can't be arsed," Mikey heard one of them say, laughing. Stoned-looking young guy. Out of his head. They all seemed to have a gnome-like appearance with their small beards, hunched shoulders, tracksuits. "Fair play to the copper," one of them laughed at his friend's description of an encounter with the Devon constabulary. They reminded him of his own crew, some of the Dolebusters Massive, now dispersed, gone on – never really a team at all. If you asked them. Nobody had actually asked them if they wanted to join.

A fifth of the world's population were women, not half as was often wrongly stated. This continued to rankle with him, nearly as much as the continuance of religious belief. There were boys and girls too. Men. And these trans people, what about them, those who'd crossed the floor and started drinking pints or, conversely, bright fizzy drinks. They were in a class of their own. What about non-sexually active people, celibate men, and women? Didn't they also deserve to be in a separate category? What exactly was somebody like Pete? What would you call him?

In time, he thought, this will change everything, this switching through. It would find new routes, much as Ada Lovelace, Lord Byron's daughter, had seen the way forward in computing. She'd made a couple of leaps forward in thought, branching off in the only possible direction. Alan Turing, so he had read on the internet, was the first to pick up her ideas, a hundred years later, at Bletchley Park during the war when he was cracking the Nazi codes. It was important in some way Mikey didn't yet understand, but he was also old enough to remember before the internet. How would he have known anything about this stuff back then? Answer: he wouldn't. Ada Lovelace, he thought vaguely, had had something to do with people like him getting to know about such things. It was change and it was important. It was good really.

In his spare room, Mikey had rigged a seat from a Peugeot, a steering wheel, a gear stick and set of pedals on a frame he'd built, which included a TV screen hooked to a PlayStation racing game. You could select any car you liked – from a Mustang to a contemporary Grand Prix car – adjusting individual tyre pressures, and get a realistic kick-back through the steering wheel relating to the handling and the dynamics of the specified track. You could also race anyone in the entire world, although so far he'd only raced against himself. It was an amazing contraption. Much the same story as chess, at which he'd beaten the built-in Bobby Fischer once or twice; Gary Kasparov, never.

He was always looking for somebody on whom to practice his prestidigitation skills. He had always liked telescopes. He had always liked card tricks. Now he learned them from YouTube, where there was some amazing stuff showing you how to do it, posted by people who had presumably been expelled from the Magic Circle.

He could do sevens and nines, find the lady, fancy cutting and shuffling, random pairs found, pennies twisted into invisibility and replaced under a glass. A whole load of other amazing feats of legerdemain. He used to try them out at work, not in the chill in

Avonmouth, but after that had ended – what a relief – in another warehouse job where they'd had plenty of time on their hands and Mikey had spent a lot of days driving one of the delivery trucks back and forth to Debenham's in Plymouth. Eventually, that had come to an end too, as all good things must, which had given him more time to practice and to buy expensive professional magician's card decks while he lived on his redundancy, and started wondering what was going to happen next.

Scenes That Are Brightest

After Pete died everything he owned was disposed of quickly: his books were packed up, sold off in a job lot to a bloke up at the airfield; notebooks of itineraries, film ratings, photographs, portfolios, poems chucked away; his clothes, knick-knacks, clocks and watches tossed in the same direction or dispersed to buyers or passed on to the unwilling as souvenirs; finally his lovely bungalow, whose new owner soon filled up a skip with two tons of brown floral medieval pattern tiles.

There were a few bequests but most of the money went to the British Legion and Guide Dogs for the Blind. Everything rippled out, dissipated, and soon the last vestige of a person's energy is gone. At first, you didn't notice, but then you did, and even the memories of that person seemed to lose definition and meaning without the presence of the one who had for years neatly recorded titles and star ratings for films and novels in those black exercise books. There was nothing left to do but produce some appropriately cleaned up audit.

Peter May was born in Park Road, in the town of East Molesey, a few doors from where the Mudie family lived after the war. He never knew his own father, had only his mother to clothe him. Crippled by arthritis at an early age, she had been able to do a little sewing until her hands seized up, her legs shrank and twisted inwards, and she was confined to a low chair indoors for the remainder of her long life. Peter, a boy lit up by the streamlined monoplanes of the inter-war era, lost in adventures, in reading, also his mother's lifelong pleasure, had to look after her.

During the war, their life was blighted by grinding poverty; Peter had gone out to work, at twelve, in a local fish and chip shop. The old lady, he called her, Mrs. May, but she was always old to most people who knew her. Her memories were of the infant playground, playing games of English and Boers, being given a black armband and a day off for the old Queen's funeral, gently laughing over dull passages in her big print library books, at how some character's socks were really more holes than sock. That's how you remembered her, often hospitalized for operations or at home in a special chair, her crooked feet up on a padded bolster, calling out to her budgerigar, her windowsills full of potted cacti.

There was a pair of heavy sticks she moved on slowly, a tap she could pry open with a claw-thing like a long-handled spanner. You were a curious child, she enjoyed company, told you stories. How in her opinion John Lennon should have been hanged publicly. But apart from that, she was a nice old lady, a light in her eyes of such cheerfulness, fortitude, she seemed never to stop laughing at something or other that remained beyond your understanding.

Peter's lot was to look after her, there being no other option. He left school at the end of the war and went into light engineering. A young man in a pair of wire-framed glasses, the serious one, hands in pockets, astride his Triumph, next to Bill and Ray in a framed photograph of the original Wild Ones. Peter May and his mother had been a fixture of your childhood.

They always came for Christmas dinner, on numerous outings, sometimes a trip on the Thames. Mrs. May was lifted carefully into place waving at our Super 8 cine camera in a sun hat, a frail old woman wobbling in her bath of summer light. Peter had been away on lots of motorcycling holidays, many of them astride his beloved West German scooter, a 250cc giant Maicoletta, on itineraries planned in minutest detail, right down to the last bed and breakfast; each photo dated, with notes on the local fauna, key words in German, Dutch, Swedish, Norwegian; prices set down, with captions: 'Steep road', 'Friendly goats!'

How many times you had shuffled through sheaves of them. Peter before fjords, next to a camel, a turban; beside his bulbous scooter. Sweeping through landscapes in lost places you had never been to in person, reliant on the precious details which this heroic moto-adventurer passed on to you: quietly witnessing the fall of Prague, the Northern Lights on Kodak; journeys punctuated by frequent brew-ups at the side of the road, AA maps folded neatly beside him, a pair of binoculars, a semi-reverted Zündapp.

For a few people in this book he will always be living a few streets away, his memories in a lock-up near Bill and Pauline, down in Devon. He didn't usually intrude much, was self-contained. The recording angel of the International Motorcycle Tour Club, a subscriber to specialist book clubs in glazed ornaments, old cars, and of course the war; a little pedantic about everything. There was your father's story of how he was once wrongly charged as a deserter for failing to report for guard duty after delivering an army prisoner. But if he didn't want to remember, why should he?

Pete was a creature of planning, happenstance and habit; stone deaf, not entirely unpleasant. There used to be some small mystery about him, but not any more there wasn't. Just something in all of them that liked the old days more than the present: a chocolate Mallard under her tree, 'scenes that are brightest'. John Hines said that. Did you know where it came from? An aria from *Maritana* by William Vincent Wallace, libretto by Edward Fitzball, an opera referred to in James Joyce's stories. Heard in a recording by Rosa Ponselle, the soaring, opulent soprano from Connecticut, a miracle girl Enrico Caruso discovered in New York. Burned out, the others fell silent. *And when they leave us, the heart is lost.*

A Lady from Des Moines

On a rare clear night the constellations were rivet holes punched in the deep blue sky. Overhead, a battered group of US Navy warplanes circled above the runway of a godforsaken place the American fliers had named Mudville. Below lay the airfield, with its groups of interconnected huts, aprons and hangars: pristine, a darkened city – and one by one the bombers dropped in to land. One of the Libs was badly shot up, mostly rear gun turret, and to one member of the expectant groundcrews would fall the task of hosing the remains of his buddy from the broken bubble. It was an experience he would be struggling with for the rest of his life.

The aircrews would be shattered, as ever, heading straight for the officers' club to down a few shots of hooch. Meanwhile, in the well-equipped camp hospital, Sergeant Platt stood by with her team of medics and nurses, on edge, ready with bandages and iodine, hoping that nothing more would be required of them. American service personnel received the best medical attention in the world, everyone knew it. Everything made in the US was of high quality and would be coveted for years to come: even the wrappers.

Eileen knew this very well. Simply to be an American was a comfort in this strange little world. The fine, rambling manor in which she was billeted, right down in the dunk of Dunkeswell, was exceptional for an English place; its owners were extremely kind to her, as they should have been, but even the crews who lived on the base knew there was something special about being an American. The way most of them held themselves in the snaps they were always taking outside their quarters said it all: something mysterious, self-possessed, confident.

But, as everyone also knew, along with all this admiration came a certain amount of envy. Not of course the unalloyed gratitude they damned well should be feeling towards men who had left their peaceful homes behind, who were giving their lives to pull them and the rest of Europe out of the hole. The boys were always getting into fights with locals, usually over some all too willing girl, although that didn't really dent their enthusiasm and pride. Why should it? After all, it was easy enough to understand these people.

Soon after the planes were down – one lost, one badly shot up – the usual in-flight injuries started to drift into the medical hut, all of them thankfully on their feet. Eileen was used to it by now, of course, but nevertheless she couldn't help being amused by how many crew members managed to get hurt during missions, not by enemy fire but by the airplane they were flying in.

Nasty cuts, bad grazes, bruised, sky-sprained ankles, damaged fingers and arms and feet and toes. Rattling around up there, scared absolutely shitless in cramped spaces, made you particularly accident-prone. Then there were bad cases of the jitters that didn't subside. Guys walked in convinced they were having heart attacks; they thought they were about to die by some sort of contagion, high as kites, when all they needed was to sit down, be calm, and watch a few men with genuine injuries getting rapid, efficient treatment from a team of well-trained American nurses. The ARC civilians and local women would take plenty good care of them.

Eileen Platt rode in a jeep that was like her chariot, open at the sides and skimming along in a soft summer breeze as her driver turned out of the airfield, passed the gun emplacement, and swooped downhill towards the church and the moth-eaten thatched pub. He turned abruptly to drop down into the dunk, a steep holler whose tight channels of deep descending lanes and ancient oak boles whose rich multiple greenery wrapped itself around everything and had the density of dappled fur. They passed the end of the ruined abbey, a community hall, a telephone box, a small church, and a beautiful old village school. Eileen enjoyed jouncing and crawling down there, her dress flapping, hair flying, as did the sergeant who was driving her. Mitch.

"Steady, Mitch," she said. "Don't hit any chickens." It was just a manner of speaking. There weren't any chickens to be hit. They lived out back somewhere in homemade wire-netted runs.

"You coming back for the Fight?" Mitch twirled the steering wheel on the jeep with its heavily-hooded, downcast eyes, swung into the driveway of Dunns End, and pulled up in front of its ancient oak door, grey but solid enough. Down here you just wouldn't know there was a war going on.

"I don't think so. I'm not on duty, Mitch," she said. "Anyhow, I doubt there'll be any blood."

"Sure," he said. "I know that's all you live for – to see good red American blood."

"Bye, Mitch." Eileen smiled her thanks and hopped over the side of the jeep, let herself into the house with her key. Mitch swung around what had been the flowerbed and past the ranks of pea-plants covering the lawn. These places never ceased to amaze him; they gave him the shivers. Not only were they nothing like Ohio, but they really made you feel weird, like a toy person in a toy world; or maybe just a clumsy, comical buffoon. Yeah, that was it probably.

He was looking forward to seeing Joe Louis fight his exhibition match tonight, sparring against the Navy's guy. Everyone would be there. They already flew Louis in on a Fortress, had him stowed in the hangar beside the officer's club where they'd rigged up the ring. Mitch's family had always listened to the fights when he was a kid. He'd heard all about Jack Johnson from his grandfather, even seen a few flickering frames of him in a boxing feature at the movies. Sugar-Ray Robinson, a fast-flashy welterweight, was the rising star now. But Joe Louis, who would've thought it, still an American for all that, coming to Mudville!

Eileen tiptoed upstairs, managing not to disturb any of the Addams family, entered her spacious guest room and closed the door quietly behind her. She kicked her shoes off, hung her jacket on the back of a chair and threw herself down on the bed. The four-poster bed. It was pretty good in there, if still a little musty. Mouse-droppings. Old mould. Who cared anyway? It had been a long hard shift and she was glad to get back into her snug little cocoon for a few hours.

After a short nap, she was on her feet again, peering out through tiny leaded diamond panes as the twilight shadows stole over the garden. It was beautiful out there, bosky was the word, and suddenly light spilled out from downstairs windows, banking the greenish darkness as they struggled to get the blackout into place. They might as well have been signalling Berlin, but instead Eileen knew she'd better get herself down to the dining room in a few minutes if she didn't want the embarrassment of arriving late to find them sitting there waiting for her politely. Possibly bickering, then going icily quiet. She pulled herself together, dragged a brush through her hair and quickly repaired her makeup, sucking her lips. It wasn't difficult, and they were so lovely to her.

All the same, she drifted through dinner, going through eating while the Dunns offered her the usual endless pattering stream of their dailiness. Mrs. B. had dutifully boiled up the cut vegetables Mrs. Dunn had picked from the garden. Mr. Dunn doddered and drivelled about ways and values and poets of the silver age. Eileen pursed her lips and inclined her head in mock-attention. The house itself was Elizabethan, double-chimneyed, all overgrown with ivy and surrounded by brambles, the oldest building in the Dunk apart from the church and the abbey. Hmmm. Maybe she should try and make it up to Mudville for the fight. She couldn't be bothered really but she had to decide. She would do so later, after the rhubarb and powdered custard, or whatever other delicacy they laid before her.

Immediately opposite her, Geoffrey, the Dunns' fourteen-year-old grandson, shovelled up the last of his potatoes and peas, glazed by a thin wash of gravy, savouring each remaining gritty bit of the faggot which Eileen had thought it better to chaw down on straight away rather than toy with for any longer than was strictly necessary.

The boy's face was flushed and raw looking; a rash of angry spots reached down the side of his neck under his grey collar. He too was trying to say something to her, but he couldn't quite get it out. Eileen noticed he was staring as though hypnotized at the front of her blouse, the swell of her uniform-sheathed breasts, and involuntarily looked down to check she was decent.

"How was school today?" she asked. "Geography again?"

"Maps of the world," he stammered. "We're each doing different countries."

"Anyone doing the USA?"

"A few of us," he said. "We're colouring in with crayons. I didn't realize there were so many different countries in America."

"They're called states, honey. Remember?" Poor kid. He couldn't keep his eyes off her. Soon he would have to make his lame excuses and run off up to his bedroom.

"Eileen is from Iowa," his grandfather interrupted. "You should try to remember these things, Geoffrey."

"Make sure you colour it in right up to the edges," said Eileen.

"What colour is it?" Geoff was half delirious with embarrassment.

She smiled at him, leaning forwards. "Make it pink," she said.

Geoff pushed his chair back and rushed from the room.

Eileen put her head down, blushing into the rhubarb. Uh-oh. She knew she'd done it again, made a giraffe out of herself.

Mr. and Mrs. Dunn seemed to retreat from her in confusion. But not for long. "Not like our Geoff to miss his rhubarb," Mr. Dunn laughed. "I expect he'll come looking for it later."

"He won't get it," said Mrs. Dunn. "Not with those manners."

"I'll feed it back to the chickens," said Mrs. B.

They laughed and relaxed together for a few moments, adults in an adult world, looking down into the murky pool of childhood, poised above it on a shared wing. But Eileen felt she was letting the side down. She'd been taking it out on the kid. She was disappointed in herself that she couldn't be bothered to go see this coloured boxer do his little turn for the Navy, to be twirled around, maybe, in the Officers' hut, chat to a pilot or two, maybe even Joe Kennedy … maybe she could pass him a canapé.

She almost gave way to an impulse to tell the Dunns about the fight, as they didn't seem to have heard about it already. But she just didn't feel like it. They wouldn't know who Joe Louis was probably. She would have to explain, and they would try to persuade her to go. But no. They were just going to have to do without her tonight up at Windsock Central.

She would go upstairs to the quiet room with the four-poster and crawl away into her own world for a few hours, maybe try to find some music on her radio. "I think I need to write some letters," Eileen said, standing up quickly, excusing herself from the table and thanking Mrs. B. for her delicious meal. "You know," she said. "You've made me feel so at home here. I want you to know I appreciate it." At that, suddenly and without warning, she burst into tears. She managed to stifle herself, pulled a handkerchief from her sleeve and dabbed at her eye as though she had something in it.

"My dear," said Mrs. Dunn placing a gentle hand on her upper arm. "Whatever's the matter?"

"Nothing." Eileen rose, scrunching her handkerchief in her hand, trying to smile. "One of the Liberator boys got pretty shot up, that's all. We lost him."

The hangar was packed out with men surrounding the empty boxing ring that had been set up in the centre, a professional ring with the stars and stripes adorning every corner, flags tightly stretched over white silken ropes, immaculately new leather fittings. It was a real taste of home alright, and when Joe Louis in his white shorts and world champion's belt and the white navy boxer in his dark blue shorts and bullet-cropped blond military hair stepped out into the ring followed by brass in a dress uniform, every man in the place started to cheer his lungs out.

There were no black servicemen stationed at Dunkeswell – something about the location and the Navy's recruitment policies had conspired against this, and the idea of a hut full of negroes out on the mud with nothing but dark mischief to get up to had anyway seemed to the navy against the interests of efficiency and good discipline. Instead, a couple of truckloads of drivers and other coloured army personnel stationed in Exeter had been brought in on a transport to see Joe Louis and listen to the Navy lecturing them about America's future.

Very smart those men looked too, each with his hair immaculately brilliantined and his cap set on the side of his head, just so, surrounding the boxing ring – ringside seats, no less – listening to the roar of cheers behind them and contributing their own enthusiastic whistles and hand-clapping at the sight of Joe Louis, right there before them, his ass as big and black and inspiring as life itself should be.

The brass with scrambled egg on his shoulders stepped out into the centre of the ring and made a speech about America's promise to the negro, the promise of full citizenship. Everyone listened silently, respectfully. But when the General – whose family, he told them, had fought for the Confederacy in the Civil War – stepped back to firm applause, the Brown Bomber and the Navy boxer circled out into the centre of the ring: Joe Louis, heavy, crouched, intent, and the blond Navy guy (who looked like a Nazi, let it be said) almost prancing, stepping out arrogantly, jabbing at him.

Joe had his head way down, just hanging there, almost still, shuffling forward. He looked like a buffalo. And all he had to do was stand there, glaring, coiled and waiting, like a big flying fortress hanging in the sky, armed to the back teeth. It was a weird thing, an exhibition of something, for sure, and if Joe Louis was the American bomber, the Navy guy was like a brace of Stukas or the gnat-like fury of ME 190s. Joe Louis wasn't striking back. He was just standing there, letting himself get hit, taking it but seeming to grow with each blow, getting angrier and angrier. The room was quiet. Joe was acting something, a part, the whole history of what a negro was supposed to be in America. And the Navy boxer – just in that flicker of a moment –was the might of the Luftwaffe, or white America itself taunting the black man, promising him everything and giving him nothing.

And then he'd shown enough of that, he'd shown enough of what he could take. He could take any shit Jim Crow wanted to throw at him because at the end of the day he was the strongest man in the world. And then he moved forward, glaring through his headlamps, the big brown American bomber, its power so obvious, bulging out of very bubble and nacelle but also hidden; and then decisively uncoiling, and he landed a couple of heavy punches. The first sent the blond bower staggering back across the ring, but he regained traction and came back at Joe like a wobbling fly, and the second short machine-like right-hand punch had put the Navy guy down flat on his fanny.

But then, of course, the Navy guy beat the count and got up again. Sparring around the ring, showing everything they had, their moves, and then it was more like they were buddies, two guys in the forces kidding around. Joe even did a little feint, a kind of shimmy. And everyone in that enormous hangar was as happy as they'd been in their life, relaxed, enraptured.

There wasn't a dry eye in the house. Guys were openly crying for home, for America, as it was and for what it would be later on. Until finally, Louis and the Navy guy broke it down and ambled there on the spot like a pair of kicking horses, and the referee, a sergeant they brought with them, held both their right hands in the air, and Joe Louis and the Navy guy put their hands around each other's shoulders, buddies now, waving to the wildly cheering crowd in the hangar, and they said goodbye, saluted and trotted out of the ring to the Sousa march, one after the other, like soldiers, Joe in the lead.

"So that was Joe Louis," Mitch said to Eileen later. "He was quite a thing, you know. You should've come, Eileen. You missed something there. I never saw anything like it."

It was a sunny morning in July and she was coming off her shift, getting into a jeep with Mitch for a drive out to Sidmouth. She'd slept most of the night anyway, so if she wasn't feeling on absolutely top form she thought it was harmless enough to drive down to the coast for the day. Anything to get away from the Dunk, even for a couple of hours. They set off straight away, both in uniform, and drove out there whizzing through the close winding lanes, rows of cottages jittering by, feeling like the most important people on the road: the only people apart from the drivers of a few tractors and horse-drawn carts and swift purposeful military vehicles, who would surely know they were playing hooky. Although who really cared?

Mitch parked the jeep in the empty carpark. They took their bags and walked out onto the seafront, nearly deserted and none too pretty. So she thought at first when she saw the wedges of scaffolding bolted together below the seawall along the whole length of the beach like some hideous modern sculpture of war. But then she turned at looked at the steep pathways of the garden that ran up from the left of the beach in a sort of reupholstered cliff and immediately she wanted to go up there, walk under it. She turned three-sixty degrees and saw that this really was a lovely little place. There was certainly nothing like it in Des Moines.

At the other end of the long sidewalk along the front she saw what looked like a party of land army girls, as brown as berries, larking about in their baggy pants and heavy sweaters. They were sure to batten onto a pair of lonely Americans, Eileen thought, so she and Mitch descended to the beach, where they could look away from the bolted fortifications. They walked from one end to the other, hopping over ancient groynes, Eileen carrying her shoes, and somewhere along there, as they walked silently, suddenly it seemed to have turned into some sort of date. At any rate, they were in it together.

About halfway along, by the time they'd scaled the central promontory of rocks, they really were in another mental place, as far away as you could be from everything once the spell of the crashing waves fell on them, a world of pools and pecking birds, their fuzzy young hesitantly finding their way after them, and beside the edge of the jagged outcrop she rolled off her stockings and paddled in the edge of the freezing, pulsing sea. Mitch was a way away looking for stones along the tideline. He stood behind her skimming them like a boy, looking past her, further out to the empty line of the horizon.

After she'd paddled, hopping in the freezing wavelets, they shared some good hot American coffee from Mitch's flask and for a moment they drew very close together, but in the event they both pulled back, carried on for another couple of hundred yards, savouring the edge of things, and then climbed up the beach, past the scaffolding and up onto the far end of the promenade. Eileen put on her shoes and they walked back along the breezy deserted seafront. Mitch wondered if there were any ice-cream parlours hereabouts but guessed not, this being England.

They passed a couple of decrepit-looking seafront hotels – one of them propped up with leftover scaffolding from the beach; it wasn't hard to imagine that good times had once been had in them. Eileen spotted the land army girls again. She fell back behind Mitch, feeling uncertain, embarrassed, as she always did in the presence of English women. Especially these land army girls. They seemed to have run wild, let themselves go, to be a law unto themselves. They had stopped being women in a way, although by all accounts she knew this wasn't the case.

Sometimes she found it hard to understand what they were saying, but they always seemed to let you know that you were in their country. To these people, they were strange creatures from the other side of the silver screen. They, in turn, gave her the heebie-jeebies. half-beings from behind the mirror of the past who just seemed to want to scratch your eyes out.

Mitch plunged in right away. "You girls know of any ice cream for sale in this town?" he asked.

"There's a little teashop along the lane on your next left," said the head girl in a surprisingly cut-glass accent.

"Not without a ration book you don't," said another, contributing what she knew, glancing around at her friends for approval.

"Don't be daft, Mary," another chipped in, and the rapid rubbing gesture she made with her fingers, coupled with the avidity on the girl's face, struck Eileen as obscene: a sign for money, the kind of gesture kids had made behind your back in Des Moines to show they knew you were a Jew who lived up on Nob Hill, which she didn't, and wasn't.

"Thanks very much, ladies," Mitch said. "You working around here?"

"Of course we are. Up to our rear-ends in shit."

"Mary! There's no need to spell it out for the gentleman."

Mitch looked as though he was about to blush bright scarlet. The land girls laughed, made as if to move on. Eileen smiled at them crookedly as she passed, and they smiled crookedly back. Not so bad then after all. Mitch darted ahead and led her to the door of the teashop, which was there, sure enough, looking dusty and lacy and half shut up, although the door was ajar. Eileen could well imagine the serving of stale scones, copious plum jam and runny acrid ice cream and poor Mitch counting bills out of his wallet. It seemed inevitable to her that Sidmouth would spoil everything one way or another, make them pay for their beautiful self-contained walk on the beach, and they hadn't even made it up to the pathways and gardens above on the cliffs. Never mind. Probably turn out to be just another vegetable patch.

"Let's leave it, Mitch. I have to get back; I'm bushed after all that excitement." She touched him gently on the shoulder. He turned, and she hugged him briefly, hard. "Thanks for bringing me."

They found the jeep and drove back more slowly, meandering, spinning it out for as long as they could manage. Mitch had grown reflective, he was rattling on and on to her. Making his sales pitch. Guys like me this, guys like me that. Eileen listened with half an ear, most of it blown away by the breeze or buried in the clatter of the Willys engine. She had pulled her jacket tight around her now, her uniform skirt held down over her stockinged knees. Guys like Mitch were great, she knew that, worth a dozen of the officer's club type. Mitch was strictly ground-crew and therefore one of the lucky ones for the time being. Until they needed them all to climb in the boats. Just somehow he was the kind of half-lucky, easy-going fellow it was hard to take seriously

He dropped her outside the ancient house, still dazed. Eileen pecked him on the cheek and used her own key to get in. Eileen realized she was well in time for dinner; she could even lie down for a while. She felt creakily tired and was sure she would manage to eat just about anything. On the hall table sat a telegram addressed to her. It was from her mother in Iowa. She tore it open. Her brother had died in the South Pacific three weeks earlier.

Eileen and her not much older brother Donald had never been very close. She forced herself to tell the Dunns about it over their evening meal. They had guessed from the telegram that something like it had happened. Mr. Dunn said he was so sorry. Mrs. Dunn squeezed her hand. Geoffrey hadn't left the table this time but stared at her dolefully and refused a second dose of stewed plums. Eileen managed to excuse herself and went upstairs to write to her mother. In her musty room a few tears came, then a lot of them, releasing a hopeless feeling that had been building all day, of being far from home, and knowing that she always would be.

She summoned up some backyard memories of Don, in all of which he showed her how much better he was than her, and a few more in which she had been shown how her parents had always favoured him. Everything had been for their handsome son, who had been athletic but also good in college, shown leadership qualities that had led him, the Army had told her parents, to sacrifice himself for his men in an assault on enemy positions. Before she went to sleep she managed to write a neat, dutiful letter to her mother in which she included a few sunnier childhood memories, and how he was the big brother she would always look up to.

Nobody up at Mudville knew about her loss, and she thought she would be able to get away with not telling anyone. She dropped her letter in the camp's mailbox and got on with the day. It was easy to feel numb. After all, it was what was expected of you as a nurse. Back in Des

Moines, crying when her brother pinched her salaciously, she had never known she would turn out to be such a callous little bitch.

The raids had been growing more intense, the shot-up fliers who limped home were patched up, the dead ones washed out of their gun emplacements; Joe Kennedy went missing, blown to smithereens in mid-air before bailing out of an experimental radio-controlled bomber packed with high explosives. Nobody cared any longer who was going to sit under the apple tree with whom. Eileen felt cut up about him, although he'd barely spoken to her. She hated her screwed up emotions and thought it better not to feel them in that case. Joe Kennedy? What was he to her? Fifty miles away, on Slapton Sands, German U-boats had sailed right in and shot up a bunch of GIs rehearsing the Normandy invasion and their bodies summarily buried in the Devon fields in unmarked graves. It was a deadly secret but they all knew it had happened.

The great lumbering planes took off and landed in Mudville, taxied and parked, and the ground crews serviced them. Sergeant Mitchell was in charge of a team of mechanics. They kept those babies in the air, changed their diapers. They were busy alright but Mitch kept an eye on Eileen, drifting by at the end of her shift, or of his when they were both finished and scrubbed up having been up to their respective elbows in blood and oil for hours.

Eileen would pass him a tight little smile, a haggard look. Once he managed to offer her a lift home as she was walking down towards the road, but she wouldn't get in the jeep. Mitch knew there was something wrong. Who would turn down a free ride with a harmless guy like himself? "What's the matter, Eileen? What did I do?"

She hadn't meant to tell him but suddenly she came out with it. Her brother's death. Her girlhood in Des Moines. How it was all gone and she knew she'd never get back there.

"It's not you, Mitch, or anything like that. I've just gone dead inside for now. I can't cope with people, any people. That's all. I've got plenty to do anyhow. We all have, haven't we?"

"Jeez, Eileen. I'm sorry. That's terrible. But you'll get back there, sure you will. Where else are you gonna go after the war?"

Poor Mitch, he took everything so literally. She smiled at him. She accepted his offer, got in the jeep and he ferried her down to the house but what she had said was true. She didn't have a thing to say to him, not a thing. He waved goodbye as he drove away and Eileen knew he wouldn't be bothering her again. It was one of the reasons she liked him, actually. He showed her respect, and at least he had some kind of horse sense. The Dunns were always waiting, always kind and a little distant. She'd grown used to that, even liked playing out their little mealtime rituals and listening to Mrs. Dunn's daily news of the carrots and runner beans and potatoes and the parsley she grew under the kitchen window to put on them.

She liked hearing about the vegetables and liked it too when Mr. Dunn sometimes talked of his role in the community down here in the Dunk. He knew a lot about the history of the Abbey (all she'd managed to pick up was that once it was an abbey and had monks living in it) and the lovely old schoolhouse and the families who had always lived here, and he sometimes told her things about the local dialect, used funny expressions from it, although thank goodness he didn't speak it all the time.

You wouldn't have thought there'd be a whole lot to organize here, but he always seemed to be organizing something, although she never quite found out exactly what it might be. Hush-hush. Probably just a drinking session of old buddies, she guessed. Once she'd picked up some news of a slide-show in the vestry of the church. Mr. Potts had shown them his collection of pre-war hand-tinted photographic plates of exotic houseplants from the Far East, and afterwards they had eaten a whole tub of his wife's mincemeat. It hadn't been a patch on Mrs. B.'s

Eileen didn't mind their unworldliness, their trivialities, partly because she was quite trivial herself given half-a-chance; but mainly because she found the atmosphere restful after the constant commotion of the base, partly because they had eventually told her all about Geoff's parents.

She'd been briefed – they all had, by those all-too-accurate, crummy movies made for US personnel in Britain – that certain kinds of English people were reticent compared to Americans, and that it didn't do to push them too hard. Never lift a Scotsman's kilt, that sort of thing. But a couple of weeks after her telegram from Iowa, Mrs. Dunn had spilled the rhubarb about why Geoff was living with them. He had lost his mother, or rather his mother had been lost to him – in an air raid on Croydon. His father, their son, was on escort duty around the Emerald Isle, the captain of a motor torpedo boat. "They're such flimsy things, MTBs," Mr. Dunn said. "Just a plywood hull with some sort of an American engine mounted in it, a Packard I believe." He had looked at some of them in Falmouth harbour, skimming across the horizon on sea trials. "You wouldn't catch me going out in one. That's what the chief mechanic said to me. So, you see, really we're extremely worried about him."

"I worry about him all the time," said Mrs. Dunn.

Geoff had been listening intently. Now he got up and quietly left the table.

"He hasn't been here for nearly a year," Mr. Dunn continued. "He says he has some sort of difficulty with Geoffrey. He says the boy reminds him too much of his mother. Of course, that's made things even trickier. Poor Geoff. I'm afraid our son may be in some sort of trouble. I know they do tend to drink a lot, pilots."

"They do," said Eileen. "I'll vouch for that."

After these revelations, the family greatly relaxed towards her, and she warmed to them. The four of them drew together under one roof; Eileen began to feel she was really a member of the household, writing her dutiful letters to her mother in Des Moines, seeing other Americans only up at the base, and then mainly when she was tending to their sky-inflicted wounds.

But when she was with these men she felt closer to them than anyone else in the world. They were all her brothers. Her relations with other nurses were cordial but a bit distant, always had been. Now she experienced a strange feeling of becoming less American, as if the most important connections in her life had become those she had formed where she lay her head; lying in the four-poster and breathing in the musty smell under fresh white cotton sheets, she found herself hoping that – one way or another – she would be able to stay in England for the rest of her life. Not here with the daffy Dunns of course, but somewhere else maybe. Somewhere she hadn't yet discovered. She didn't miss Iowa.

Mitch lay on his bunk in hut A46GR. He was thinking about Eileen. Who else? He wondered whether he could change his game plan a little, just adjust the stroke, tweak the jets. Maybe leave good old Sergeant Mitchell on the bleachers for once and try out that new guy, Willie the Weasel. But he'd racked his brains. Naw, he was crazy to think about her. He knew it already. He knew why he liked her and why she wasn't going to go for him. It was a selfish way of looking at the situation, but the situation brought that attitude out of you. He took the last Chesterfield from a pack, crumpled it, and threw it accurately into the bin. He lit up and inhaled deeply.

Eileen was classier than him, that was the trouble. He knew jack about Des Moines, but he knew that if they'd both been there, or even in his own hometown, she would never have looked at him twice. Whereas the English girls ... they liked Americans just for being American. We had something for them. Money. Sure. But something else. But it was different for American women. They seemed to keep to their own kind. He would like to do that too, given his druthers. You couldn't beat an American girl. They were home. Sweet as apple pie, for sure. When an American girl gave her heart, you knew she really gave it. But you never knew exactly what the English were after. It seemed to him you always had to try and out-guess them.

A lot of guys felt the same way. It would have been impossible for him not to know it. Those busy nurses out in Mudville must have been the most desired women in the world, but actually they were always just out of reach. The Navy liked it that way, which is why most of them weren't around much, which is why they were billeted off-base, and only came up for their duty rosters and social occasions, mostly in the officers' club. For their own protection from all those woman-hungry U.S.N. males. Reporting for duty, sir! Too bad these apes didn't know how to behave around girls.

Mitch rolled over on his side to extinguish his cigarette, lay on his elbow and gazed across the ground crew's quarters at the small window. It was sunny out there: a miracle. Eileen was right about one thing. They all had plenty to think about, and as the pressure mounted and the number of raids increased, pushing for victory everyone hoped, their need for any and every distraction had peaked into a sort of frenzy and then suddenly died away.

All leave cancelled. Life parked in the sky in its forever holding pattern. Just fucking airplane engines twenty-four hours of every day, and for the aircrews a near-nightly duel with the big man death. They were really hammering the Kraut cities now. Joe Kennedy gone. Who would believe it? A member of a blue chip American family giving his life to protect this dump. People had often said that he might be President one day.

When the Flying Fortresses came down after a raid, Mitch and his team and the other guys were all over them. Trying not to get burnt, listening to the pilot's instructions, the flight engineer. Anyone else who thought they'd spotted a problem. One of the port engines losing power, not running right. A nicked fuel-line. Ailerons shot out. A gun turret with a buddy splattered all over its shattered bubble; because when the guns were spitting it was like a lighthouse for ME fire. If the German planes were armed moths, the ground crew were worker bees: they crawled over every cell, painstakingly healing each one for the queen – a broken con-rod, a new set of pistons ready to go in, faulty wiring traced, sometimes a whole fresh loom fitted. Except in the case of Joe Kennedy's rigged PB4Y-1 Liberator; it was like somebody had taken the safety off a gun with a hair trigger and a full payload. Fortunately, it hadn't happened on Mitch's watch, but the guy who was supposed to have checked over the electrics on that baby – an experienced guy too, out of New Jersey – felt pretty sick right now. Just another grease monkey who fucked up.

Maybe that's all Mitch could ever be for Eileen: a grease monkey. He tried to remember if she had ever said anything about her brother. Nothing much. Just that he was in the Pacific someplace. Her big brother. Poor kid. He realized that's how she'd been treating him. Like a brother. She was his kid sister? Had they been close? It was hard to tell anything about Eileen's deeper feelings: she was so guarded, so secretive. That was what she'd been looking for from him, he thought. He'd known it somehow, played it that way. Maybe she still was but didn't know it. He rolled out of his bunk, walked over to the door, and went out to savour the sunshine, maybe try to rustle up a cup of joe before he had to go back to the hangar and strip down another eight 1200 hp Wright Cyclone GR-1820-65 radial engines from Hot Tamale and Sleepytime Gal.

Mitch was in luck. They had a fresh urn of hot on the go in the canteen. "Gimme a proper cup of coffee," he said amicably, "otherwise I'll just take tea."

2.

Eileen looked up at the covered statue of Diana above the shrouded fountain. She didn't know what it was, muffled up like that in camouflage tarpaulin and wide netting, although obviously a fountain of some kind. She walked on towards the American base at the far side of Bushey Park. She actually liked walking, had been doing a lot of it since her arrival at her new posting. She lived on the base, for now, in the nurse's quarters, but her duties were laughably light – band-aid anyone? – compared to what she had gotten used to. It was impossible to believe the war was over, more or less, also that she wouldn't have to go back to Des Moines – at least for a couple years.

She knew she had to put the recent past behind her. She seemed to be always trying to do that, first Des Moines, now the airfield, and the Dunns in their fusty little English world, especially Gerald Dunn. Geoff's father, when they'd finally met, had turned out to be quite a handful. It wasn't easy but she thought perhaps she was getting used to it. For several weeks she'd been wandering around the gardens of Hampton Court Palace, stripped of railings and ornament but open to the public, their wide, intensively tended beds bursting with forced-on blooms. She enjoyed looking down at the Thames, sitting beside the Long Water, although the maze hadn't tempted her. It reminded her of Mitch. The Tudor tennis court had been closed, like most of it, for the duration, but the palace was slowly re-emerging. Eileen had no doubt that the puck of Elizabethan tennis balls would be heard once again, propelled by long-haired people in doublets and hose. There would always be an England.

Ah well, at least you could get an ice cream down at the Jolly Boatman. Quite a lot of the guys from her new base went there, in fact: an old ice cream parlour, soda fountain type of a place that reminded them of home. Jeeps from the Base were often parked outside. Americans never went anywhere except in a jeep with the officer in the back and a sergeant riding shotgun beside the driver. Then they ordered double scoops of everything. This place seemed largely untouched by the war, as though it had just bobbed along with a few ducks floating on it, although there were a few jagged holes here and there. But compared to the total devastation shown on the newsreels, and the shot-up American flyers she'd nursed, it was like nothing important had happened to these people. She knew it would be the same in Des Moines, the calendar flipping over as usual month by month, factories opening or closing, the batting averages of the Cubs and the Oaks and the college football teams, births, marriages and deaths, a boring round of social occasions her mother would dream up until she had found her the right guy to marry.

It's said that anyone who didn't have something seriously wrong with them was having sex on VE day. Eileen was no exception. She finally had sex with Mitch Mitchell. It was in the medical hut, to which only she had the key. They had both been drunk of course, and she had to admit it was exciting to do it there on a narrow hospital bed with their clothes on. Afterwards, Mitch had broken down and cried and made her promise him the earth. All she could do after that was avoid him, stay down in the dunk, refuse to take phone calls, and ignore his circling jeep. He soon got the picture and moped off, but Eileen had felt bad about it, as though she had done something bad to him, or him to her, as if some sort of apology was in order. She would have liked to explain but it seemed better to say nothing. It was her way, around guys who were too interested in her.

The Base was a large compound surrounded by high walls and barbed wire. It covered a considerable area, although nothing like as large as Mudville with its multiple runways and hangars. Eileen reached the gate and the long white pole swung up and the pole operator stood to attention and saluted. She walked straight through without acknowledging him, her bearing instantly more military as she crossed the immaculate raked parade ground to the camp hospital. It was considerably newer and bigger than the corrugated hut she'd left behind, breeze-block built and full of new and little-used equipment.

Eileen oversaw its day-to-day running. Her experience – combat experience they called it – had swung her posting right at the last moment. They knew she had what it took to lick a team of civilian nurses into shape as most of the American girls had fled back across the Atlantic in search of their sweethearts, or something like that. Eileen was clearly committed to a career in military nursing, and she desperately wanted to stay on in Blighty. She had presented herself as a fierce, hard-bitten character. Her references had been top-notch, impossible to fault. She would be working for the Marines and the Marines did everything by the book. On the other hand, there wasn't a whole lot for them to do except endless precision drills in their white dress uniforms and shiny helmets. Face it, this was one easy posting.

Trained nursing staff were easy to come by, particularly as the Americans paid better wages than any British hospital or private client. Most were local women, two were Irish. Eileen had trouble understanding any of them at first, even after all her years in Devon, but soon discovered that informality wasn't appreciated, so she cracked the whip over them somewhat (you're working for the US Marines now!) and they soon started to shape up. Everything in the hospital building was new and sparkling. The nurses' duties of care included making sure it stayed that way: twenty beds in two wards, gurneys, screens, a fully-equipped operating theatre, and some equipment that hadn't even been unpacked. The floor was a burnished skating rink from which any spillages or rubber marks caused by swivelling shoes were removed as soon as they occurred by a nurse on her hands and knees.

Eileen found the nurses were competent, and well-trained, although she hadn't anything to do with employing them; but some of the American patients had had trouble taking them seriously. Of the twenty beds, only three were currently occupied. Sergeant Beynon was flat on his back, his leg in traction. Private Weisz had sustained burns and shrapnel wounds from an exploding flare on the Base. They'd tried to send it up on November 5th as the US contribution to Guy Fawkes night. Weisz was on the mend, but his torso was still bound up in dressings that had to be changed regularly. Lieutenant Wallace had been offered his own room but preferred to hang out with the guys on the ward. Mooching around in his dressing gown and playing cards with the guys. Beynon and Weisz liked playing cards with the Lieutenant, a languid, haggard man who had been given three months to live and spent a few hours a day inside some new machine that was supposed to help him. They gathered around Beynon's bed, playing poker for small change. After three years in the country, Weisz still referred to threepenny bits and silver joeys as nickels and dimes, but the others patiently helped him figure it out. There would have been no enjoyment in mocking him as they might have out on the Base. In fact, they would never have met, except in hospital.

Eileen was popular, as she always had been – after five years she had the touch, although nowadays her team of Brits did most of the actual touching. They had soon got to like her too, especially the younger nurses, who as always wanted to know about the USA. When she told them about Des Moines they wanted to know if there were cowboys there. She told them not many, not any longer, but there had been a lot of factories, which had all closed down in the Great Depression. Not everyone was poor though – it was just a dull, boring place and she didn't want to go back there too soon. She admitted to preferring England to her part of America, and after that, they liked her more. The two Irish girls didn't want to go home either, for much the same reasons.

At the end of her shift, she went back to the nurses' quarters. She lay on her bed – her flat was self-contained and had its own shower and small cooker – thinking about Dunkeswell and smoking a few Luckies. Gerald Dunn came to mind, as he did so often. He had been there one morning when she got up and went down to breakfast. He was on leave and had motored down the night before to see his son before the 'big show' started. A tall, slender man, striking in his naval uniform, he had looked up at her from under a mop of dark hair, streaked with grey, and smiled rakishly. He and Geoffrey had been racing one another through boiled eggs and soldiers. The boy was obviously awestruck by his father, who despite his long absence had won him over in about five seconds flat. Eileen could see why. He looked a little like Ronald Colman, she thought, the English actor she had always liked best. *The Prisoner of Zenda* had made it to Des Moines, and foolish as it now seemed her heart had lurched at the sight of him.

How childish it had all been! Eileen put out her cigarette in self-contempt. Mitch would have been a better bet than that bastard. Still, how could she have known? It was all still churning around in her pretty head, as he'd called it, and if she was being honest she'd known from the start how it would be and what sort of man he was, exactly. Oh dear, oh dearie me, as her grandmother used to say.

"Sergeant Platt," he'd said, offering a lazy American-style salute in mock deference. "I'm Gerald, the absent father." He had been embarrassed then, turning back to the boy and his half-eaten egg.

Eileen was smiling down at him. "Pleased to meet you at last. You've been missed." Then it had been her turn to be embarrassed.

"Don't mind me, I'm just parachuting in for a few days," he said, "my parents have been telling me all about you – it's been a real help to them having you here." He looked serious, then smiled again. "If Geoffrey likes you, I like you."

"Me and Geoff get along very well," she'd said. "Don't we Geoff?"

"Sure."

Eileen sighed, remembering it all on her bunk in Bushey Park. At first she hadn't seen much of him. The Navy had lent him a car and he had taken Geoff down to Sidmouth in it. They had wanted her to go with them, but that was impossible. Anyway, she'd already seen Sidmouth.

It was strange to think of a boy and his father on a pleasure jaunt as American bombers droned thickly overhead night and day on their last great killing spree. It had seemed strange to all of them, the sky was black with aircraft and underneath the optimism of having the Axis on the run, a feeling of dread and desperation seemed to hang over everyone. Could it be true? Gerald behaved as though it was, he was determined to celebrate in advance, to make up for lost time with a boy he might never see again. He was overwrought, that was for sure. And Eileen, coming in and out of the house, exhausted from her rotating shifts, seeing him perhaps for a few minutes or half an hour at mealtimes, quickly become overwrought herself.

How long had the whole thing lasted? Five days? On the third day, he had whispered to her after Mr. and Mrs. Dunn and Geoffrey had retired from the dining table. "Do you mind if I show you something you might be interested in?"

"I'm sure I'd be absolutely fascinated," she'd replied, or something like that.

"It's in the garage," he said. "Very hush-hush."

"You're sure you haven't got a bomb out there?"

She had followed him outside. There were still a few hours of daylight left and the garden looked very fetching in the late afternoon light. A funnel of midges was revolving slowly under a cherry tree, bees were buzzing languidly around the small white blooms on the rows of propped up pea plants and the gnarled branches of ancient fruit trees were immobile while their leaves rustled faintly in a breeze that was no more than warm air falling back into the dip of old dunk. But first, he had gone to the trunk of the Navy car, unlocked it, and taken out a jerrycan of what he called juice which he had brought up from Falmouth. Nobody was going to miss it. He led her to the garage, semi-derelict, half-collapsed under ivy – she had seen it but thought it was an annex of the potting shed – opened the rotting door and revealed a small English sports car. A Riley, he said, which looked to be in remarkably good repair for something that had been garaged for the duration. He'd said something Mitch-like about how there was going to be plenty of work for mechanics after the war replacing the perished rubber hoses on cars and cleaning engines clogged with jellied petrol, but Gerald had thoroughly flushed out the Riley in 1940 and set his father to watch over the car until he could get back. Eileen hadn't noticed him doing so. However, she said nothing as his son poured in the gas through an old funnel he found on a shelf, opened and smelled a can of oil and poured that in too after checking the dipstick under the hood. It was the pungent, already burning smell of that oil which had done her in, or did they say undone her.

She'd stood there silently, barely breathing as she watched Gerald Dunn work on the dark, gleaming little automobile. He had stood up.

Wiped his hands carefully on a rag. When she still didn't say anything he asked, "Well?" She remained silent, stood perfectly immobile against the bench, and then he had come towards her. He was all over her in a second, and she was willing it all to happen right then, and it did.

Afterwards she had sat in the driver's seat of the Riley while Gerald started it with a handle – quite easily, she remembered, and how they had both been unsurprised, and then Gerald got behind the wheel as she clung to him and they inched out of the garage to race around the lanes of Devon in the last hours before nightfall. They had both been as high as kites already, but Gerald produced a flask from his jacket pocket, took a pull on it and passed it over to her and she had done the same. They'd pulled out of Dunkeswell the back way, longer but straighter, roaring and making a hell of a racket as they plummeted between dense overhanging woods on a winding upwards gradient, past hidden houses even grander and more secluded than the one they'd left behind.

"Know who lives there?" Gerald shrieked above the Riley's engine. "A fascist writer! An Irish fascist writer! Do you think he cares how many people the Krauts have killed?" She just about caught what he was saying, then she saw tears were streaming from his eyes. Gerald Dunn, whose wife had been killed in an air raid, who might well die himself on D-Day in his plywood MTB, was laughing his beautiful head off.

Up out of the woods and onto the Taunton road they'd turned left and after a short while, with Gerald changing down and opening her up, they'd skirted the edge of the airfield, and Eileen had looked across at the hangars and the darkening bulky shapes of the Liberators and Fortresses, airborne tin cans the fliers called them, that were all we had to try and stop it, death machines to put an end to death. Beyond the edge of the huge American camp they'd turned left again and dropped, almost in freefall, down through a long series of zig-zag hairpins with mopping trees, until Gerald had stopped the car abruptly and they drank the contents of his flask and made love again, more slowly this time, more awkwardly in the front of the car, and it had seemed to her – and she'd thought to him – that this was the kind of thing that might, just might, bind two people together for all of the time they had left on earth.

For a while they sat together holding one another, then they'd put themselves together and Gerald drove on a bit further, into Wellington, but the light was fading fast by now so they didn't stop, just turned around and headed back to the house, meeting nobody and nothing on the shadowed empty roads, and showing no light. When they got there he had neatly returned the Riley to its dilapidated quarters. "That warmed the old girl up a bit," he said unnervingly, and they had kissed in the hall and parted to sleep in their own beds.

Eileen had gotten up early next morning – no-one else was awake – and walked up to the airfield to go on duty. She had been unable to sleep but had poured plenty of American coffee down her throat to get through the shift. She remembered Mitch had been there, had spoken to her. She'd managed to shrug him off. She didn't know how she did it – just grit and sleepwalking – but the heavy shift had passed without accidents. Gerald hadn't been there when she got home. He'd taken Geoff out in the Riley and they didn't get back until after she was asleep. On the fifth day, she'd seen him again at dinner, which was frustrating to say the least. Obviously, they hadn't been able to speak. She'd kept her head low over tasty English meatloaf and managed to escape soon afterward. Later that night, Gerald had come into her bed stealthily. They lay there all night, made love, talked quietly about all sorts of dumb stuff, and she'd fallen asleep in his arms and woken to find him gone, gone away, back to Falmouth. She hadn't seen or heard from him since. Bastard. Eileen had never given herself like that to anyone and she vowed once more that she never would. Mitch, she didn't really count. She turned into the pillow of her single bed in the nurses' quarters, and muffled her sobs.

Not long after her encounter with Gerald, the Normandy landings started, and she and the Dunns waited every day to hear that he was dead. Americans were still dying. So was everyone else, civilians and military. It was horrible that so many people were still dying – it seemed to rise into a sort of frenzy – but by that time they had all just come to accept it. *He died because I loved him.* A crappy line from a crappy British movie kept nagging at her. Then a call to his parents. He was alive but couldn't get away. Italy had fallen. Then Paris. Then it was all over in Europe. Then the Enola Grey had dropped a couple of Atom bombs on Japan and that was all over too. Everything was over. Everything she had known through most of her adult life.

Bushey Park was a sunny place most of the time. It wasn't all bad, hell no. Sun shone, rain fell. She had gotten to know some new people, wandered in the gardens of a real palace and got to know the nearby town of Kingston-upon-Thames, which was no bigger than

Des Moines, smaller in fact, probably not much more exciting, but she enjoyed wandering amongst the Saturday crowds.

It felt like it was slowly coming back to life. People were waiting for things that had been unavailable during the war to reappear in the shops. Eileen felt she should be coming back to life too, and perhaps she was in a way. She certainly told herself it was so. Sometimes she went to one of the pubs along the river with a few people from the Base, but mostly it was her fellow Americans she saw; the English – who had once seemed so strange and exciting – revealed themselves as dull and standoffish and without a great deal of curiosity.

Sometimes, on Kingston market, men would approach her and tried to sell her things. Cheap nylons or underwear. But, if she said anything to them, it was simply no thanks. The river was beautiful, much more deep, compact and attractive-looking than the Des Moines River, or the Raccoon River, which crossed the prairies and, in the past, had sometimes risen up and swept away large tracts of her native city.

Occasionally, she sat there and wrote letters to her mother, but the replies were always similar. Pop was doing this and that and when was she coming home. She didn't miss it, not at all. Instead, she sat on a particular bench along a towpath beside the Thames and watched the coal barges, rowboats, and bus-like double-decker passenger boats. The people of Kingston, it seemed to her, were growing giddy and taking to the water in droves on a gentle lapping flow of forgetfulness. Why not? Let it all wash away, up through the great city of London and out to sea.

Mitch wrote to her sometimes, but she never replied. There were plenty of Mitches, she thought rather cruelly. Plenty of guys on this new base who wanted to run her around in a jeep and take her to secluded places. Sometimes she went, other times she didn't. She knew she was selfish – but she enjoyed reading his news. Not much to report – Mudville was being dismantled and would soon be handed back to the lucky RAF. Mitch would shortly be heading back to Ohio. He would always remember her and the times they spent together. Sure, so would Eileen. She would remember exactly what she wanted to remember, that was about the size of it, as far as it would ever go.

After about a year in Bushey Park, Eileen began to feel like a prisoner at the Base. The covers had been taken off the Diana fountain, water squirting only feebly from its lead orifices. The corpulent woman rose up splendidly enough, but around her the whole thing looked dirty, chipped, in need of attention. She was trapped here in this bogus place and she knew she wasn't getting any younger.

Her mother had given up on trying to persuade her to come home; instead, she nagged her daughter about her men friends or lack of them. An old maid! It was starting to feel true to her. Twenty-six years old and without a husband or babies of her own. Sometimes she went out with the guys who worked on the Stars and Stripes, but she could tell that her attractiveness to men her own age or older was fading fast. Good old Eileen, fine for a night in the pub, maybe a tumble (if you were lucky!) but just a little too stiff and serious, and kind of stuck up. She always seemed distracted in the company of American soldiers, as if she was looking out for something better.

In the *Stars and Stripes* office men who had never grown up fawned over their young English secretaries, churning out bland, flag-waving stories for the troops in Germany, often illustrated by photos of pretty girls who worked right there on the Base. But although they'd sent a photographer round to snap Sergeant Platt in her nurse's uniform, and it had been duly printed, she herself hadn't been quite satisfied with the result.

Around that time an unexpected letter arrived from Dunkeswell. They missed her! That was damned nice of them. Mrs. Dunn's handwriting looked like it had been done with a quill pen. Nothing could have been nicer. They were all doing fine. Mr. Dunn was spending more time in the garden (as usual) and Geoffrey was growing up fast. They wondered if – they knew it would be too boring for her – if she wouldn't like to visit them soon, before they all lost touch. They had liked her enormously. If so, they would be delighted to see her sometime in the first couple of weeks in June. It would be a real treat for them.

Strangely, there was no mention of Gerald. She wondered if this was some kind of tactful omission on Mrs. Dunn's part or if she'd simply forgotten to mention her son. Perhaps it had slipped her mind that they'd met, that might be why, but it definitely implied that he wasn't around.

She had misgivings but she really had come to love the Dunns. She thought it had been that eccentric couple who had made her want to stay on in England, way before mad Gerald had barged in on the scene. She would go, dammit. It would be great to see the dear old Dunns again, maybe lay a few ghosts. She replied straight away and arranged to go down on the first weekend in June when she had some liberty due.

When the day arrived she simply got the Hampton Court train up to Waterloo and changed for Honiton via Salisbury. The journey seemed interminable, far longer than it had during the war, although she could think of no particularly good reason why except that on her rare trips up to London she had never been in any hurry at all to get back to Mudville, and so the journey had passed quickly. When she did get into Honiton she reached through, opened the door of her compartment and stepped down onto the platform with her weekend bag. There at the far end by the white gate stood Gerald Dunn – and Geoffrey, his gangling son.

Geoff seemed to have grown about a foot taller. He was kicking at the ground awkwardly: some things never changed. Gerard was tall and hollow-cheeked, as ever, but it looked as if D-Day had snowed on his hair. As the train clattered on towards Exeter, her heart started to do the same. She had been cornered by the duplicitous Dunns. She walked slowly towards them. "Geoff," she exclaimed a bit hysterically. "How you've grown!" She put down her case, pecked the boy on the cheek, extended a gloved hand to his father. "Gerald, Gerald."

"Good to see you, Eileen," Gerald simply said. He led them round to the battered car. Geoffrey got in the backseat with her weekend case. Gerald drove in silence as they sped back to the house for tea.

Nothing had changed – it was an odd thought, given that she'd only been away for just over a year, but as the car rose into the Blackdown Hills, then plunged down into the fairy glade of Dunkeswell and dipped right into the short drive of Dunns End, the whole magical scene of the Elizabethan house and its garden seemed to explode upon her in all its shady beauty, enclosing her in a spell she couldn't resist. Not this time, brother! she thought. But the Dunns were welcoming, the table laid for tea with scones and jam made with the admirable assistance of Mrs. B., and tea hot from the spout in their best blue bone china, each delicate cup of which had a slender band of gold laid around the rim. Milk and clotted cream too. Soon it was as though she'd never been away, and she managed to avoid looking at Gerald throughout the whole performance as the Dunns chattered away about life in the village and how the airfield looked bleak now they'd all gone away, as a plain of mud, and the poor old RAF apparently didn't know quite what to do with it.

Rather a lot had been going on locally, according to Mr. Dunn. The series of talks he helped to organize in the village hall had resumed with vigour; more blooms were becoming available by the day. A funny old

Irishman who lived down the lane had produced a bale of black wool in the form of a novel about the American servicemen at Dunkeswell. He'd published it himself but it had been the most unreadable rubbish, downright offensive, so most of the church committee had thought.

Mr. Dunn was such a dear old man in his floppy gardening hat and worn corduroy pants, but in the eighteen months or so since the war had ended he had aged further. Gerald too was … not exactly ancient, but sat stiffly silent at the tea table, and bore himself with a quiet dignity she did not recall having seen in him earlier.

After tea they brought out some old family photographs in a leather-bound album and showed them to her, thinking rightly that as an American who had spent so long in this country now, she would probably be interested. Eileen flipped through them dutifully, lifting up each page's covering of grey tissue paper while Mrs. Dunn sat beside her and offered a running commentary. The photos were small, with deckled edges, and each page seemed to reveal another dimension of their connectedness to the past as streams of relations in hooped skirts and high collars appeared were identified and folded away. One of the photos was of a boy in what looked like a strange old priest's cassock and a square squashed cap.

"Who's that?" she asked guardedly.

"That's Gerald at his school," Mrs. Dunn replied.

Eileen glanced towards him, quietly said ah yes, she could see a likeness now.

After the photos were put away they drank a little brandy and toasted Anglo-American friendship. "We could never have done it without you," said Mr. Dunn, to which his son added a quiet hear-hear and to her surprise Eileen found herself becoming suddenly heavy-lidded, maybe from the drink or the country air. All what? she wondered, and following a round of goodnights, plump Mrs. B. ceremoniously showed her up to her old room, which, she pointed out, she had freshly aired that afternoon. Eileen was both exhausted and relieved. She put down her weekend bag, determinedly turned the large open key in the lock and flopped lifelessly into bed.

She woke up in the familiar fresh-musty smell of clean-but-old bedding but instantly realized she was back in her bed on the Base. Worse, she'd been dreaming about Gerald. She turned off the clattering alarm clock and forced herself to get up. A jumbled series of images: things that hadn't happened, some that had. In the end, he had been walking away from her down a long corridor in that strange priest get up, and she was flat on her back with her uniform skirt hiked up, waiting for some sort of internal examination.

Stupid! Her weekend at the Dunns' had been some weeks ago now. Although the situation between her and Gerald had changed quite a lot at that time, she was distressed to have it forced upon her that he was still a figure of distorted fantasy and mystery in her subconscious mind. She shook the dream away and began to dress for work. One thing that had happened during her visit to the Dunns – right from the beginning really – was her realization that she had indeed, in the year since she left Devon, changed quite a lot.

The spell had definitely been broken and being confronted with the place again as she had brought that home to her. When she'd returned from that weekend, it was to discover that the Lieutenant had died in her absence. Lieutenant Wallace. The rest of the card school – Weisz and Beynon – had long before recovered and been discharged, but their sad Lieutenant had stayed on to continue his treatment, had tried to make friends with other patients, and slipped away on Saturday night.

The kidney machine had kept him alive, but he was growing weaker instead of stronger. Finally, he had decided of his own accord that he had had enough. There just wasn't anything left for him to keep on living for. She had returned to find her British civilian nurses in tears. Some of them had grown to love him in a way, and Eileen had been forced into a position of trying to cheer them up, stressing the importance of professionalism, carrying on. Their sentimentality annoyed her.

It had been a strain, but this had pulled her away from Dunkeswell and Gerald Dunn and all that, reinforced her feeling that she was a different person now, no longer the girl who had lodged with them when all hell had been breaking loose. She told herself she had better take her own feelings with a grain of salt too if she was going to move on and live her life in a sensible way.

She brushed out her hair, applied layers of make-up, headed out and walked diagonally across the parade ground to the hospital building. Nothing particularly challenging awaited her. The four current inmates were eating their breakfast. At the back of the building, duty nurses were bustling around, getting ready for the doctor's visit, and for her.

One or two of them said "Good morning, sister" and she plunged straight into the business of the day.

What had really happened at Dunns End? Eileen had simply got up in the morning to be told they were all going out on a family picnic. She had put on a pair of slacks and they set off at ten in the black English saloon in which Gerald had picked her up from the station, with a hamper in the trunk.

Mr. Dunn had driven, Mrs. Dunn beside him, Eileen and Gerald in the back, separated by Geoffrey, whose behaviour seemed distinctly awkward. Mr. Dunn marvelled at how much room there was in the car – it was black, a new family model – and Mrs. Dunn turned around to chat as they went along. Mr. Dunn was a surprisingly good driver, as smooth as the English car would permit, displaying none of the demonic characteristics of his son at the wheel of that flivver of his. Eileen asked if they wouldn't mind her opening her window a fraction, and when they said of course, she sat in her corner looking out at the high reeling hedges, glimpses of fields. It had been quite a long drive, to a little cove on the coast none of the Americans, at least those stationed at Dunkeswell, had ever discovered.

Abruptly, they turned right along a narrow lane and soon came out on a dappled hillside on a road that led in a series of lazy zig-zags down to a wide secluded bay. There was an old pub tucked in at one edge and the other rose straight up in cliffs from the pale sandy beach, a white thread of path climbing through stiles across their highest point. Mr. Dunn parked the Standard Eight. Eileen thought it was the most beautiful place she had ever seen and said so loudly. Mr. and Mrs. Dunn seemed pleased.

They got the hamper out of the trunk; and a soccer ball, with which Gerald and his son scampered off to the beach, like a couple of small boys. Mrs. Dunn spread out a tartan blanket on the edge of the deserted beach and they sat down to look out at the sea.

Mr. Dunn asked her how her new posting down at Hampton Court was getting along. "I know that part of the world," he said. "But from a long time ago. Before we were married. I may have chased a few young ladies around that maze, I can't remember."

"Don't be ridiculous, Ernest." Mrs. Dunn turned to Eileen. "We thought you were very brave, Eileen. All you Americans. But you especially. You helped us a great deal. More than you could know."

On the beach, Geoff and Gerard were kicking the ball back and forth between them in great curving arcs against the breeze, running to retrieve it and carrying on mindlessly, as if for her benefit.

"You know, to be honest, seeing the way you coped with your duties up there, never a complaint, and all those badly injured men to cope with, made me think that American women must have something we don't."

"Hey, that's just not true," Eileen laughed delightedly. "We've got some great British nurses working at the Base. Some of them worked in London hospitals during the blitz. There's a couple of Irish nurses who... "

"I don't suppose you've heard of Florence Nightingale?"

An actress maybe?

"The lady with the lamp," Mr. Dunn chipped in helpfully.

"Just a nurse we were always told about. A girls' heroine. In the Crimean war."

"Oh, we had a whole bunch of them," Eileen said. "Clara Louise Maass. She was all over the place, in the Philippines, the Spanish American War. She died nursing yellow fever."

She had been told about this woman in nursing college in Des Moines, and her name just popped out. At the time she had seemed like a sickeningly pious, self-sacrificing character, impossible to connect with her own life. But she had been a career nurse. Eileen didn't like the idea that she had turned into such a person.

Thankfully, they let the subject drop. By and by, Mrs Dunn opened the hamper and they each ate one of the small sandwiches that had been prepared, took a scone, and sipped hot tea which Mr. Dunn poured from a flask into thick china mugs. Geoff and Gerard picked up their ball and came over for refreshments. They sat around quietly, looking out towards the brightness and the sea. Eileen felt easy and relaxed, she felt what she had wanted to feel, like she was a relation of theirs, part of the family.

Soon she stood up and herself broke away from them, picking her way down to the sea. Halfway down the beach she kicked off her flat shoes and pulled off her socks and paddled at the very edge of the soft, lapping waves. And, in a while, Gerard walked down beside her and stood there skimming stones as Mitch had on their illicit jaunt to Sidmouth. She had felt more comfortable with Mitch, she thought suddenly. He was more of a gentleman than Gerald Dunn ever would be, perhaps one of nature's gentlemen as she had once heard somebody say, whatever it meant. She looked down at the water dribbling over her sandy painted toes. Maybe Gerald had thought she was some kind of prostitute, she thought.

"I really wanted to get in touch with you," Gerald said. "I missed you like crazy after that weekend. It frightened me."

Eileen hadn't wanted to hear his excuses. She turned away and walked along the margins of the sea, picking her way over ribbons of strewn kelp.

"Look out for jellyfish," Gerald called after her. "Don't get stung!"

"Don't worry," she called back. "I won't get stung twice."

He came up beside her. "So, you missed me too."

"Of course I did," Eileen said. "Until I realized you were a heel."

"Eileen," he said. "Can't we try again? In a different way?"

Something about the pleading in his voice almost convinced her. They stood facing one another. But she didn't want to touch or be touched, not with the family doubtless taking it all in from their blanket. They walked back slowly side by side, saying nothing, and as they did one or two things dropped into place for Eileen. It made sense after all that this tall, gangly Englishman with greying hair would want her. He was a widower, and like her, a veteran. She already knew he meant a lot to her, but the reason for that clicked into place as well. Didn't seem so crazy, seemed to fit together. Might even be the reason she had stayed in England, why she had hung on.

She could see why he might want a young American wife. They were both quite lonely people, she realized. Both had been sort of backed into the same corner whether they knew it or not. As for the Dunns, she suspected they knew very well what they had been doing when they'd asked her down here without mentioning his name. She peeled away from Gerald's side to pick up her shoes and socks from where she'd left them, leaving him to wander back alone and sit down beside his parents and his son.

As the day wore on the weather became a little unsettled, a few clouds blew over and the sun was quite pleasantly intermittent – two or three further cars arrived. Another family stationed themselves next-door, nodded and set up camp; a couple of small children were tottering and darting forward at the shoreline, three hikers strung out along the white path over the cliffs. They eased back, basking like the dogs they were and talking about nothing. Some pieces of chicken appeared and were gobbled up, a bottle of soda. After they'd finished everything in the hamper, they packed up and wandered over towards the pub, which was looking livelier than it had done, open anyway.

There wasn't to be another chance to talk to Gerald. He seemed quiet with his parents, but once they were lined up on a bench outside with their drinks, the conversation picked up. Eileen felt she was understanding something new about family life, that it was a sort of performance they seemed to want you to admire them for. That's how the Dunns were – putting on a show in which the parts seemed only intelligible for them.

They always expected her to find her way into their world, she thought. It was all they knew, so in a way they had no choice, they were left vulnerable; on the other hand, they were genuinely offering themselves. What else did they have to give her but who they really were? And why wouldn't you want to join in the game? At the same time, she felt insubstantial when she was with them, as if she didn't really exist for them, and they, in turn, seemed to melt away into nothing the more layers of themselves they stripped away in the cause of this friendship.

Eileen turned her attention to Geoffrey, remembering their old conversations over the dinner table. "I'll bet you know every country in the world by now – eh Geoff?"

"I know about every state in the union," the boy replied in a voice broken and well-modulated. "I hope to go to America one of these days."

"Well, you're welcome to Des Moines," Eileen said. "We have a saying there – Iowa a quarter."

"What's a quarter?" the boy asked.

"Half of fifty cents."

"It can't be that bad," Gerald smiled. "After all, they produced you."

"They have huge farms," Geoff informed her. "And before that cowboys and indians."

"Des Moines is a city," she said. "It has more than farms – they had mines, factories, then the Great Depression. They moved the Indians out a long time ago. Not long after the French. Iowa used to be part of Louisiana."

The old man nodded sagely.

"I'm sure you must miss it really," Mrs. Dunn said.

"No, ma'am," said Eileen in a non-native accent. "I don't."

But she didn't want to talk about home. It had been so long since she saw the Des Moines river. She felt like this was her home now, although it obviously wasn't so. Since shipping abroad she'd met Americans from all over the States, and many of them had gone blank when she mentioned Des Moines, Iowa.

"Your father works in a bank, doesn't he?" Mr. Dunn ventured "Or have I misremembered?"

"Not exactly. He's a land agent."

Nobody was exactly sure what that was. Eileen was forced to give a brief explanation. He sold land on behalf of whoever owned it. As before she tried to give them the impression her family was a cut above the average, which was true. But it was her father she most didn't want to talk about. She had recently received a letter from her mother to say that Pops was ill in hospital. Sounded bad. But she was damned if she wanted to go back there for the funeral when it came. They would never let her out again. She had written to them telling her news, such as it was. Pops had written back a note in her mother's reply saying she would always be his baby girl. Also, that they were both proud of her.

She thought of them in that house, the house they had bought to raise her and Donald. Before long, her mother would be completely alone there. Eileen felt terrible about it. Her father's death and the weight it would place on her was speeding towards her like a bullet she wouldn't be able to dodge. Instead, she raised her glass to the Dunns. They were nothing like her family. She thought her own mother must be the loneliest woman in the world, but the idea of being near her, sharing her fate, knotted up her insides. Her fear about Gerald, she realized, was that he might turn out to be a man like her father. They said you were attracted to your father – God forbid. They also said you could tell the English anything you liked about America and they would believe it, but she herself had never had the urge to spill any of those particular beans.

As if sensing her reserve, feeling his ground, Gerald asked if she'd got to know any of the countryside around where she was stationed presently.

"Not really," Eileen said. "Only the park, and the grounds of the palace. Beautiful places. Oh, and Kingston-upon-Thames. That's an interesting little town."

Geoffrey said that he had read that it rained a lot in Iowa and it was also incredibly hot there.

"That's about the size of it, Geoffrey my boy. Really cold too in the wintertime. It's a land of extremes – extremes of frusration."

From looking at school maps, Geoff had gathered that Americans had a huge continent to roam around in wherever they wished. He couldn't understand how anyone could possibly get bored there. Wide-open spaces appealed to somebody who had grown up in a hole in the ground. Being without tact he bombarded her with questions all the way as they drove slowly back to Dunns End. Gerald didn't intervene but leaned into his own corner of the backseat, so he could enjoy her evasive replies to his son's interrogations. Eileen could see his father in his face, which had cleared up nicely. Why couldn't she have still had a nice cute little brother?

Apparently, he had done quite well at school in Exeter but had decided not to go on. In a couple of months, he would be starting work, as an apprentice to a law firm in the town, where he was supposed to work his way up. Dull work for such a lively kid, she thought. She wondered how come he hadn't been sent to the same school as his father, which she had gathered was one of the oldest in the country. They made the boys wear skirts. Well, but she supposed his grandparents had known what they were doing. Gerald's war seemed to have been one long lost weekend. She wondered what he was going to do with himself now it was over. She didn't ask. It was a question she was still asking herself and couldn't answer.

The following day they lazed around the garden in the morning. Gerald tinkered with his beloved Riley in the old garage, but this time Eileen didn't follow him inside. They ate a good roast lunch prepared mostly by Mrs. Bailey, and then it was time for their guest to depart. She kissed them all goodbye. "Come again!" said Mr. Dunn. "It's been delightful my dear, completely a pleasure."

Gerald had driven her down to the station to get the 3.15 train to Paddington – in the Riley. It was strange to be sitting again in the small front seat of the tiny rattletrap with this tall man beside her. It brought back memories, quite intoxicating ones, as Gerald had no doubt hoped it would.

He pulled up outside the station, put the handbrake on and as the clattering of the engine died way, leapt from his seat, went around and opened her door, and handed over her neatly repacked weekend bag. It was then, with the train due in a few minutes, that he made his big pitch.

"Eileen," he said. "I know I've been a complete fool – probably always will be."

"I'll not argue with you there," she said.

"But look. I want you to come on holiday with me. A river trip, down near where you are at Hampton Court. There's a place I want to show you – near here I went to school – I know you'll love it. And ... if it doesn't come to anything, no problem. No strings. Just a few days on the river with yours truly, to see how it goes. Maybe in a month or so, or whenever your next leave is."

"You have a boat?"

"I can get one – I'll show you the most beautiful spot you'll ever see in your life."

Eileen looked at him sternly. "I'll think about it, Gerald."

"Think about it? What's to think about?"

"Okay," she said impulsively. "Gerald Dunn, you're on."

They were standing on the platform by now. She extended her hand to shake his, but then by mutual assent they embraced and then clung to one another tightly, too tightly, until the train rolled in bang on time and she got on, and shakily took her seat in an empty compartment with tears welling into her eyes. Feeling like every kind of fool herself, but incredibly, ridiculously happy all the same, as if a giant ice floe that had been stuck in her heart was calving, dropping away in huge chunks, sliding shelves of ice, Devon cliffs falling into the sea.

The main business of the day on which Eileen had awoken from her disturbing dream about Gerald Dunn, turned out to be hearing of her father's death. One of her mother's telegrams was delivered to her on duty, simply saying he had died during the night in Iowa Methodist. It was the hospital where she had done her training, before joining the U.S. Cadet Nurse Corps. She pleaded with her daughter to call her long distance, and to come home to Des Moines for the funeral.

Eileen decided on the spot that she would have to go. She called her mother, who sounded as if she was in the next room, and cried tears of joy that she was coming home. She also called Gerald to tell him their boat trip would have to be postponed. He offered his condolences, he understood. The Marines were actually very helpful. As soon as she applied for compassionate leave to attend her father's funeral, not only was it granted but her liaison officer, in light of her service with the Navy (to whom she was still attached) arranged for American military transport to take her all the way there. They would fly her to New York from Bournemouth, from where she would be accommodated aboard another US Navy plane to Chicago and pick up a connection for Des Moines early the following morning. It wouldn't cost her a dime – courtesy of Uncle Sam.

Thirty-six hours later her final aircraft, actually of all things a Liberator converted for civilian use, finally touched down on the wide pan of Des Moines airport. The humidity hit her in the face and she felt sweat prickle on her torso as she walked towards the passenger terminus, which looked slated for demolition, like something from an old movie. Dear old Iowa. I owe her five farthings said the bells of St Martins. She was back, where she'd never felt she belonged, and in the middle of a heatwave.

The carfare into the city was extortionate, but what could you expect? And as she dragged her baggage up the steps to the front door of the house she'd grown up in, Eileen had a queasy sensation – underneath her exhaustion – a feeling that she wasn't ready for this, she'd arrived too soon, or too early.

An old woman soon answered her knocking. Eileen immediately burst into tears; her mother had aged a great deal in the six years since she had last seen her. A once formidable lady, now stooped and white-haired but resplendent in ancient mourning clothes heavily embroidered with jet, she seemed to descend upon her daughter like an enormous bat.

The house had been full of people she didn't know. Marjorie Platt, as though Eileen had just been for a stroll around the block, insisted she must come in and meet them right away, so she dropped her baggage in the hallway, repaired her face in her compact and followed her mother into the front parlour. A glass of wine was put into her hand. "This is Eileen, just back from England."

Her mother did the rounds, introducing her to colleagues of her father, some of whom claimed to remember her as a little girl; a cousin or two she might have played with in the backyards of long ago; two aunts and an uncle, parents of either or both. These she did remember, Maud, Dorothy, and Ed. The relationships clicked into place suddenly, more shockingly than if she'd never been away. Dorothy was her father's sister, rarely seen; Ed was her stringy husband, owned a hardware store in Sioux City, and the two cousins were their kids. Maud was her mother's sister, whom she did remember, of course, a poor relation who had always resided in the shadow of her older sister, never married, and seemed intimidated by her still.

"Eileen," she said. "You're such a lovely girl. Your mother never stops talking about you." She raised her glass shyly and nuzzled into it. Several of them complimented her on her British accent. One of the guests was, like herself, in uniform. He had once been a protegé of her father at Bingley's: a promising young realtor who now wore an air force uniform and Flight Lieutenant's stripes. They were left together, but they couldn't immediately find much to say to each other. She learned he had fought the Japs in the south Pacific, just like Donald, but was now based at Des Moines airport, which she knew was still the principal USAF base in Iowa.

"You'll have to excuse me," she said. "I'm totally exhausted. I've been in the air for most of a day and a half."

"That's quite a long haul," he said. "I hope we can catch up later. You know, your dad really helped me as a boy."

She excused herself with apologies and retreated to the hall. Her mother followed her out, calling after her as she climbed the stairs with her bags. "I've put you in Donald's room for now, honey. Yours is full of Pop's stuff. He turned it into an office a couple of years ago."

Eileen pushed open the door of Donald's room with her foot and dumped her luggage on the floor. She was feeling dizzy now. The wine had helped, and she knew she would go under as soon as she hit the bed. She pulled off her clothes and lay on top of it, sweltering in the heat. The room, which she supposed he'd returned to more often than she to hers, had been turned into a shrine to him, untouched. When she forced herself to get up and turn off the light, she noticed his mitt lying on top of the dresser with a baseball resting neatly in its palm, never to be picked up. On the wall were crossed two pennants of the Des Moines Demons, with their red devil and pitchfork, which she had once found so frightening, and on a bookcase stacks of the cards he had collected as a boy.

Just before she passed out she remembered the Demons had merged with some other club, or gone under, and for a while some pitchforked demons fought it out with a big brown bear in a stupid dream she was having, picking up from Don maybe, still tormenting her. Later she was dimly aware of the door opening, her mother looking down on her, but thankfully she went away again before Eileen's sleep was interrupted. Eileen had always been a light sleeper, and so had her mother.

In the morning she felt a whole lot better, but she couldn't wait to
get out of Don's room. The bookcase still held the books he had read as
a child, and she had read them too, Hardy boys mysteries and stuff like
that. On the windowsill, half-hidden behind the drapes, she spotted
a flat-bottomed speedboat he had made one summer, out of spruce,
with a motor whose copper coils she remembered him winding himself,
painted in yellow and blue. She removed the hatch carefully and saw
the battery was still in place, its terminals corroded. She remembered
how she had gone with him to launch it on the pond in Gray's Lake
Park, and how the motor hadn't really been powerful enough to push it
along. It was beautiful all the same, and she was glad that it at least had
been kept here in this room, safe from harm.

At breakfast, the ordeal began to unfold in all its glory. Before she
had finished her pancakes and coffee, it was clear that her mother was
unable to address her without a note of recrimination entering her
voice. Her flat mid-western voice. Even her question: "Did you sleep
okay?" contained a rebuke. That some people had been unable to sleep.
For various reasons that would naturally be of little interest to her.

"Yes, mom. Thanks. It was quite a journey." She reached for her
mother's hand and squeezed it to reassure herself and her mom that,
well, here they were again, together, just like mother and daughter.

Mrs. Platt returned her finger grip. "Your father asked for you at
the end. But of course, you had more important things on your mind."

Had her mother said that? It didn't matter much if she did or not.
Eileen could read the gist of her thoughts quite easily. Anyway, in a way,
in every way, what she said was true. She'd been working at the base,
thinking about the Dunns, going down to visit them, and thinking about
Gerald. She had been trying to live her own life, thinking about her own
future, her own happiness. She was entitled to do that, well wasn't she?

"You can say what you like about Tommy and Iris, they do an
incredible amount for their parents. When Ed was sick and couldn't go
into the store, Tommy used to practically live in the place."

"Donald never showed any inclination to go into real estate," Eileen
stated flatly.

"Iris lives just around the block, she's always available to help. Do
you know, during the war Iris and Dorothy plumbed in an entire water
closet and bath on the upper floor of their house. Pops said it added
greatly to the value of the property. She still comes around to see her
mother every day, just to see she's alright."

Any response could only lead to another twist of the knife, but she hazarded: "Why wouldn't she be alright? Doesn't she have Ed there?"

"He's not what he was," Mrs. Platt said. "Couldn't you tell last night? That man's like a wilted runner bean."

"Mother!" Eileen laughed aloud. "Now you know why I miss you sometimes."

But her mother didn't laugh, she didn't think it was at all funny. Tomorrow she would be burying her husband, just as she had buried her son three years ago, and this stranger who sat across from her thought she was an amusement. She went quiet for a while, then got up and started fussing at the sink. Today was Anna's morning off, but she would be around later to help with the preparations for the funeral. A few people would be coming back afterward to pay respects after the church service and the graveside committal, which would be for family only. It promised to be a difficult, tiring day. Her daughter looked very different now, a grown woman, past her prime by Des Moines' standards. At some level though, she registered, if only negatively, that Eileen was another person now. The war in Europe had cost her a lot, she thought. It had taken their children or altered them past recognition, but she and her husband hadn't been altered by it. They were part of what had gone before, too old to enjoy the money and the new wave of building that would soon change the town.

Old Bingley himself gave the eulogy, saying how he'd recognized in Henry Platt from the start a young man who had a keen eye for detail, and who really cared about Des Moines. He told several fishing stories, made reference to Hal as a family man and the kind of guy who had built this town and made it what it was. Eileen sat in the front pew beside her mother, feeling the eyes of the mourners on her back, and bowed her head, remembering the other Hal Platt. The drunkard who had made her childhood a fearful misery, struck his son often for no reason and made her mother cry out in the night. He loved the town alright, explored every rotten corner of it and twisted very penny he could from its poorer tenants on behalf of his employers.

Pops had had a finger in every pie, but Eileen realized now she hadn't really known him, nor seen the full extent of her father's true life. Her parents had been so caught up in their social standing, her father with a kind of fierce, boisterous pride in being somebody people should look up to. A wealthy man, recognized by the local board of trade. You had to go along with him, had to be seen to enjoy yourself in his presence, or he turned nasty. How she and Don had despised his petty cruelties, his bullying. He had first turned them inwards, and then away from him. Their mother had been his yes woman, fronting the operation. As a kid, she'd understood little of this, only that she and Donald had better keep out of his way, but now it was perfectly clear.

Afterwards, they walked grimly from the hole in the ground into which he'd been lowered and returned to the house to receive those mourners who wanted a drink. Eileen recognized some of them from the night of her arrival, but her uncle, aunt and cousins had to take off early to drive back to Sioux City. It had been a joyless gathering, as though Old Man Bingley's oily peroration – which had been mainly about himself – had drained even his most ardent sycophants of any remaining spirit. Mercifully, they didn't stay long. She talked to the USAF Lieutenant she'd met earlier, an uninteresting young man who wouldn't have minded getting fixed up with Platt's daughter, and maybe using her as a lever to get back into Bingley's and out of the Air Force. At least, that's how Eileen interpreted his well-mannered friendliness and extravagant compliments.

Once they had all gone she helped Anna and her mother clear away the plates and glasses and wash everything up. Her mother cut an eccentric figure after all, up to her elbows in suds at the sink, then stacking plates in the absurd ancient mourning dress she had inherited from her own mother. One last duty as hostess to her husband's business connections. Perhaps she would be happier now, be able to relax and unbend a little. Perhaps. She could maybe hook up with some of the other board of trade wives she had been gushing over and play bridge, or canasta. She still had a hand to play. Eileen wasn't sorry she wouldn't be around.

Sleeping in Don's bed, she realized that for all their problems in getting along as children, she and her brother had been on the same side in this loveless house; they just hadn't always known it. She wished he were still alive, and they had managed to get to know one another as adults, but it was all too late now.

The following day she walked down to the Des Moines river. Walking around brought it back to her that Des Moines was quite a city. It surely beat the pants off Exeter and Kingston-upon-Thames, but you didn't necessarily notice things when you were a kid. You had nothing to compare. Still, a lot of it was built around the same time, and Des Moines had been lots of different kinds of a place over the centuries since the Indians traded with the French monks, and thousands of years earlier when (she half-remembered a teacher saying) there had been great cities all over Iowa. It was odd to look at her hometown through expatriate eyes, but that is what she had become. Everything was now shadowed.

There were buildings in Kingston you could compare to the turrets and the five-storey tower of the house the first Des Moines millionaire had built on Turret Hill, now the governor's mansion, though none were quite so elegant. She'd seen nothing as beautiful in England as Des Moines' pre-war fire station, she remembered that going up. Her father's excitement had failed to ignite her at the time but now she could see he had been right to enthuse about it to his offspring.

Des Moines was old but modern and the whole attitude to life of the English was going to have to change quite a lot before they had any chance of catching up with even this American backwater. The Des Moines river at this point was a lot like the Thames at the point where it thickened and everything got dumped into it, even the balustrades she walked beside and leaned on to look out across to the other bank were like those at Hampton Court and Richmond, only a little newer, a WPA project her dad had thought was a waste of public money and too fancy for here. It had been the depression. They were middle-class, seen as, though not really, rich folks. As a child she could feel the resentment for people like them; but all the same, as a kid, you were given the idea it was their fault, these workless poor people. She had felt afraid of them because they were the ones responsible for trying to turn Des Moines back into what it seemed to want to be: a flyblown dump instead of a great city as people like her father had thought it should be.

A couple of days later she arranged to hitch another ride on a Liberator back to Chicago, picked up her connections easily for the long ride back to Bournemouth. Her mother cried, and she did too, but she didn't produce any hysterics; they would keep in closer touch in future, of course she would be back, silly. She meant it too. Soon it would be easy to hop back and forth between countries. The war had made it possible. "You could come over easily," she said. And she felt her mother finally let her go, as though she'd been trying to get her out of the house all along.

Stepping back into her English life with relief, Eileen threw herself into work and a new social whirl seemed immediately to present itself. She even went out to a nightclub in Mayfair with the guy who'd written the story about her in *Stars and Stripes*, and laughed at the terrible floorshow, and tried to put a distance between herself and Des Moines, her childhood, her mother, and everything else that wasn't strictly about herself in the here and now.

That was Ron Tupper, from Delaware. Boy, that fellow had every angle covered on the professional expenses racket. The American taxpayer was bankrolling some big nights for Ron. Who was a funny person, she discovered, although he always seemed kind of anxious on the Base. But he liked taking her out, she liked going and other things followed. The Stars and Stripes people had the use of an apartment overlooking the river on Richmond Hill, and they spent a few nights back there, guzzling hospitality booze, doing what came naturally.

You could say she had developed a swift grasp of relations, but after the third visit to the same swank restaurant in Richmond followed by a night in the apartment getting sozzled, she recalled her mission to pull for higher things. It was just something she needed to do, as much to find out if what had happened with her and Gerald would happen again given the right amount of abandon. But it hadn't. She and Ron weren't going anywhere just jumping around like kids on a trampoline, except they were big kids susceptible to sprains and bruises, bright-eyed and over the edge.

Even this little adventure threatened to get more complicated than it had needed to be. Ron started to ask her out increasingly often; he had schemes to visit the Lake District, near Scotland. He wanted her to come to Paris with her in September. What was she doing for Christmas, maybe she'd like to meet his folks in Delaware? Ron's love strategy was to push everything as hard and fast as it could go. He thought he was romancing her but he came over as an increasingly desperate character.

One day when she was assisting Stevens, the base surgeon, in an emergency appendectomy she had almost sewn up a swab inside the poor guy. No harm was done, but Stevens and the rest of the team had seen her fumble and hesitate, and afterwards she found herself trembling, mainly at the thought of her reputation as a nurse being on the line. When she thought of all the men she'd stitched up! Eileen had to give Ron the big heave-ho, so she did, nicely but firmly, comforting him when he cried. Hey, don't take it so hard, big man. After all, there were plenty more fish in the typing pool.

3.

Gerald Dunn had found her and pulled her back to him quite easily. He'd thought she might decide to stay in Des Moines, once she got there, but arrogant as he was he decided that if she did return to England it would mean it was for him. Guessing she must have returned by now, he didn't want to seem to be chasing after her but instead wrote a thoughtful letter of condolence and offered her his true friendship. The naughty schoolboy who had once so rudely accosted her, that sort of thing.

He didn't hear from her for a few days. He thought she had definitely given him up or decided to stay on. Her letter arrived on a Saturday. He read it lying on his bed at Dunns End. There was a sweetness in the way she thanked him for his condolences. She was glad he cared for her. She briefly described her trip home, said she would like to tell him about her hometown someday. She gave all her love to his parents and to Geoff, and in a quick, stabbing p.s. she asked him if the boat trip was still possibly on offer. Half-an-hour later she telephoned and he told her it certainly was.

Eileen still had a week of unused compassionate leave owing to her, and plenty of unused compassion to go with it, so it wasn't hard to arrange another break in her routine. Everyone in her chain of command recognized losing a father was tough and her request was immediately rubber-stamped.

Gerald came to pick her on in the Riley and half the base seemed to be on hand to watch her climb aboard the flimsy, noisily rattling vehicle with one crazy-looking Englishman behind the wheel. What was wrong with Americans? Eileen tied a scarf over her hair like a movie star and they set off on their grand adventure to the ends of the earth.

As they hammered down the Portsmouth Road in the vibrating death-trap, she began to recapture some of the excitement, the knot of anticipation in her stomach she associated with her first ride in the Riley, which in its own way was as much sex on wheels as any Buick could ever be. She wished Gerald might put his hand in his breast pocket and pull out his silver flask. But he was intent on driving, and half-an-hour later they were skirting Guildford, another old town to be held up against the template of Des Moines, but this place seemed to bust out of the lush countryside that had cradled and fed it, and then lain quietly dozing and complacent for centuries.

They turned into some narrower, more twisting lanes, reminding her of Devon, except here the little towns and houses laying back along their route were better tended, less picturesque. A bare hour and a half after leaving Bushey Park they pulled up beside a small humped bridge on a water meadow that stretched away to a nearby glinting spire. "Only one really famous person ever came from here," Gerald told her. "And that was the radio operator on the Titanic."

"What was his name?" Eileen asked him.

"He isn't famous for his name," Gerald laughed gaily. "Which means I have forgotten, by the way."

He led her down to an old boathouse and club building to a narrow boat tied up with others, where he told her a Navy friend of his had bought into a business hiring them out. He was there to meet them: a vague but sensible seeming person in a ragged jersey. Half-an-hour later, the Riley tied down under her cover, a box of provisions Gerald had brought to keep them going and their luggage safely on board they set off slowly into the narrow tunnel of greenery with the sun still high in the blue English sky.

There were children sunbathing on the towpath, electric-blue dragonflies, midges funnelling beneath overhanging trees, paddling ducks, swans gliding, swooping herons, and every time they reached an ancient lock another boy would appear out of nowhere to bum a few pennies for helping them through it. Gerald got out to help them wind the handles that raised and lowered the sluices and pulled the boat along, and left Eileen in charge of the ropes and tiller: a task she felt more than prepared for by her earlier exploits on Grey's Lake and on the Raccoon River. Pointlessly, and partly because she knew it couldn't be so, she wished her brother Donald had found this spot instead of the godforsaken island where they hadn't even recovered enough of his body to send home to Des Moines.

If she had been with Ron or even Mitch, she would soon have tired of being under their scrutiny, she thought, but Gerald was nicely preoccupied with running the engine and pointing out hazards (there weren't any) and he left her to flop around at the front of the boat in some old slacks and a pair of gym plimsolls he had told her to bring along.

Before long the green cocoon of the navigation began to wind itself around them, the clustering houses on the towpath fell away and bigger houses backed down onto the trough-like watercourse; the stream arced around islands guarded by the skeletons of old barges tangled in the roots of ancient frozen trees in the crumbling banks, long crooked weirs sucked off surplus flow, small foot bridges spanned the narrow main stream, and further along the lawns of greater houses dipped in their corners as they inched the narrow boat around the hairpins like a trapped matchstick.

They weren't alone on the river: a few skiffs and small rowboats appeared, and as they neared Guildford there were working boats too. A boat similar to theirs on the opposite bank was more down at heel and pulling harder, a whole family, ragged children at every station, thin elderly parent, shabby and worn out looking, a cargo of coal, clothes pegs, who knew what, a poor old tired horse plodding along the path. Obviously poor people, some kind of water gypsies, they refused to glance at Eileen and Gerald, whose craft had been vaguely tarted up, endured the indignity of paint, and was now a pleasure boat to be ignored with contempt.

Eileen started to jump out first, engaging the rusty old handle and vigorously winding the lock sluices down and up.

After an hour or so they tied up on the riverbank. Gerald pumped up the primus stove in the galley, put on the small tin kettle for a cup of tea and they munched their way through corned beef and tomato sandwiches he methodically assembled from his box of provisions. Eileen was practically speechless, as though some witch who lived around these parts had cast a benign spell over her vocal cords. Gerald Dunn, on the other hand, grew quite chatty for a change.

The idea, he explained, was to spin out the journey for as long as possible. But not too much longer, she thought. When they had finished their sandwiches and drunk their tea, Eileen interrupted what sounded like it was going to be a long and interesting story about Gertrude Jekyll, a garden designer and the second most famous person from Godalming, by putting her arm around his neck and pulling him gently towards her. They climbed down into the boat, forrard to the stifling cabin, and began to make love.

"I need a drink," she said hoarsely as they were fumbling in the initial stages. Gerald found a bottle of brandy in his box, they slooshed it into mugs with some Crabbie's green ginger wine, and sweating in the close cabin they did what they had done that night out in the breeze in the Riley, again with most of their clothes on. Eileen would have to say it was just as fine.

"This is like having the honeymoon before the wedding," Gerald said.

"Steady on there, boy," Eileen said. "Not where I come from it ain't."

But if the idea was to spin out the journey for as long as possible there wasn't really any reason to carry on right now, and nothing very pressing to talk about either. They sloshed down some more of the brandy until they were properly drunk and quite incapable of driving a boat anyway. Eileen found it easier that way. They rolled around in the cabin until darkness fell, then crawled back out to the stern to bathe in the night breeze for a while, Eileen wearing nothing but his scratchy sweater until it was too cold out there and they went inside again to sleep it off.

In the morning they felt a lot easier, bonded with each other, lolling around like a pair of old lovers. There was water on board and a crude water closet of sorts. Eileen was relieved she wasn't expected to piss and evacuate in a bucket like some Iowa farm girl. She brushed her teeth in a little water and washed off the remains of her make-up. Gerald had even brought some instant coffee for her, so she drank some of it in the glorious, slanting morning sunlight. A family of early-rising ducks came quacking around and Gerald tore up a couple slices of yesterday's bread to toss for them.

They set off efficiently, once everything had been thoroughly ordered and settled, which took some time. If she'd had to say one thing about Gerald, it would have been that he knew how to run a boat. But Guildford was just around the corner. It would have been foolish to pass it by without a look, so they tied up at end of the public wharf, where a couple of working boats were loading up with foodstuffs to be rushed to the best hotels in London – at least that was Gerald's idea of what they were doing. They walked around the town for an hour or so. It was a Tuesday, but the wide main street with its ancient clock, amongst the first in the whole world, jutting from a timbered building to keep everyone going, was full of mid-morning bustle. Tradesmen were rushing around, English cars were queuing to get somewhere, and surprisingly many people like themselves, who seemed to have nothing better to do than walk around looking in the windows of expensive shops.

Normally she would've been interested, but today the place felt like a horrible interruption. They perched at a table on the pavement outside a small cafe, and here at least she was able to procure something approaching a real cup of coffee. In an old tobacconist's, dark brown, with the horn of plenty spilling shag in the window, she was able to pick up a carton of Luckies.

Seeing the cigarettes, he began to ask her about her trip, how her mother was bearing up. Des Moines, it was a great name. Sounded exciting. Did she think she would be moving back home soon? But Eileen found it difficult to respond to any of his tender enquiries with anything but polite evasions. There was something in his tone, his solicitousness, that made it feel like she was being asked to describe her life on the surface of the moon by somebody who only knew about pruning roses in an English garden. She tried to say something. "Des Moines and here are similar in a way," she began, faltering. "They're parallel worlds, maybe identical, just in a different place and climate. My father used to be quite a big man in Des Moines. We were the rich folks. We didn't really get along though." She broke off. "I don't know, maybe you'd like it there. Used to be prosperous, then very poor. Now it'll be a go-ahead place."

"I'd like to see it sometime," Gerald said quietly.

Once they were underway again, pottering out into the green shade of the navigation, navigating, the past enveloped them, suspended them. She wondered what they would make of him back home – not much. But he was like her people in a way, an apple which hadn't fallen far from the tree. She asked him then about his school, she'd heard it was very old and very distinguished. The way she said those words made her sound like a mock-credulous, sceptical American, which she still was at heart.

If Gerald was at all offended, he didn't show it. "It is," he said. "It's the kind of place prime ministers and admirals go. Charterhouse school is a world of its own, it goes back hundreds of years. Houses with strange names. One of the old masters looked like a frog. My grandfather was an admiral, you know. I suppose that's why my parents sent me there. But I'm afraid I wasn't one of its brightest stars. They have some nasty old-fashioned little ways of letting you know you're not quite the thing. But I'm still an old Carthusian."

Eileen didn't ask what nasty little ways were. That she already knew, her father's cruelty – the sneer, the back of his hand.

"To be honest with you, I was damned lucky to get any kind of commission."

They fell silent for a while, sitting side by side in the stern, the engine throbbing below like a steady low pulse. Gerald kept pushing the throttle off so they could drift slowly forward for a long stretch carried by the momentum of the heavy iron hull in the narrow wood-banked channel. The silence then was almost total, just birdsong and murmurous plashing, and she felt, absurdly, as if they were on a fantastic voyage of discovery. They were certainly both refugees, in a sense, misfits at least. Gerald had been right to think of bringing her, to be truly alone together and to discover this ground.

The navigation had been built around 1650, when Cromwell and the Roundheads were in power. England had been a republic for a few years ("Big deal," said Eileen) and these public works were an attempt to recover from the civil war, build a new commercial infrastructure using state of the art technology. There were sluices each with its own rack and pinion to raise and lower it, like the locks, flooding wide low water meadows where crops were forced on, grass grew and cattle grew fat. Near Weybridge, where they were going, some early communists tried to set up their own society where they farmed and all lived equally on the land, which they claimed was owned by the people. The Cromwellians built this instead. There were even the remains of old factories beside the water, seventeenth-century factories making pottery, porcelain for the tables of London, ironmongery, and God-knows-what.

Eileen looked up at their eyeless, semi-derelict windows. "Somebody should do a few repairs," she said. "Before they fall down."

"When I was a boy," Gerald said, "I used to sell the *Daily Worker* at Godalming station.

"Many customers?" Eileen was a little shocked by the seriousness of this. She remembered Don and his baseball cards and models.

"A few, yes," he said. "Mostly they just laughed at me."

But they were in no hurry, and after a couple more locks and rickety bridges which looked like they should be guarded by someone bearing a musket, they nuzzled in under a tree and tied up for the day. They made a rough meal of fresh buttered bread and a large pork pie Gerald had bought in Guildford and drank a bottle of his father's wine he pulled from the provision box like a rabbit from a magician's top hat.

"Gerald Dunn, you are a thief," she laughed at him. "And the most unconvincing communist I ever met."

Before they could settle own, just as the light was falling, an angry mob of wasps invaded them. There was a nest high up in the tree and they'd decided to swarm down and spoil their evening meal. There were hundreds of the little bastards. A dozen of them immediately clustered at the rim of her wine mug, and when she reached to snatch it way, one flew up enraged and stung her on the arm. They had been invaded by pirates, they were creeping everywhere, swaggering little buccaneers.

Eileen ran through the cabin and up to the prow of the narrow boat. She grabbed the long pole lying on the roof of the cabin, managed to cast off and push the front of the boat out into the stream, away from the immediate source of their guests. Gerald did the same at his end. She heard the engine start, then a sickening thud when he engaged gear, followed by silence.

"The prop's tangled in something," he shouted angrily as if it was her fault. "You'll have to pole us away."

Eileen did her best, taking up a position in the middle of the prow, swinging the pole from side to side and digging it into the riverbed. The channel was only a few feet deep even at its centre, and she found she could control the boat quite well, feel it moving sluggishly underneath her soles, knowing which way it would go. At that moment another working narrow boat appeared around the next meander, pulled by a horse plodding along on the opposite bank. She had to push mightily into the bed, the pole digging in, to swing the prow around to give them room. They passed smoothly by, plenty of room, their faces averted in scorn.

When they had gone she lost control briefly, the boat yawed across the river, blocking it completely, the stern pushed around mercilessly by the current as Gerald leaned over the back of the transom attempting to pull away whatever was tangled around the propeller. Then they were drifting quite fast into the far towpath bank. They hit it broadside on with a loud bang, Eileen leaped ashore with the painter, held onto it, and ran back to where Gerald finally managed to toss her the stern rope. When she had made safe he got into the water, pulling off a stream of tangled weed, and after further struggle, a glistening length of ancient frayed rope was dragged up for display, the strangling past, the remains of the shed skin of the serpent in the Garden of Eden.

Most of the wasps had returned to the safety of their nest, but a lot were still trapped in the cabin, settled in by now. Gerald found an empty milk bottle, rinsed it in the river and poured some sugar into the bottom of it, swirling it. He placed it on the galley table and soon they began to crawl and fly into the bottle, from where they were unable to find their way out. He lit a hurricane lamp and they drank wine and watched drowsily by its light as the wasps climbed over each other into the milk bottle, sacrificing themselves, until it was tightly packed with their tiny cadavers.

The incident brought them closer together. It was amazing, they thought, how well the two of them had co-operated. There had been no tantrums, no screaming nor recriminations. They laughed and congratulated themselves, kissing and cuddling like teenagers. What a team! But, after all, they were both used to teamwork. They set off at a leisurely pace the following morning, moored at a riverside inn at Pyrford, drank some beer and ate some pork scratchings. What in hell were they, Eileen wanted to know? They played a game of darts in the dank parlour, until a stinking old labourer came in and stationed himself at the bar, gawping at them in idiot fascination. No hurry. They pulled on a bit further and found another pub by Byfleet lock.

Wildly looking out from their floating domain through a screen of trees to port, she glimpsed the ruins of what looked like a huge cathedral just hanging there across a wide water meadow, on an island amid the farmed fields. "Newark Abbey," Gerald informed her. "Used to control the whole county in the middle ages. It was a powerful place."

"Newark? I thought it was in New Joisey." To her, it looked craggily classical – and completely desolate. "I hate to say this, but most of Europe looks like that now."

This thought – that the war had completely wrecked a lot of the world – damped their spirits for a while. Eileen didn't want to stop again, nor to see any people or things outside their moving space.

It took them two more days to get to Weybridge, by which time a brisk, efficient staff nurse and a pinched demobbed widower had been changed into a reckless female river pirate and her leering, loping boy companion. It wasn't so much they felt they owned the place, but they owned their own space and they defined it. They crept along, a burst of power, a long glide; by far the worst, laziest slobs on the navigation, they just had fun and wondered what they were going to devolve into next. They drank wine and brandy at night, made love by the light of the hurricane lamp, beside which stood the dark milk bottle crammed with dead wasps, a grim reminder of their triumph. In the morning they cleaned up a little, Eileen brushed her teeth at a dribbling tap on the riverbank, and they drank instant coffee, black, to which she had managed to convert her English lover.

As if to thrust down their throats the comforts of life along the Wey, there were more stretches of beautiful old houses, really old, their lawns backing down to boathouses where large cabin cruisers bobbed gently in their wake, and sleek low speedboats with varnished decks and chrome fittings promised quick getaways. Gerald sprang his big surprise – he had been hinting at it all along – just as they were getting to the edge of Weybridge. "There she is," he said. "We'll pull in ahead of her. Make ready with the rope, your ladyship."

It was a military boat, still with a red and blue roundel on its side, painted light grey. A circular platform on the foredeck no longer held an anti-aircraft gun, and the torpedo tubes had also been removed. It looked forlorn, useless, still with the remains of last year's rotting leaves compacted on her decks, like advanced rust.

"She's mine," said Gerald. "What do you think?"

"What do you mean, yours? This the boat you ran?"

"Not this actual boat," he said. "One like her. I bought this one from the Navy – through the back door as they say."

They stepped aboard and Gerald showed her around the ex-MTB. Chained up, spooky, deserted, but in closer inspection solid, intact. He undid the padlocks and chains and showed her below decks. An empty space mostly – and ghostly by torchlight, but she could see bare metal bunks and bays where armaments had been stacked, and a huge engine, which looked like it could have powered the craft through the air.

"I can get across the English Channel in a couple of hours in one of these," he said. "Civvy paint, a refit, and I'm in business for myself instead of the Royal Navy. And as for the coast guards – catch me if you can." He laughed drily. "This is my meal ticket, Eileen. I can't lie around in Dunkeswell for the rest of my days. Probably couldn't sit behind a desk to save my life. Kenneth – you met him – found her and asked me to go in with him, run the show. He can find the clients, I run the ship. Good chap, Kenneth. We were at school together. First class failures, the pair of us."

"Gerald! So, you really are a pirate. A smuggler, that's what you're planning to be, or worse." She laughed aloud at the sheer audacity, the craziness of his ideas. But, she supposed, they must know what they were doing.

"There are people, believe it or not, who'll pay good money to get across to France in a hurry, or back the other way."

She had to hand it to him, she was surprised. She'd vaguely imagined him staying in Devon, going into real estate like her father, or selling insurance. The same kind of thing Mr. and Mrs. Dunn had planned for his son. Gerald was deadly serious. The whole plan was to go into action in a couple of months when the nights grew a bit longer, and they'd have their work cut out getting her shipshape by then.

He locked up the chains again and they returned to the narrow boat. She knew he wanted her to tell him how marvellous it all was; instead, she said: "You're actually going ahead with this, aren't you?"

He looked at her seriously. Obviously, he was. His mad dream. Oh, Gerald.

They set off again for a short distance until he brought the boat in on a towpath beside another water meadow on the opposite side of the stream. They were near the end of the navigation. "Let's tidy ourselves up a bit," Gerald suggested. "There's a hotel up on the road. We can get a room for the night and scrub up properly."

Eileen was reluctant to break the spell of their marine idyll, but the promise of hot water and a soft bed was too much of a temptation. She changed her clothes, brushed out her hair and put on make-up. Gerald managed to make himself look semi-respectable, and they were easily given a room at the Bridge Hotel, signing in as Mr. and Mrs. Dunn. They used up a lot of hot water in the bathroom, made love on the creaking double bed and ate an indifferent meal in the dining room. The spell hadn't been broken; a kind of magic was still strong between them, but it was difficult not to feel a little furtive under the eyes of the black-clad waitress and a couple of respectable-looking families with children. They hung around in the saloon bar for a while, sipping drinks and looking out at the widening river. When the bar started to fill up and get too noisy with the harsh voices of Weybridge citizens, they retreated to their pleasant brown-panelled room and their freshly laundered sheets.

In the morning they ate stiff porridge and drank stewed orange tea, and afterward went back to the boat. They didn't have much further to go and they'd be out on the Thames.

The last lock was a double-lock, wider and with higher sides, a double step to jump the navigation up to the level of the great river and to withstand its enormous pressures. The water ran heavily down its slimy, greenish stone walls, and as it flooded through the opened sluices created deeper turbulence that threatened to bounce the metal-hulled old narrowboat around like a paper straw. You didn't want to fall in; it was easy to understand how easy it would be to drown, as children and adults often did in the Des Moines and Raccoon rivers at their confluence, whose frequent flooding sometimes used to wash away the low-lying parts of the city.

Here, the lock-keepers weren't boys but older men with pitted iron handles hung permanently over their stooped shoulders. The ancient gates, cut from great English oaks that had once withstood the tusks of wild boar as they truffled for acorns, swung open slowly, Gerald and Eileen cast off their slack ropes and her pilot gunned out into the wide expanse of the river.

The light seemed to change suddenly, as the sky opened out, for a moment as wide as anything in Iowa, flooding over them as Gerald shut back and nosed the narrowboat out to the middle of the stream, which parted here in a wide bulge around a densely-wooded island with derelict Edwardian houseboats around its edge, places where criminals and river gamblers must once have lived, had vaguely heard.

Eileen leaned back on the roof and took in the view. Hampton Court Bridge was only a few hundred yards upstream, she guessed, which meant she was actually more or less facing the American Base, hidden of course behind the lawns of the houses rolling down to the river, by the smaller houses behind them and a few meaner streets she vaguely remembered or imagined must come before the edge of Bushey Park.

The river was surprisingly full of traffic in this wide, turbulent basin where the narrow stream finally emptied into the Thames. A few scullers; a six-man rowing team skimming along; a pair of empty black barges stinking of coal, returning to a yard somewhere in the city, she guessed. One of the filthiest men she had ever seen – who seemed to have been carved out of anthracite – petted a little dog, which seemed to bark at her. Gerald dodged them all with ease, turning in a wide arc across the London river, which she had to admit did have something – and they circled back towards the lock, as they'd agreed, because there was no time to go any further, and nothing to do really but rethread their slim craft through the eye of the needle.

Toy Town

Jack Mudie felt he was a shadowy figure to his family, obscure even to himself. He put down his phone and sat quietly at the desk in his bedroom. The bamboo blind was down but sunlight filtered through its slats, lending a little warmth to his dusty living space. His papers were strewn about the floor, teaching materials mostly, unpaid final demands for council tax, water rates, and what have you. But what exactly did he have? A view, for one thing: a room with a classic view, if he cared to look out at the trees and what have you, the da-da-da, and opposite the lit windows of other living spaces.

The blossom and the leaves had come quickly this year, as if squeezing themselves violently into existence following a long period of turbulent weather: unseasonable snow, icy winds, bursts of tropical heat. What was going on in the eco-system of the world as they had known it? Frankly, he didn't care all that much. In between scuttling forth on his journeys across the city, Jack had spent the past few months assembling memories, fancies, and splurges of invention into something he was calling, to himself, a novel, although in some quarters there might be disagreement about this appellation.

As his fingers flew over the keyboard of his laptop or scribbled out his inspirations in notebooks, he'd been wondering how he had the cheek to call what he was doing invention, imagination, storytelling, or any of the other fudgy terms for composition, narration, scribbling, and moulding into unity. Theirs had been in his estimation a whatever period in human history, and in his own life as he spiralled on towards his final years. Perhaps this was it, and that was that.

His mother was dying in hospital, not at home as she would have wished, and his father was refusing to visit her. No amount of bullying or cajoling by Mikey, his brother, was going to make any difference to that. Jack had sat quietly beside his mother's hospital bed, spooned ice cream into her dry, sunken mouth, and tried to make out words in the faint mumbling sounds which sometimes came out of her mouth. Dad was in bits. He'd sat with his father, listened to his brother hammering on and on. Sometimes he thought the sole purpose of his brother's rivers of speech was to batter him into submission, bang nails into his head, and to prove for the last time Mikey's superiority and dominance in the family, his greater worthiness of the name son. All this 'man-up' shit. Telling his poor stricken father to 'man-up'. Fuck that. His need for authority. Basically, he was a pain in the arse, they both were.

Jack wanted to abandon him, once and for all to leave them all behind, his clinging family with their tedious repeating loops. But he spent a lot of time alone, and his own repeating loops were not much more beguiling. Is that all human beings were made of? A few strips of worn out tape spooling around the brain's playback heads forever, a few tones that beat out 'me, me, me, me' forever, until the game was up? People were pushy, more or less so, but few were truly reflective. This went for Jack Mudie himself. Wasn't it possible that what he passed off as hard-won wisdom was merely the recurrence of opinions and attitudes he had arrived at sometime near the get-go of his conscious life, or before, and that he now ground out fresh-minted as points of final destination? More than possible!

One thing his writing had taught him was to be aware of how little he himself knew about anything – things he was supposed to know, for instance, like his supposed nearest and dearest (though he could make a stab at them, he felt), and beyond this a whole murky world of relationships, systems, and ideas that others seemed to dance through with such confident aplomb. But he could only sketch them in vaguely, in accordance with some ideas he'd inherited from somewhere or other – and it was always the worst ones which stuck firmest, occluding earwax muffling the world, leaving him with vague sonic guesses that invariably turned out to be wrong.

When you were wrong it was like being locked out, losing your key, or even worse being supplied with a replacement key that didn't work. This had happened to Jack very recently. He'd dropped his keys he knew not where. After ringing his downstairs neighbour's bell, he got into the flat by removing the cardboard he'd put up and reaching through the window he'd broken with a large stone last time he'd lost his keys, a wire-reinforced pane which he hadn't bothered repairing because he knew it would sooner or later happen again.

At the Housing Trust, there had been a bit of an argument. A rather stern, moralizing woman whom he had never seen before but who seemed now to be in charge, informed him that his request to borrow the master front door key to the house was out of order, just not possible. His downstairs neighbour had told him that the keys were impossible to copy anyway, she having tried twice to have hers duplicated for her son, who had stayed with her for six months a few years ago. Jack duly told her story to the woman at the Housing Trust, which seemed to have changed her mind, if only to contradict him and his ill-informed neighbour. What she had been lacking in was this woman's permission to cut a key.

Meanwhile, the younger woman, pretty, mixed-race, well-dressed, who sat at the front desk, smiled wryly and said it wasn't a problem. She fetched the key (which he had to promise the older woman he would bring back before five o'clock) and took the master over to their designated locksmith ("Extortionate!" said the younger woman) by an unfamiliar bus they helpfully suggested to him.

These were smaller buses than the usual kind, and the journey he made to the locksmith (a journey which was to become familiar) followed a long and winding route through hilly North London streets. It was a beautiful journey, the small bus half-full of women and young children, friendly, chattier than they would have been on a full-sized bus, and the dark orange houses were residences he would have loved to have owned. Who had originally lived in them? What class of people, and what had their lives been like? These were questions he had often asked himself but had always been unable to answer satisfactorily. This didn't prevent them from popping up again.

When he reached the locksmith's, the man behind the counter took the passkey from him, found a blank and fitted it to his cutting machine. He popped the correct holes and grooves into it mechanically, without removing his mobile phone from his cheek. Jack paid fifteen pounds by card and was shortly handed both master and a duplicate along with a receipt. He enjoyed the return journey on the half-size bus more than he had his outward trip. This time a small boy had waved at the driver, standing with his mother and sister at the side of the road and waving until they were out of sight. Jack had waved back shyly.

However, once back at his home address, he discovered without real surprise that the new key didn't work – although the master did, perfectly – and he wondered if perhaps the downstairs neighbour hadn't been right: somehow the keys were actually uncopiable. She had also remarked that Turks were untrustworthy; they would say anything. Jack wondered if there might be something to this, although the man at the locksmiths, the locksmith, in fact, had not been Turkish.

Nevertheless, he made an immediate return journey on the miniature hail-and-ride vehicle that pushed through the same sloping avenues of attractive villas, again admiring the filigreed decorative flourishes in the brickwork of some of them, their overwhelming design-grace, as always preferring those with the original window-fittings. This time another man was also riding on the bus, pricing a minor building job on his mobile. Jack could not tell exactly what it entailed, nor did he particularly care – but he heard the man pointing out that he and his partner had been doing similar work for years, suggesting politely that his prospective customer could phone around for more quotations and, if he was still interested, get back to him. Middle-aged and dressed in working clothes, the man got down at the next stop, leaving Jack to his anxieties.

He was worried that – five o'clock fast approaching – the locksmiths would be closed by the time he got there. But when he did arrive the key-cutter was no longer speaking on his phone, and he carefully compared the master and duplicate keys before refitting them to his cutting machine.

"Sorry about that," he said after a couple of minutes, casually handing them over. "Should work now."

"What was the problem?" Jack asked.

"The first cut wasn't deep enough."

"The first cut is the deepest, hmm?"

"Now it is perfect," said the locksmith.

He trudged back to the bus stop outside Sainsbury's to pick up the return bus to where he normally resided. While he was waiting there for it, a small man with long dreadlocks sprinted past them across the carpark, his arms full of clothes on hangers he had evidently stolen. The thief kept glancing behind him, without slowing his pace, but he wasn't being chased. All the people at the bus stop turned to watch him pass out onto a further road and make his escape.

This time a young West Indian woman boarded mid-way through the journey. Wearing a pair of loose men's trousers, struggling on crutches but with a radiant face, she addressed the other passengers.

"Is it just me or has it got a lot colder today?"

Several of them agreed vigorously, shivering, turning up the collars of their coats.

"It's freezing!" she exclaimed, smiling at all and sundry, obviously feeling that she was giving voice to some closely-guarded secret, speaking of something about which they had as usual been misled by the authorities.

She found the weather mysterious. So did Jack. Would they wake up in the morning to golf-ball-sized hailstones? He remained sceptical about the key until he pushed it into the lock and found that, this time, it did indeed work to perfection. But he was too late now to return the passkey to the Housing Trust. It would have to wait until the following morning, he decided he would drop it off there on his way to work. The downstairs neighbour had remained behind her own locked door, unavailable for further questioning about the misinformation she'd blatantly proffered earlier on.

Keys were indeed a difficult business, and once you had one available you would be wise to keep it close at hand, if not firmly within your grasp, at all times. He kept his in his left trouser pocket and felt the top of it with his thumb frequently. A few days later he ran downstairs in a hurry to fulfil an obligation in Chingford, only to find he was locked in: in a further mysterious twist, the front door lock had jammed. The neighbour spoke at length, as usual, then phoned the Housing Trust whilst he sat on the stairs to wait. Within the hour, as promised, a representative of the designated locksmith had arrived to repair the defective mechanism, but Jack had already called Hazel Miles to cancel his tutorial session with an overlong explanation.

Travelling back and forth between the town he lived in and the rural place where his parents and his brother resided, Jack had begun to notice a strange but interrelated series of phenomena. It was as though the reality of one place was partly obliterated by his being in the other. When he was in his parents' bungalow he found the details of his urban life and the places it took place in started to become vague generalities about the places and people in question, and when he was at home the reality of their place, his parents' place, darkened like a map withdrawn from torchlight.

The effect was certainly one of darkening and lighting up, but being in the lit-up place obscured the details, almost blotted out entirely the place that had fallen into shadow. As if the existence of one precluded the other, although there was no proper relationship apart from the long thread of railway track running between them. Therefore, to think or speak of one place whilst in another was difficult, to say the least, and certainly different than speaking or thinking of the place you were actually in.

But then, he realized, this was no more than a subjective phenomenon, amounting only to an experience of how little real detail he retained, how quickly it decayed and floated away, how little he solidly knew about either place or the people who lived in them. Out of sight, out of mind. The mind, his anyway, really was feeble when you got right down to it, although powerful as well since it was able to generate a whole cartoon version of imaginary places to replace them in their absence. How completely the reality of other people dropped way when they were gone, leaving only shadow puppets in a theatre of his somewhat lacking imaginings.

It was a disappointing insight into himself, for all that it was one that he (and others?) had gone on living with for quite some time. It was a matter of picking up and putting down, stepping into a set of half-familiar relationships, or trying to hop from one place to the other. An act of mental reconstruction was taking place every time, he realized, an effort which produced poor, softened, self-serving reflections of those people and places he was trying to bring to mind in his recollections, putting them in order as he went, giving them a final so-called 'life' in his so-called novel.

All his became particularly obvious and painful when it was his own particular mother dying in her generic hospital bed. She was slipping away forever without ever having been known, or so it seemed, and conversely it became difficult for Jack Mudie to believe that he himself had ever – except perhaps in childhood – been anything more to her than a dimly apprehended shadow, a glitch in her mind, an irritating shadow moreover which frequently angered her by not behaving as it should in her own puppet theatre version of the world, as they had watched it slowly disintegrate under the onslaught of her growing dementia. But he knew, they all knew, that she had always been mad, and furthermore he believed that they had been the main cause of her insanity.

Anyway, this is perhaps why the towns he dwelt in remained strange to him, and why he remained an outsider in them both. Running through the strange town, surviving due to inefficiencies in the administration, the lack of mesh and cohesion to be found in their hollow notions of community and representation. Did he believe in any of this ridiculous crap? How might it have turned out for the best?

In the winter, his father used to take the gearbox off a car and carry it upstairs to their council flat to work on in front of the fire. Newspapers were spread on the carpet, and a sheet held over the fireplace to get the flue roaring, until it finally caught alight and flew up the chimney, and all those words flew up with it, glowing for an instant then grey flakes drifting away: that was their world, it had gone forever, and good riddance to its facsimiles, thought Jack.

Fitting cogs together, scrubbing wire brushes in petrol baths, worn bushes all carefully replaced, reassembled, all to make ends meet. Except they didn't always, they sometimes flapped loosely in unrealized, unsingable songs, and at the end of a week he and his mother scoured the flat, looking down the back of the red settee for pennies: worn or not, twelve of them would buy five Players Navy Cut, and he'd been sent down to Iris, in the middle shop, to hand them over. He'd felt no shame in this. On payday, a comic he'd eyed for many weeks would at last be his: Classics Illustrated, *The Black Tulip*. It was a rare flower, coveted by all who saw or heard of it, grown in a greenhouse in old Amsterdam by careful selective breeding.

One snowy Christmas day he'd unwrapped his first guitar. How its tan sunburst had shone! He'd started to strum on it tonelessly, slowly learning to play *Silent Night* and *Old Black Joe*. Gone are my friends, from the cotton fields away. Keith Steel, a merchant seaman, lived in an upstairs flat with his mother. Here and now, in the strange town, Jack remembered him in his sailor suit. He'd given Jack an old guitar of his own, a slightly better instrument, darker anyway, with ancient varnish that scraped away in powder under his fingernail. Keith's guitar had a battered air of having accompanied a drunken merchant seaman over the seven seas.

He'd tried to learn 45s, destroying them one by one on a wind-up gramophone. Jack needed lessons. His mother suggested he should ask Mr. Hopkins, from the last shop, the grocers. A lucky guess. Behind his white coat, cheese wire, whirling bacon slicer, and a jar of broken biscuits on the counter, he was a retired amateur jazz musician with a grey goatee who played guitar and soprano sax. He'd taught Jack on Fridays, early evenings. Chords, simple classical pieces. Jack's fingers had been too small for the fretboard, Mr. Hopkins' wife always knitting an endless cardigan, and towards the end of the lesson she had brought in unbroken biscuits on a plate, coffee in small green cups. Once, after much persuasion, Mr. Hopkins had taken out the treasured Soprano and played them his tune. They'd sipped and listened, listened and sipped. *Ain't Misbehavin'*. Mrs Hopkins glinted behind her winged spectacles, knitting, because he was savin' all his love for her.

If you really wanted to be a drug dealer in London, not just a fake one like Gay Tony, your best option, the best job you could possibly have would be as a bus driver on one of those winding hail-and-ride routes. They could just put their hands up with a couple of twenty-pound notes in their palm, and the driver would stop and pull a wrap out from behind his counter. The mayor could issue you with a special licence to carry a weapon. Nah, said Maleek. That's clever, but you would soon be caught. They got cameras all over them buses. Not the little ones. Hmmm. Tyrone a no show. Sally put him in the sitting room to wait. Again, it was an experience of being locked in. She'd removed the inside handle. It was her punishment room, Tyrone said after he'd turned up and been debriefed about his mock exam performance.

Jack hadn't minded being Sally's prisoner. A beautiful, sexy woman whose harsh tongue inflamed his Wednesday evening sessions with an (as always) half-reluctant boy, she had put in only the briefest of appearances, just enough, more than enough, to make her a ft. She looked like Kelly Rowland, Queen of Nellyville. Did she think of him when she was with her boo? Jack purposely spun out each and every conversation past its tolerable limit: a few seconds before she slammed the front door in his face.

When he went down to be at his mother's bedside, he had noticed Mikey's head was shaped like an unopened bulb, bulging but tapering away at the top; a sprig of hair remaining on its summit formed the wisp of a question mark above his large eyes. They were sitting in the Highfield Social Club. The place was half-dead. *Don't Look Back in Anger* played on the jukebox, put on by the clutch of twenty-somethings clustered at the end of the bar; to them a classic of twenty years ago, it reminded Jack of the woozy, unhappy hedonism of the daft university students he'd been teaching at the time. It put him in a place he didn't mind remembering.

The barmaid sent over a couple of glasses of something that tasted a bit like anisette. Brought to them by a thin, youthful woman from the Midlands. She had four grown-up children and had been one of their mother's main carers. Maybe it had been her idea. She was a lovely woman. At last Little Richard came on and Mike told him something he'd recently read on Wikipedia about his career. Jack felt at a wrenching distance from it all, as perhaps did Mikey, but no, he had been playing tapes as usual.

Peace to him, peace to all of them. After all, they hadn't asked to be related to him any more than Tyrone or Maleek had demanded he give them English tuition. The former polite and thoughtful, although completely uninterested, the latter bouncing off the walls of Hackney Youth Hub. One of the naughty boys as his mother had described them to all her carers, with one of the last of her smiles, her face alive with irony.

Earlier on, his brother had shown him the latest of his dioramas, constructed of model cars and accessories he'd bought over the internet or had found in Taunton. It was a scene from the late forties of a woman standing beside a silver Airstream caravan, looking obliquely out with her arm raised to shade her eyes towards what might be a horizon. Her husband, in knee-length shorts, prepared to throw a frisbee for a jumping, excited dog. Behind him was a Nash Countryman of the correct year and a downloaded wraparound photo of the landscape of the Rocky Mountains, below them a piece of Astroturf cut to fit the top shelf of one of his car cabinets. The other held his reconstruction of a Studebaker garage, with two Golden Hawks in different states of repair, one of them undergoing restoration on a ramp. Mikey had got him to try out his virtual car racing set-up in the spare bedroom, and also performed a couple of magic tricks.

They sat and drank until closing time, and as usual Jack felt his brother's slight irritation when he turned down his tilted-glass offer of one last drink. He'd had enough, enough so that he felt a bit unsteady as he tottered around to their parents' bungalow. His father was still listening to the radio in bed, which struck him as a good sign of something. Jack had fallen asleep straight away in relief, as he usually did after one of these long, strained sessions.

Now he was back in town at his desk in front of the sticky keyboard at which he wrote his dirty little books. Jack Mudie. The man without a story. But there was a wisp and a wire curled up around here somewhere, a final connection always to be made, at which point the whole gizmo would light up like Christmas and begin to whirr a little bit. The windmill on the music box would turn again. The Antelope would leap from its signboard and become a real antelope, running like hell to get away from the two White Lions. And so it would all come out straight and true in the end. Suddenly, through the fog of this belief, he remembered the absolute certainty with which his father once demonstrated the action of a magnet upon iron filings, the unerring patterns they made, the invisible field of astonishing forces, and the important idea – held to have a mysterious explanatory power – that like repels like and opposites attract; leaving him to pry the two magnets apart for himself with his small, grappling fingers.

Dad remembered, those special moments that seemed to define something for him. Do you remember when we worked on that Buick? Comes out of nowhere with that smile, and Mum used to curate these moments of his sometimes, mentioning them, imbuing them with further portent and significance. The lord had spoken. And it wasn't even that she particularly revered his defining memory moments herself, although he 'often mentioned' them, just that she thought that he, Jack, should mark them, remember them, guard their meaning. Do you remember when we worked on that Buick? As if that was the only moment of contact they had ever achieved, was it really the only significance his eldest son's entire life had for him?

It wasn't, of course, but there was always something irresistible to him about the way these things fell out, offering themselves up for meaning like the wishbones of Christmas turkeys they had eaten long ago in his childhood, prised apart between his father's short blunt finger and his own pink twig. But who would get the bigger half, who would be allowed to make their silent wish?

Making somebody else listen to your memories was like showing off your gold filling. A way of registering your contempt for them, with a none-too-appetizing treat. If you are noticed at all it is as a denied influence at first, doomed anyway to become memory's tool in one way or another; automatic cheerleader to their inner theatre of recollection, internalized approver of dubious exploits still at a planning stage. For every Saturday afternoon sports watching armchair ham there was a mum on hand with an ever-replenishing round of ham sandwiches. Without her dark energy to drive them, they would all flop down, like broken puppets.

Dad, always with a smile on his face at the thought of a car, a bike, lighting up in company like an extension-lamp plugged into the grid, the grid. Jack had always admired him for having a job he liked, being a mechanic, which he might deny, but it was the whole of the best part of him, finally what had made him be like himself.. Not so chirpy nowadays, devastated by mum's death, he held *Motorcycle News* in his mottled brown hands, he read all day long, not trying to reconnect, watching the rebuilds on the rebuild channel, rubbing away at the hours until he himself was rubbed out.

All these ridiculous things were prodded towards you, and fatefully, faithfully, you picked them up. His father had always got the main part of the wishbone, and it had turned out just the same this time. The lion's share of suffering was perhaps his final prize. It had been more than he could possibly bear, yet somehow or other he had done so. He appeared unchanged, the only way they could really accept him. And at the end of the last day, he was alive to watch cars being rebuilt on telly and read the motorcycling papers. Mikey brought them around for him, kept him talking.

Stationers Park was a long narrow piece of ground which tumbled down between two nearby streets, amongst the most agreeable in all Toyland, red and stately, suitable for Christmas cards, framed by processions of alien pollarded trees on the steep hill from the top on which Jack had recently taken a photo with his phone, only to be asked by a passing woman if he happened to be David Icke, or 'ick' as she pronounced it. Finally, the penny had dropped with him, who she was referring to, but fearing she might be a follower of his instead simply said that no, he wasn't the lizard-fancying conspiracy theorist. "But you are him," she had insisted. "You look exactly like him." Jack had descended the hill to his assignment in the beautiful Christmas card house, actually a well-appointed foster home: a surly runaway of a boy who was determined not to be inspired by anything, not even stories about space and long multiplication.

Jack was back there today, wandering around the park, biding his time, drinking an Americano at a trestle table before his weekly torment with the lad. It really was a pretty little park, locked up at night, a river of brightly dressed children continually streaming around it from top to bottom, either in school uniform (he had once seen his tutee hiding under his jacket passing through), or gambolling at the side of responsible-looking young middle-class parents wearing whatever they had now instead of cagoules, carrying those modest frayed bags stuffed with anything sensible a child could possibly need, their awkward, slightly frail looking bodies obviously bursting with inquisitiveness and intelligence. The park had everything – a dried up rocky stream with a muddy pool at the bottom end, a stony bridge you had to clamber across, holding on, a couple of tennis courts, the back end of a mid-Victorian church now repurposed into fifteen flats, the vicarage still next door, and at the top of the park a trio of bowl-like baseball and football courts in which a few boys wearing sharp sports strip practiced in the early summer evening. A few groups of mums and adolescents sat around smoking and chatting at folded steel municipal picnic tables.

Something about the place, its continual ambulatory circular traffic, reminded Jack of the cliff top garden at Sidmouth where he and his brother had scattered his mother's ashes, partly at a bench looking out to sea, partly beside some shrubs planted in a clump around a secluded bower. Both had a certain holiday gaiety he supposed, something worn-in and reflective, public memory gardens with open lockable gates. She would have liked the park, Jack thought, as he tried somehow to mentally attach her to it, but she would not have wanted to stay long or come back. It was a pleasant place, lovely enough, but mainly for young people not old ones like herself and Jack. He would do just as well to avoid it himself in future, and probably would not be returning often to the Sidmouth cliff garden either, much as mum had loved its fragrant borders, its mini-amphitheatre, its old potting sheds and greenhouses for bringing on cacti. Maybe there was something about places where you scattered ashes. You didn't really want to go back to them. You had a kind of secret with those places – not a public memory. Mr. Jinx flowed down from the shoulder of her ruby dress, a river of tortoiseshell fur.

Huguenots

Charlie Russell was born in 1901, in Dorset. The years of his childhood coincided with a great agricultural recession, and his birthplace seemed to offer few prospects except for a lifetime of ill-paid and insecure day labour in the fields around Dorchester. Lucy Goddard, also of Piddlehinton, was from a family of Huguenot descent and by profession was a glovemaker. Recognizing that the young man possessed both ambition and nerve, she married him, and the young couple immediately decamped in search of a new and better life.

And so to Croydon, where Charlie joined the Metropolitan police force. Their only child, Ivy Marie, my mother's mother, was born there. My mother, God rest her, owned a big solid silver Metropolitan Police medal which commemorates the coronation of George IV in 1911, with Charlie's name, initials, and rank engraved around its edge. She was thinking of selling it on eBay. But didn't.

He wasn't particularly a kind man, she says, he often took the strap to my mother as a little girl.

In the late thirties, he had been injured in the line of duty by a man whom he had just prevented from committing suicide by jumping off West Croydon railway bridge, while attempting to place him under arrest. This desperate man, who was wearing hob-nail boots, had kicked him several times in the shins, broken his skin, subsequently making good his escape over the railway bridge.

Charlie received no treatment for his injuries and soon gangrene set in. Finally, too late, he was hospitalized, and his damaged leg had to be amputated at the knee. As if this hadn't been enough, his remaining leg was left unexercised during convalescence, and, because of this neglect, curled up beneath him and grew crookedly backwards to match his stump at the right knee. PC Charlie Russell was never able to walk properly again.

Their cottage in Hampton Hill was owned by the police, paid for by his police pension. Charlie moved slowly around the cramped place on his knees – but even semi-truncated he was an imposing, fearful figure to his pretty little granddaughters. My grandmother made him some special strap-on knee pads out of old hot water bottles, which made his shuffling method of locomotion a little more comfortable, and he lived on into old age: a large man with a bristly police moustache and a mop of thick white hair on his grave, equine head.

Lucy Goddard had died some years earlier, but his daughter still brought the little girls to visit their grandfather. Charlie would often walk up to the garden gate on his knees, carrying a basket of fallen fruit to offer them from his trees, a peace offering perhaps, intoning: "Haaave a haaple?" in his low Dorsetshire accent.

I have already mentioned Lucy Goddard was once a glovemaker, but that is really all we know of her. It's difficult sometimes not to think of the whiteness of the gloves she made as being in some sort of correspondence with those later worn by Ivy, her daughter, in her occupation as a telephone operator in London, at the Mayfair Exchange.

To get a job there you had to possess two things: a super-clarity of diction and a pair of white silk gloves. The first was easy enough to put on, but the gloves required a considerable investment. Their purpose was to completely insulate your fingertips, so you wouldn't earth any of the surplus electricity spilling through the wires. Some of the conversations you heard on those headsets might give you a nasty shock. And when Ivy spoke at home she often gestured with her hands, as though words in themselves weren't enough to convey her full meaning. "It's the French in you," her husband, my grandfather, always said, and she turned away from him impatiently to the keyboard, and began to play a beautiful, dreamy tune.

Fire in the Hole

Eileen could see it flittering just above eye-level from the square tower that protruded from the ground, half-buried down there, as they approached in their hired car. They still flew the Stars and Stripes from the Norman church in dear old Dunkeswell. Her heart lurched at the sight of it, but they drove on up to Mudville, which of course wasn't there at all, not really, although it was still an airfield of sorts. Who would have thought she'd ever be ninety years old? Longevity wasn't something she'd bargained for, or even thought about, but there, it had happened anyway. She had learned how to take care of herself, unlike most nurses she'd ever known.

When they said your mind was as sharp as a pin, you knew you were fading fast. Comes a time when all you can do is remember, but it's all you can do to recall a damn thing. Which is why she'd agreed to come on this trip, apart from the hope of seeing some people she remembered. Deep in her heart she knew they were all long dead, but why not kick over the ashes and see if there was a spark still glowing under the grey stuff, the cold cinders? Why not? In reality, it had all been Delphine's doing.

"You remember any of this?" Delphine sang from the driver's seat of the silver Peugeot. "This is about the prettiest place I ever saw."

"I didn't want to leave." Eileen spoke quietly, but she'd said it so often that Delphine didn't hear her grandmother.

"You didn't want to leave, did you?"

Eileen said nothing, looked out of the window, which was half rolled down so that a warm breeze might tickle her nose. These hills were beautiful in late spring, but it was at this time that the hedgerows suddenly and completely put forth and obscured them. A green blur. They dipped down a lane, turned up past a pub that didn't seem to be there any longer, and around the final bend into emptiness. She'd known that Mudville wasn't going to be there anymore, but in her mind, it was still that buzzing city, a fractious, intense sort of place, stressed wasn't the word, they hadn't heard of that then, and yet all around that sleepy, syrupy stillness of countryside. She was unprepared for the wide open breezy park, the Aileron, a homely little bar and grill, the Sunday fliers, parachutists overhead and light aircraft bobbing down the runway like brightly-painted toys.

The warehouses – one or two were rusty relics she actually recognized, most were modern units – reassured her that people actually still did some work here, but before long she had repeopled the place, and Delphine, who had known this was going to happen, just let her be and stopped her prattle whilst her grandma looked around her at the jeeps, the rows of huts and hangars, anti-aircraft gun towers, silo-like fuel tanks, taxiing Liberators and Flying Fortresses. Where was the hospital? Gone west, old woman. The officer's club? Ditto.

The museum turned out to be a two-storey walk-up prefab in one of the smaller warehouse units. They were going to close it down but this would be one last opportunity for any surviving veterans to go and look at it. After a quick circuit of the other attractions, Delphine and her partner helped her out of the hire car and they proceeded towards the entrance of the memorial display. The welcoming party consisted of a few local volunteers, and an old woman she didn't know who'd settled around these parts. She was soon led towards a desk where they gave her a name tab, immediately offered her a seat. Eileen didn't want to sit down now she was standing up.

Glenn Miller was toot-toot-tootling softly through small speakers as she walked around the cases, looked at the wall displays, pieces of shrapnel and old spare parts nobody could identify any longer, faded from the earth. She moved slowly but didn't linger long in front of each item, though some of the photographs of airplanes stopped her in her tracks. The photographs were best, and a copy or two of the old camp newspaper. There seemed to be nothing about the medics and the nurses. Everyone was hale and hearty, flaring up at her. She was staring fixedly at a group of enlarged snaps when suddenly she noticed, in a picture her eye had glanced past several times, that the bright-faced young woman was herself. She wore her sergeant's uniform, smartly buttoned up, and stood beside the curved corrugated wall of a Nissen hut – next to a soldier who was considerably less formally dressed, grinning sideways, pulling a dumb face in a practiced way that told you perhaps that he was a sergeant as well, off duty. Then there was another photo, a bare-chested guy out on the field, from a few yards back, captioned 'Master Sergeant'.

She saw him again in her mind's eye as he had been that day in Sidmouth, but most of all reaching across from behind the wheel of his jeep with an open-palmed gesture that welcomed her to her carriage, her ride. Mitch was a lot of fun, a good sort. Their moments of closeness raced upon her, raced up her body like an electric charge. She felt a terrible pity rushing into her brain, forcing her to cry out her eyes but she blinked it away. Those damned pictures. They were all anyone ever seemed to have, and they tore your heart out. She fought it back and turned away with no expression, walked stiffly on. Eileen didn't want to be discussing any of this with Delphine. But then it struck her that Mitch must have had children. Where else might they have gotten the photographs?

Hurrying around the corner, she came upon an old wooden cabinet dedicated to Joe Kennedy, some medals, an old newspaper article mounted on cardboard and propped up. She glanced towards it but moved straight on towards the stairs. Thankfully there was a stairlift such as she had at home, which whisked her up in no time. She looked around for Delphine, who was nowhere to be seen. She'd lost her, raced off like a greyhound on her own. That's not exactly how Delphine would put it. Eileen felt a sort of childish glee for a moment. Again, she pulled herself together and headed in the direction of a knot of people who were gathered at the far end of the gallery.

Old people mostly, as old as her, and still going. A tall slightly stooped gentleman was standing in front of a wall-mounted display of blown-up photographs, a sequence of a Liberator that had exploded on the runway while being refuelled fully-laden. And standing before her was the guy who had been on top of the plane with a hose, refuelling it when it went up. Incredibly he had survived, after years in hospital, and rebuilt his life. There was something a little twisted about his face, as stiff as any of them, but there he was, relaxed and fluent, telling them about it. He had no memory of the incident until he woke up in hospital, and in a very bad way. Eileen listened in fascination. She had no memory of the incident either, yet she thought maybe someone might have spoken of it. Maybe it was before she arrived at the base, a few months ago.

It didn't matter either way. The man, Howie Feather, talked on and on, laughing and joking about his lucky escape from an inferno in which the aircrew had perished. But what could you do? He'd had to come all the way over from Flagstaff to bear witness to it. He was wearing a pale blue windcheater which hung off his wide frame, smartly dressed in American casual clothes. A prosperous old man, not much hair, a little wild. You just had to love him, everyone did. He certainly had a story to tell.

Eileen wanted to ask him a question, but she couldn't think of one for now. She enjoyed listening to his voice, the way he described parts of the refuelling routine, of course they'd never found out what caused it to go up like that. They never did. Faulty wiring probably. She looked along the photographs, taking in the hellish ferocity of the blast as it developed, sliding over everything like a hood until at the last there was nothing but brilliance. Everything was gone.

How in the hell could Howie Feather have survived that? Plainly he was lying. Eileen wanted to say this, but she didn't have the heart she supposed. She felt a little confused for a moment. Howie Feather had stopped speaking and stepped towards her. He peered at her name tag.

"Eileen," he said. "Nope. Don't recall that name. Wait, you were a nurse?"

"I think I must have come later. I'm sure I'd remember the incident you describe. I patched up a lot of GIs in my day."

"You saved my life!" said Howie. "I loved you girls!"

"But I wasn't there," Eileen insisted. "I was there when Joe Kennedy got killed, when Joe Louis came over. Right to the end."

"Sure." He put his large hands on her tiny shoulders. "Sister," he said. "I'm so glad to see you! I'm so glad I had you in my life."

Oh dear. He sounded a bit mad to Eileen. He'd obviously just floated way. She smiled back at him. He was, after all, in spirit, one of the men she had nursed. Not that she had ever been the type to hang on to memories of that sort. Once out of her ward people were generally out of her mind.

"Well, I'm very glad to meet you too, Mr. Feather."

They began to talk, and it transpired that Howie had indeed returned to Flagstaff, invalided out of the war, and it had been there he'd gotten into real estate with his brother. No more aero engines for him. He'd ridden a bicycle to work in the downtown office for forty years, to which he attributed his longevity. Unlike Eileen, he had never married. Strange. To her, he looked like he had been tended by women throughout his life. How else could he have survived so long?

She asked her about herself and she told him she had hailed from Des Moines. But she explained with a triumphant gleam that unlike him she had remained in England. She had married an Englishman and she had stayed here. Howie was delighted by this news, astounded but happy to discover such a great thing. This woman had stayed here in the place where she had served. She had become English, more or less. He was damned if he would have guessed she was from the mid-West.

Just then Delphine bounded up to them like an overfed Labrador. "There you are, grandma. I see you've made a new friend already." She smiled warmly at Howie, a buxom American girl of about thirty-five in a billowing flowery cotton blouse, a pair of capacious denims, a Southern Belle. No-one in a million years could ever have guessed those two were related. That's what Howie thought. "I hope you haven't been getting her too excited," Delphine blurted out.

Howie didn't reply to this remark, nor look again at the woman who had made it. He was in his own world, though still standing over Eileen, a pale trembling streak of a man who was just happy to be there. Delphine noticed the wall display of the sequence of the exploding Liberator and soon became absorbed in examining it closely. Howie joined her, pointing out the dark smudge on top of the plane just before it caught fire. "That's me," he said. "I was there."

"Grandma," she called over her shoulder. "You've been holding out on me. Did you see this?"

"Just now," Eileen replied. "I don't remember it. I don't think I was there. Was I?" She looked at Howie, who had turned, but he just stared at her. "They must have rebuilt it all so fast," she said vaguely. "Like they did after the war."

Delphine gaped at Howie Feather. She too was astonished he had survived this incandescent immolation.

"Did they give you a medal?" she asked him.

"No, ma'am."

At the reception proper, which took place in the dining room of the Aileron, Eileen was introduced to more of the other attendees, one or two of whom were in old uniforms that didn't fit right. All of them were old gentlemen, all praised the nurses, but none of them seemed to remember her. She was still popular though. There was something about the small woman who stood there so firmly, appraising you with a sharp eye, which drew people to her.

Afterward, Delphine drove her down into the dip in search of Dunns End. It was there alright, although she knew for a fact there were no longer any Dunns living in it. Gerald had sold it soon after his parents died, a considerable nest egg to revive their flagging fortunes. Eileen saw that the name had been changed. It was now The Manor, and a freshly painted black iron gate was firmly closed across its raked gravel drive. Eileen didn't, in any case, want to go in there. Better to remember the place in wartime. Almost falling down, ragged with leaning beanpoles and clucking chickens, which Mrs. B. had reared from tiny chicks. Then Delphine drove them back up to Weybridge.

The house was made of wood, stained with dark creosote to stop it rotting and falling to pieces. Eileen and Gerald had brought up their children here. Miraculously the place hadn't burned down. It was actually a beautiful house, had been relatively cheap, but with the downside that it had proved hard to resell at a decent price. Not that Eileen cared particularly. She didn't particularly care but on the other hand, there was now a lot of space for her to rattle around in.

It wasn't until a few days after Delphine flew home to the States to rejoin her partner – another woman she was in some sort of business with, although Eileen could never understand what it was: she'd thought her oldest grandchild was a grade-school teacher – that things started to slide a little bit further down the slippery slope to Mudvillle.

It had been Benji, their eldest, who'd decided to go back to America, to be an American like his mother. He would have been in his mid-sixties now, but had died fifteen years ago, not long before his father. She always said one thing about Gerald – she was never bored when she was with him. Benji had tried to live an adventurous life but had wound up working for Shell in New Orleans. It was there, in the French Quarter, that he had met Delphine's mother, a fellow barfly, and there he had emptied so much alcohol and seafood gumbo into his body that it turned into cancer. Delphine had loved him. Delphine had always wanted to come to England. And now she had come and gone home again.

Susan had always been a homebody; but even plain, intense Susan, who had inherited some of her father's darker moods, had eventually moved away, got married to Tom from Derby and produced three grandchildren, whom she had sometimes brought down to see her. Now they too were grown up and gone. Eileen resisted all attempts to dislodge her from her home and move her up to Derby. She thought Susan had been relieved – her mother was perfectly willing to spend Christmas with them, or to have grandchildren to stay from time to time but drew the line right there. After all, she had the carers coming in three times a day and had found these tattooed, no longer young woman – one girl in her forties had four almost grown-up children of her own – to be good company, in brief if frequent doses. Apart from her carers, there was always the bridge club to keep her on her toes, should she feel the need for mental exercise.

Eileen no longer made any effort to keep the house. There were cobwebs in every corner, some hanging down in ribbons from the lampshades, but she didn't even notice them. The carers – it wasn't their job to do that kind of thing, they had Eileen to look after, and each was responsible for several other elderly people on her rounds. Cathy sometimes brought her dog with her, a narrow-nosed, stocky creature, tan and white, which looked as if it had been bred for fighting, although Cathy had assured her this was not the case. The dog, whose name Eileen could never recall, was a friendly enough creature and didn't; mind Eileen vigorously stroking his ears. "You're a handsome devil!" she would say, bending with enthusiasm to this task, and the dog's long mouth would crack in a wide grin that ran almost the length of its narrow head.

Eileen never found herself looking forward to the dog's visits, but was always pleased to see the animal nevertheless, and disappointed when Cathy didn't bring him along on her rounds. Eileen had trouble with everything nowadays. Worst of all, she felt a mounting dread. Not of death itself – she'd seen too much of it not to feel as calm at the prospect of her own demise as she had at the bedsides of a thousand others. But, like all of them, she valued her independence, and she dreaded the day she would no longer be able to get up and hobble to the toilet, and more than that she dreaded losing her marbles, although when they did finally roll away under the Chesterfield she knew for a fact you soon forgot they were gone.

She heard a tapping at the door. "Come in," she called waveringly, recognizing the knock of Joy, one of her dog-less carers.

"Hello Eileen!" she said. "Time for your medicine. What shall we have for dinner tonight? How about some soup!"

"Thank you."

"Thank *you*, Eileen. Thank you for thanking me."

Joy went through to the kitchen to pop Eileen's medication out of its bubbles and place a can of soup she emptied into a small saucepan on the hob. Eileen didn't own a microwave, she didn't trust them "How was your trip down to Devon?" Joy asked her.

"It was splendid," Eileen said. "Absolutely splendid. I was there during the war, you know. The big one."

"Yes dear, you told me. Well, that was a nice quiet place to spend it." Joy was the younger of the three carers, quite the glamour girl in her pale blue nylon trouser uniform with its swallow insignia flying over her left breast.

"It wasn't always quiet," Eileen murmured.

She wanted to tell Joy about Howie Feather and the exploding Liberator, but suddenly she felt tired and realized as she opened her mouth to speak that she was fuzzy on the details. Had Howie jumped for his life? Had he been killed? No, he'd been right there in front of her. She tried to remember what the planes sounded like. Like a convoy of big trucks driving low across the sky. As she framed something to say she noticed that Joy had gone back to the kitchen to pour the simmering soup into a bowl and bring it through. By the time she arrived Eileen had forgotten what she was going to say. Joy perched on the sofa and watched her spooning the soup into her pursed mouth. It was too hot, but Eileen kept at it, glad to demonstrate that she could at least feed herself.

"Did your granddaughter enjoy herself?" her carer enquired brightly.

"I hope she did," Eileen said. "I think so. She's gone home now."

"She didn't stay long, did she?" Joy's tact.

"Long enough."

"Come on, Eileen. Let's get these tablets down you." She gave Eileen her tablets with a glass of orange juice from the fridge. Eileen didn't feel like taking them, but she didn't make a big issue of it.

Delphine had done a lot of sightseeing in London, with the help of her walkie-talkie, and Eileen told her a few stories about how it was in wartime – and how later she and Gerald used to take her father to Hamley's – the toyshop on Regent Street – every Christmas to watch the trains running round and round. Delphine said she would check it out, but Eileen didn't think she had bothered. After all, she didn't have any children of her own, not as yet, perhaps never at this rate.

After a few more attempts to make conversation, Joy took away her soup bowl and left. She would be back on Friday, she reminded the old lady.

What a mad old woman she had become, Eileen thought. Sooner or later she was going to have to give in and move up to Derby into Susan and Tom's granny flat, as they called it, none too enticingly.

Their dark wooden house with its draughty spots, its nooks and crannies crammed with half-forgotten junk, was still so full of Gerald's presence, like a coat left over the back of a chair. Eileen still half-expected to hear his key in the door late at night, but most of the time she managed to drift off to sleep before getting too fretful about this, staying quite comfortably cocooned in her routines and her memories.

Gerald's boat scheme had come to more or less nothing as she had expected, as she told him it would not long after their marriage, but not before he'd sunk what little savings he had into it. He'd done a few cross-channel trips alright but being out there in the dark had given him the heebie-jeebies, always half-expecting a U-boat to break surface on his port bow, or perhaps it had been the stuff he knocked back to get himself through his crossings. Also, he didn't like having to be nice to people, the passengers, and frequently he wasn't polite to them.

But he'd managed to offload his half of the boat onto his partner. Poor Gerald. He'd been like a cat with fleas after that for a whole year, trying anything, drinking too much, until eventually, the old Dunn connections had paid off, strings were pulled, and he was found a place at Lloyd's in Leadenhall Street as a shipping clerk and from there became an underwriter, an assessor of other people's risks.

When the base had closed in the early fifties, Eileen ceased to be a nurse and became instead a trainer of nurses at the Royal Free in Hampstead. Later on, she graduated to lecturer in the nursing school, then senior lecturer. Specialist subject: bones. She'd worked damned hard in those early days of their marriage, often felt she wasn't being appreciated for it. Gerald spent a lot of time away from home in all phases of his career, whether supposedly lashed to the yard-arm or allegedly meeting an important shipping client.

Still, their life together had always retained an element of fun, that's how she preferred to remember it, and when she had fallen pregnant with Benjamin there could have been no two parents more delighted than Eileen and Gerald Dunn.

She sat there remembering, a small dark figure in a chair beside the only light in the room, next to her on the small table; and the darkness covered her, like a rough, blanket. Geoff. Geoffrey. He had grown up so soon to be such a fine young man. He had been a comforter, and as his father grew older, his son had gradually come to replace him in her affection. Something hurt and then it didn't, but in the space where it didn't – purely relief at first – a small feeling of bright emptiness persisted like a heartbeat.

Red Leicester

Rich Mudie wasn't the last of the Mudies, not by a long chalk, but sometimes it definitely felt like it: a chalk long enough to draw several times around his huge body. Richie they none of them wanted to take the measure of. Chalk and cheese. On his own, since mum died.

He trailed his menagerie of broken-down Jags and Daimlers from unit to unit up on Dunkeswell airfield. Luxury cars of the 80s, big rolling tanks with a spongy ride and luxury interiors of walnut and creamy leatherette. They were later models of the dinosaurs his father had driven as a chauffeur from the sixties onwards; cars he'd borrowed to take mum and the four kids down to the seaside whenever his boss, Mr. Merit, was out of the country. Merit – he had some things to recommend him, Dad used to say. They'd all piled into the Daimler. Richie loved those motors. They were imprinted on him. A ledge to perch on. Beautiful things not going anywhere. But they must be worth something to somebody, he would've thought, especially if he got them running.

For a while, he lived in a small caravan tucked inside a big warehouse unit: a closed space in a closed space, a bug in a rug. He moved up onto a wide ledge near the roof, a cosy little nest up there, a bit draughty; then moved to an old USAF repair hangar left over from the war, fraying corrugated iron paper thin, perforated by rust mites, full of left-hand drive jeep ghosts. Boxes of parts, boxes of his mum's ornaments and family albums, electrical fittings, furniture, bits and pieces, plus a considerable number of motorbikes, another accumulation of non-runners; and the cars.

Whatever happened, happened. There wasn't a day went by he didn't think about his mum and dad. Both gone now and the rest of the family scattered across the South of England like rotten fruit on the ground with no-one to pick it up. Leading separate lives as they had done, done for years. Anyway, they'd all had enough of him. All that. It was the realization he was on his own, not just for a while (he was alright with that) but for the rest of his life. France? Spain? His plans rose and collapsed: geysers prickling the surface of his brain. On the plus side, he had money in the bank. And his heavy plant licence. Plenty of work, yeah – if you thought it was worth doing.

He picked and chose, put in a couple of weeks on some site – digging on the sandy beach along Newton Abbot way was a nice one – but mainly he found himself choosing to stay at home and spend his downtime picking out more useless things to buy. A Bedford van, a Luton same as his brother's, a space heater, a set of golf clubs, a radiogram well past its humming days; but he wasn't going to put his money into a house on the estate. He much preferred it up on the airfield, where there was a bit of life.

Plenty of people around, all busying away. A decent breakfast to be had, and if worst came to worst, watching the microlights and light planes taking off and the parachutists blossoming high up, drifting like tiny puffs of smoke, getting bigger as they fell back to earth. If you could be bothered to watch them. Because of the time. Because of the time it took. Grubbing around, looking at this, looking at that. Weighing it up like. The big bloke. Was it a good deal, a sound investment? Or was he wasting his mum's money, which should have been rightfully all his to spend as he wished, however he wanted?

But he was forced to split it with them or else he'd have had no family, and he had to sell off mum's bungalow, and clean out the garage, because they owned it too, and he moved to Dunkeswell because it wasn't far away and he had relatives there who might put up with him for a while. They wanted him to come, uncle Bill especially, and well, he wouldn't turn away his brother's son, would he? So, he did in a way have family there, and it had appealed to him when he scoped it out from the motel perched at the top of Honiton.

Richie had enjoyed living in the motel, getting dinners sent in, spent most nights in the bar, hassling whoever was around. He wasn't a troublemaker. More a big matey bloke – and some people expected trouble from people like him. They didn't want anything to do with him to be truthful. What was wrong with him? This was where he tried to be careful, but sometimes he wasn't careful enough. It didn't matter. Really it all bounced off his thick skull anyway, they'd always said so.

He lay in the double bed he'd fixed up in the rafters of the second rented storage unit adjoining the airfield. There was a metal staircase leading up to wide shelf, further storage space which he'd arranged into a little flat for himself, full of all sorts of stuff but giving the appearance of being almost empty due to its expanse, open on one end to the emptiness of the large unit and a fierce drop to the ground below. Fortunately, he had a space heater up there to take the edge off the cold.

The table lamp beside him didn't penetrate far into the blackness but rather built a dark wall around the bed where he lay on his back under two duvets and a pink candlewick bedspread. Nothing penetrated except a faint patch of lighter darkness pricked by stars above and in the pitch-black shadows to his right the red filament of the space heater, which he'd just turned off prior to hopping into bed, faded like dying coal. He snuggled over on his side and watched it retreating, a collapsing red planet, a tiny speck of almost-light, far off then invisible in the freezing velvety infinity of deep space. He felt himself drifting away in his warm cocoon of stuffed polyester, his eyelids falling shut. A deep droning sound lulled him further into sleep. In the airfield hospital, a group of uniformed women stood at the ready.

He wasn't dreaming about any of that, although he'd had a look around the small war museum and admired the sheer enormity of the Liberator prop planted in the ground outside, as though it had sprouted there. It gave him a sense of connection to things his father had always loved. American things. And when he'd first arrived he was delighted to find out that the few remaining hangars and workshops were owned by someone and available for rent. He discovered quickly that they were more hole than sock by now, decided he'd be better off in one of the new units on the nearby industrial estate, which housed every conceivable kind of small business and secluded rural sweatshop assembling boat fittings and trinkets and electronic doo-dahs. You weren't supposed to stay in them overnight; it was against the tenancy agreement. Richie had decided to ignore this and make his unit into a home. Until he decided on his next big move. He had a few quid in the bank; the last thing he wanted to do was get lumbered with a house down on the Highfield estate.

He wasn't dreaming of anything. His dream-life took place mostly during the hours of daylight. Often he stationed himself on a chair in Pauline and Bill's living room for hours, holding forth with a cooling mug of tea that was dwarfed in his fist. A big cuddly giant who lived at the top of a beanstalk. "It never happened, Bill," he explained. "Not like they said it did, anyway. How'd they known them planes was going to fly into the towers? Which they did know, it stands to reason they did. The CIA. All of them. They were behind it truth be told. In other words, it was the Jews behind it. And behind them ... the Illuminati. The Illuminati, Bill. That's where it starts getting a bit complicated." He frowned as he delivered this coup de grace: "The Illuminati!" he whispered.

There was a parched feeling, a dryness produced by empty words hammering about the room for hours that had always been, historically speaking, associated with setting the world to rights. Bill worried that a load of Pikeys were going to move into the mobile holiday homes being erected on land at the bottom of the road, right at the edge, just before the land tumbled down into a forested gully, but so far they hadn't arrived. "Who are they?" he asked. "It don't make no sense to me, Richie." He hadn't heard of the Illuminati.

"They are – how can I put it – a secret group of people who control everything. They're super-powerful and they can do anything they want. Make us believe what they want us to believe, far as I can tell. Jews, most of 'em are." He held up his splayed hands, minus thumbs. "Eight people who control the world. Don't bear thinking about, do it?"

"You do talk a lot of rubbish, Richard," Pauline said. "You want to sort your own problems out before you start talking about things you don't understand. That's what Ray and Viv would have said – I know that's what they'd want you to do."

Pauline and Bill were side by side on their settee. Bill had been yapping on for hours too, a small man with brown, leathery skin, telling stories of when he and Ray were boys in Molesey, pulling Miller's Thumb out of the River Ember, or young men in Canada wondering what they'd got themselves involved with. It was all too involved, she'd heard it all before a thousand times. Pauline sat in a fug of cigarette smoke with a cold cup of tea beside her and an overflowing ashtray on the small table, resigned to listening to a lot more rubbish. But she liked him, she couldn't help liking him for being family, a connection going back through him to Ray and Viv, to family, and to her judgements of them. It was a mystery to her as to how anyone could think in that disgusting way. All she could say was that it wasn't how she'd been brought up herself, properly, in Priory Road, Hampton.

He put down his mug on the stool beside him, trying to rustle up a more detailed explanation, but abruptly and mysteriously thought better of it, sitting back as far as he could manage between the narrow wings of the dun green armchair.

"You're very welcome here, Richard," Pauline said. "But I'm not going to listen to this sort of rubbish anymore."

"Sorry, Auntie Pauline," he had said contritely.

For somebody with such strong convictions, opinions which seemed to make perfect sense to him, it surprised her to see how he worried so much about giving offence. Now he sat uncertainly, looking like what he really was: a strange, large child with nowhere else to go or be.

Richie pulled his car over to the side of the road, attracted by the sight of a man sitting up there on a big digger, trying to grapple and pull the stump of an ancient oak out of the ground. It was snagged deep by its roots in the dense, stony soil. He stepped through a gap in the hedge and picked his way over towards the bloke, attempting to keep his jeans and trainers out of the muck of the stubbly field in which the man was working alone.

He stood there, commanding attention like a visiting superintend-ant of works, and called up to the bloke with the levers in his hands: "How much they pay you to do that then, buddy?"

The driver didn't notice him straight away. He was wearing his big yellow ear-protectors, sealed in behind the perspex panels of his cab, extended grippers wobbling at the oak stump like a great stubborn tooth stuck in the ground.

Richie stood there grinning at him, hands on hips, waiting to be noticed. The driver didn't stop though, just redoubled his efforts until the stump was torn free of the earth with an almighty grinding of gears and a final groan, and hung aloft, swaying above the desolate field, an exhumed once-living thing whose dangling, twisted roots continued to brush the ground from which they'd been wrenched. At that point, the driver left it hanging and turned off his engine, pulled off the ear-protectors and wall-eyed Richie with a jerk of his head. Richie was applauding him in mimed slow-motion, about as irritating as he could be, oblivious to any effect this might be having, protected by his sheer size, as the oak might have thought it was protected if oaks were capable of thinking.

"How much they pay you to do that then buddy?" he repeated. "Hundred pound a day?"

The other man didn't reply, just sat there, looking down at him.

"Hundred? One-fifty?"

Again, the driver didn't answer.

"I'd want at least that," Richie continued. "Two hundred then? That's what I've been getting over at Newton Abbot just for moving a few piles of sand around"

"Good luck to you, mate." The driver called out suddenly above his grumbling engine, then turned away, shaking his head. He was contemplating the oak stump, immobile now in mid-air, an impressive sight dangling its long roots above the massive hole it had left behind. He felt annoyance. The plonker who had arrived in his field had taken away all the pleasure in shifting it finally, stolen his moment of victory; it was twisting now, none too miraculously or securely suspended in the air in front of him.

"Just asking like," Richie laughed as if he'd made some sort of joke. "Alright, buddy? Don't seem fair, do it?"

The driver grabbed the levers abruptly and swung the stump to one side, not away into the corner of the field but over in Richie's direction, where it hung high in the air and looked for a moment like it might easily break free of the grippers and crush him to death. Richie saw it coming, not very near him really, but stepped back sharply, nearly losing his balance on the grassy furrows. He stumbled, managing to keep his feet under him. "Whoa there!" he shouted.

Now there was mud all over his new brown-tasselled brothel creepers and the bottoms of his jeans were soaked in it, bespattered with shit. He thought he'd like to pull that bloke out of his cab and stick one on him, or several, but that would have entailed getting even muddier. Instead, he retreated through the hedge, got back into his parked car and drove away down the lane.

He hadn't gone fifty yards before he was laughing, a big idiot grin spread across his face as he thought of the bloke sitting up there in his cab wondering what to say back to him. What a wanker, he thought. There really were some absolute tossers driving the heavy machinery in these parts. He had a good mind to report him for that kind of behaviour. You had to chuckle about it though. For some reason, Richie thought he'd "won" this encounter. For some reason, he couldn't stop himself laughing.

East of Dunkeswell the airfield gave onto a long road across the plateau of the Blackdown Hills, not the deep green impassable lanes of Devon but a scrubby plain on which a nylon windsock still bellied and a few hundred yards along a dusty beaten track ran back to a now-defunct racetrack owned by a famous driver, where Formula Three car racing had taken place from time to time, celebrities only, just as on the other side of Dunkeswell, on the way into Honiton, a fairly new stock car stadium stood out over the flat empty fields that strode away on either side of the road that connected to the main London throughway always deserted-looking but buzzing with activity on race nights.

Richie was driving his van along the edge of that long spinal column that made its way towards Taunton, fast and arrow-like, but nevertheless soon fell away if you took any of the turns offs, to small villages consisting of a church, a British Legion hall, a pub or two and possibly a fish and chip shop that opened on Tuesdays and Fridays. Upottery, Cullompton, names like that; places of concentrated settlement that fed tucked away congeries of newer but still old housing, long cul-de-sacs where the buses turned around, places full of old parlours where everything had always been kept miniter, spick and span, with small brass ornaments, Toby jugs on doilies and tiny dark mites of transplanted furniture dusted regularly and polished with beeswax. The jazz singer Joss Stone had come from one of these places before being shot to stardom as a yokel teenager with an astonishing larynx and still used to pop into the shop on the Highfields estate for a few packets of fags and a six pack, until an almost successful plot to kidnap her for ransom by a couple of stoned fans from Sheffield had put paid to her relationship to her roots.

The Taunton road was a fast one and the continuous winds, sliced across by driving rainstorms, had generated a kind of tumbleweed trapped at the edges of the wide fields, made of sheep's wool, and torn up hanks of thin coarse grass, against the square wire fences and newish-looking log posts. At intervals between them, often at crossroads, Richie passed the written-off wrecks of red and yellow hatchbacks, crumpled as if for the crusher, but nobody had even bothered to pick them up, tow them away, grapple them up onto the bed on a big truck. It was a job he wouldn't have minded doing himself if the price was right. But no. There they stayed, looking like someone had died in them, most probably had, and no-one could even be fucked to pick them up. They were death warnings.

It made him angry for some reason. It was typical of the mentality around here. Who wanted to look at that? The families? The effect on him was to make him put his foot to the floor, turn the van's wipers up and keep barrelling through to the other side of the plain, where thankfully you did have to turn down, slow down to plunge past the edge of a wooded precipice hung with mopping trees, braking on the long, twisted way down towards Wellington, more of a small town, schoolkids in bright yellow and maroon blazers flocking along neat pavements and a music shop from the fifties full of brass and woodwind instruments for them to play on.

Out of there quick, the landscape changed again, a straight bit them a plunge leading out into beautiful views of mini-castles set back, which Bill and them always tried to turn into a game of deciding which one you'd like to live in; but since they lived in little bungalows on the estate he couldn't take it seriously.

He had his money and he had to decide what he was going to do with it, realistically not in some ridiculous fantasy. He'd been surprised to hear such crap coming out of Bill's mouth. His mother and father would never speak like that, and he thought there was more love between them too. France? Houses were cheap out there. He'd had a look round out there, seen a few, but he knew he'd never be able to speak French. Would that matter? Of course, it would. No plumbing. Fuck that. With such thoughts teeming in his mind he wound down the last stretch into Taunton itself, where he stuck the van in the town centre carpark and went off to strut around the shops for a while, which is what he'd come for.

He strutted around town, he was still fucking angry. There were quite a few people on the streets, teenagers, mothers and children – it was going home from school time, and being Friday the whole place had a knocked out, can't be bothered feeling to it. He looked in the windows of the shops and found himself getting annoyed with the thin people in them, and the assistants, just sitting around, getting paid for dossing through the last of the day. He wanted to wake them up. Make them run around for him. It was shoes he was after, he remembered now. A good pair of work boots with steel toecaps, size twelves. You'd think that would be easy enough, wouldn't you? And yet every time he went into a shop – be it Clarks or Millets or some such place – he found that all these idle little teenage assistants were suddenly nowhere around to be seen. They miraculously found something more important to do than serve him. What was wrong with him, for fuck's sake? He even spotted a shelf full of boots of exactly the right kind in one place, and stood directly in front of it, but did they come over to serve him? No, they didn't. They all seemed to be out the back suddenly, having a good laugh at him. See that big bloke? You go and serve him. No, you go. And he started to think he heard them laughing about him out the back, in their little cubby holes, and he thought fuck this and walked straight out of the shop. He tried again. This happened two or three times until he thought he must've been giving off some sort of signal whereby they all scattered and hid when they saw him. Like a bad smell. Until he thought fuck this again and gave up on the work boots altogether and went into Wetherspoons for a quick drink.

He bellied up to the long bar, ordered a pint of Stella and copped a look at the menu. He already knew what was on it, knew what he was going to have, but even at this time of the afternoon, the place was heaving with drunks, bar swimming, beer towels sodden. Richie looked down with disgust. The place was filthy and all around him scraggy-looking scumbags were jogging at his elbows, trying to get in front of him, waving their dole money in the faces of skinny couldn't-give-a-shot teenagers moved around at a snail's pace, logging in and out of the tills with their keys and as often as not punching in the wrong numbers. He drained his pint and managed to order another, put in an order for cheeseburger and chips, giving a table number he'd memorized near the door.

But they were still there on either side of him, particularly a man with long greasy hair and a torn, stinking tweed jacket who kept jabbing at him as though he had some prior right of way, to shift him over. On his left side was some sort of mate of his, lanky disgusting alky-type with a big distorted purple conk on him. What the fuck did they want? Richie inflated himself, stood up from the bar, bringing up his elbows hard as he did, managing to clip both of them, so they were knocked back, the tall one holding his face. Richie stomped hard down on the little bloke's foot. "Oh, sorry mate," he said. "I didn't see you there." Then he turned around and marched away with his second pint of Stella and his bar receipt in his hand, back to the front to find his table before some other piece of shit jumped into his seat. Luckily it was empty, he didn't have to turf anyone out of it. So, he sat down, facing the bar, and surveyed the mayhem he'd left behind him. He sat there, upright, looking down at them. Yes, here I am, he was thinking, come on down and have a word if you've got a problem.

The little one was still hopping around, then he seemed to collapse against the bar and slide down onto the brass rail. His mate, the lanky bloke, was standing there gesticulating wildly as blood dripped off his face, and behind the bar the teenagers were dithering, pretending not to see what was going on, but because they'd stopped serving a ruck of customers had built up, and they were looking down to where Richie sat, some of them pointing down to him. Come on then come down and have a word you fucking wankers. He saw one of the bar staff, a slight boy in a waistcoat with a shaved up blonde top knot sneak down the end and through the back door to the kitchen. Something was going to happen, he thought. That little rat's gone to fetch someone. Let him come. The big manager bloke, maybe. He wondered if they had a bouncer tucked away out there. He sat waiting for it all to kick off. Otherwise, he would just eat up his cheeseburger when it came and piss off back to the airfield.

Things had settled down a bit up at the bar, although, even to Richie, it was obvious they weren't going to let it rest there; they never did. He kept an eye on the door to the kitchen, waiting for a big black bouncer to come cannoning through the swing door – and he was thinking, yeah, he was up for the crack of that, if they wanted trouble. But when the door did swing open it was to let out a small manager of some sort, in a greasy suit, about fifty years old, and he just walked straight over to Richie. And said: "I'm sorry sir, I'm going to have to ask you to leave." And when he objected, the manager said. "You leave now, or I call the police." And he stood back, crossed his arms over his belly, waiting for Richie to say something else.

"What?" Richie asked him 'as if he didn't know what. But he did know what. For some reason, he remembered Mikey telling him about the bloke who'd gone rampaging through a pub he was in with a pair of knuckledusters, and he'd done a lot of damage to people. They just stepped back, as though he was invisible, and carried on with their conversations. The pub management had done fuck all about it, and the police took ages to come. Meanwhile this mad bloke – local, everyone knew him – had gone on lashing out, cutting random people's faces open with his knuckledusters. A real animal, like.

And then something seemed to clear in his mind as if he was suddenly able to stand back from it all. He realized he was being offered a good deal and sank his pint, got up, left slowly and calmly without looking over his shoulder. It wasn't until he was halfway down the road, back on the jostling five o'clock pavements of Taunton, he remembered he hadn't had his cheeseburger, nor the money, and he missed a beat while he thought of going back and asking for a refund … but, fuck it, he managed to fight that one and carried on around the corner, up towards the bridge, and turned into the small carpark and his van.

The sun was out, shining brightly, but it was quite cool and fresh. A bit blowy. Richie lumbered towards the carpark, tired, sagging, feeling regretful. The castles and spires and serried ranks of Taunton's wide streets and twisty little alleyways were lit up from above by an even light that seemed to have broken through from heaven; but it was his parents, Ray and Viv, gone now, and he was thinking of them. They weren't coming back, he knew that, but they weren't up in heaven waiting for him neither, and how he wished they were. He tried to think of them looking down on him, telling him what he should do, and he knew it wouldn't be what he had just done, but he couldn't bring himself to think of them up there because he knew they were nowhere of the fucking sort.

And when he got up to the van he noticed it was sagging a bit and saw straight away that someone had slashed one of his front tyres. Good and done properly. God, it might've been, the big bloke telling him off for being a fucking idiot, or just some kids on their way home from school. He got his jack out and quickly fitted the spare, looking around him warily, half-expecting some gang from the pub to run out and ambush him. The place seemed deserted. Out in the open. It had entered a lull before Friday night proper began. Everybody was having dinner and watching the news. He drove back shaking, his hands gripping the wheel tightly. The entire experience had given him the heebie-jeebies.

About halfway home he flicked his headlights on, although it wasn't yet dark just drifting into twilight. He didn't want some clown of a boy-racer to come haring round the bend and smash into him as he carefully climbed up again through the deep wooded hollows and low mopping branches back onto the fast main drag that led to the safety of the airfield. When he got there, he parked the van alongside his unit and scuttled inside, retreating as far as he could, up and towards the back, cocooned himself in darkness and fell asleep listening to crap on the radio.

He'd been banging back and forth across a deeply rutted field for three hours, perched atop a small dumper shifting tack from one spot to another, ferrying half-loads of sand and cement towards the hole they were trying to plug. What remained of the earth's oxygen-supply was being sucked down it into a giant cavity in the centre of the globe where these weird self-replicating insects were feeding it to their young. It was a race against time, but worthwhile all the same. After tea-break, they'd be handing out oxygen masks. Actually, they were repairing a giant underground sewage pipe. They had the lid off it and a team of workers in orange overalls supervised the mix and ferried it down in buckets to the lucky underground operatives.

The dumper groaned and shuddered, strained and spun its wheels, spilled its load across the already near-impassable track, and he could feel the ground banging up through his spine as he perched on the bare metal seat of a machine which he dwarfed like a child's toy. Fuck this for a game of skittles. Fuck it, he was done.

"I'm done, buddy," he called over to the site manager when he reached the edge of the field again, turning off the motor and tossing his liver-coloured gloves onto the warm seat. "I said, I'm done." He walked away from the site and back to his car without waiting for a reply or turning around. He didn't have to do it, did he, if he didn't want to, and this was just a waste of his time to no good purpose. He could do without it, at the end of the day. But as he drove home, he knew that it couldn't go on forever. The money his mum had left him was dribbling away. He had to make his move, do something with it that would be an improvement. For now, though he didn't have to take any shit the agency happened to offer him.

It was about three o'clock when he got back to the airfield. He thought he'd pop into the Aileron and see if they'd sell him a drink. No way. The place was all locked up, a chain across the door. He banged and rattled, peered through to the bar. The lights were on back in the kitchen but no-one was coming to serve him. What was the matter with them? They had the drink in there, why couldn't they come out to sell it to him, where was the objection? He had a few tinnies in the fridge back in the unit, but it wasn't the same without company.

The trouble with drinking on your own was the trip down memory lane it always sparked off, which he remembered two hours later as he lay on his bed amidst a litter of Fosters cans, sobbing his heart out. Poor Rich. He knew he would never have nothing like what his mum and dad had, the sheer amount of love they'd had between them. The way his mum had looked after Ray for years and years, long after his head ballooned out literally out like an elephant's head and he couldn't do anything except sit in the back garden in a camping chair. He didn't even say much. Not a lot anyway. But he did keep cheerful, insofar as he could. All that was true and he knew it. And in earlier years Ray would always spare Viv a thought when he was out. He always remembered to buy her a packet of fags, bring her a bunch of flowers or something, a tea-pot warmer, some trinket.

He was just a human being who wanted what others wanted and in some cases already had. It wasn't hard for some people, and yet for him, these were impossible, impossible dreams. It wasn't hard to hear Viv laughing at something he said, encouraging him, and trying to make sure things were okay for her youngest, who had never flown the nest, that he got everything he could out of his life; and in his mind Richie often saw Ray turn his great baggy turnip head, swollen by his illness, towards him, as if he was trying to pass on something important to his son: the key to everything, how to achieve love and peace, especially, and to be what he himself had been, maybe by sheer luck: a husband and father; but he hadn't succeeded. He thought of it as being like some final fatal line from Buddy Holly.

Richie had been sat next to him in front of the TV when he finally let go. "You alright, Dad? You alright?" Watching his hand rise and fall slowly, as if he was trying to point at something or reach out to his glass of water, but he hadn't wanted it really. Suddenly his hand had stopped moving, and Richie knew, he thought that's it, he's gone. But when the medics came a few minutes later they managed to bosh him back into life again. Amazing how they did it. Amazing to see him come back around, just a bit dazed. But not for long though. Not for long.

Finally, he managed to pull himself around, wash and brush up, and headed down the Aileron, wondering if they would let him in and serve him. You could see they didn't like it, but they did serve him a few pints and he sat at the small bar down the other end from the dining area and looked up at the football match alongside the usual crowd who got in there on a weekday night, nothing special none of them, but struggle as he might he could not get more than half a grunt from any of them, and the eye of the pretty barmaid, about fourteen, skated away every time he tried to catch her by it.

After they'd taken his money, at the end of the night, the manageress – her mum – came around from the other side and told him not to come in again. That was when he got himself banned from The Aileron.

Luppitt ... Smeatharpe ... Combe Raleigh ... Broadhembury ... Mumbai ... the big black pods of hay were being collected from the corners of mown fields and towed away behind tractors; thin, dirty-white cows slumped hopelessly on the wet muddy grass in a field glimpsed through a hedge, a row of bare trees in winter months, before the leaves sprouted and unfurled and hid everything in the deep lanes.

Sometimes he drove over to see Barbs over on the other side of Devon. Apparently, according to her, Princess Diana had been assassinated by the royal family, personal orders from Prince Philip. Richie didn't find that hard to believe. It made sense to him. Diana had secrets, she knew all the dirt on them, all the dirty stuff they got up to which was hidden from us, and she'd been just about to spill it all. Plus, Dodi was a Muslim, which they didn't like at all. An MI6 agent, who was just about to die, had been the one to do it – for queen and country – but she'd lost the link. She thought he'd sabotaged the car or something like that. It had all come out, except it never would. Richie nodded, sipping his tea. He knew where he was with Barbara, with any of his family if they deigned to speak to him. They all lived on the same planet. They shared things. It all fitted together and made sense – the 9/11 cover-up, the moon landing, and now this. It had been well known enough for a while, but Barbs said they had proof. Here was the bloke who'd actually done it, confessing on his death bed. Convincing or what?

"It makes you think, don't it Mikey?" he asked his cousin later on.

"Yeah." Mikey knew it was crazy stuff, madness, pure madness. But Richie was so convincing on these subjects. It was almost impossible to argue with him, and Mikey had learned not to bother.

Mikey listened as he was listening now, half-incredulous, half-swayed. At the end of the day though these were the opinions he'd been listening to most of his life. It was the people who knew that a lot was being hidden from us versus the other people, the majority, who thought everything was as it seemed. Okay. Kind of. The people in the social club liked the Royal Family, for example. Richie certainly didn't. Nor did any of his family. Pauline and Bill and their lot never had any time for them, although their sedentary senility had given rise to a half-hearted participation in televised state occasions. At least it was all familiar. The Queen and Prince Philip had got married in the same year. Their own ceremony and reception had been seen in parallel to the affairs of royalty, you could tell from the photos, full of ladies in waiting, a lounging Falstaff and a flash young prince peeking in, and Graham, soon to be married to Carolyn, and small white ancestors trussed into their costumes, half-obscured by a drooping rack of cherry blossom. Eclipsing the royals in every way. Especially in the beauty of the bride. And they were all still alive. But even that sense of identification was dying away. They weren't all still alive. Some were. Most of these guests, even those who'd arrived too late to be photographed by Pete, were gone now.

"What do you think of the Queen, Richie?" Mikey asked out of the blue.

"She's no mug, is she?" Rich replied glumly. "Put it like that." But he couldn't really see what Mikey was driving at with his question. He started to mentally drag his own opinions of the monarchy across the threshold of speech, pursing his lips, but realized his cousin would share most of them. Except for the conspiracy stuff. Mikey was somebody – same as the rest of his family – who or some reason only wanted to know half of the truth. Why not the whole truth? Anyway, he held back.

I was the only one who wasn't like that, Richie thought, looking back on his own family. Some of the things they thought were - okay - wrong, but all the same there were basic truths about the world you could – and should – never let go. But when Barbs had started talking about Princess Diana's assassin, just soon after he got there – he didn't stay long – as he was sitting on her deep couch, putting his mug of tea down, spreading his arms along the back of the sofa, it was music to his ears, a glimmer of light came on in his head. And for a short space of time, it was like being at home again.

He played with his lovely little nephews, good as gold, listened to Barbara moaning about her ex.. She was still hurting bad, he realized. She was never going to get over it, especially because he'd left her for another bloke. Just walked out on her and his kids and set up home with this feller. What sort of a man was he? A middle-class wanker. He said he felt guilty, but he'd left her in bits. Barbara looked away though the large picture window, tears filling her pale blue eyes.

It was while he was driving a hundred miles or so across Devon, back from Great Torrington to Dunkeswell, that he had thought of Mumtaz again. It was after her husband had died that she took him first into her bed. And it had been okay. He liked it. He liked going round there. He'd always got along quite well with her kids. He was their big uncle Richie, despite everyone knowing very well what was going on. So did his family. They didn't like it at all. Jokes about little brown babies. And worse shit, much worse, his mother screaming at him. Anyway, after they'd upped sticks and moved down this end it had quickly fizzled out. Fft, right out.

Mumtaz was a bit older than him. She had been married, a neighbour of theirs back in Frimley, a family so respectable, so relentlessly friendly that the Mudies had been forced to get used to them. Although she was difficult to understand due to her accent, she was a well-spoken, educated woman. Richie had always liked them. What was the matter with them? Nothing, so far as he could tell, but he'd been gradually worn down by the attitudes of the rest of them on the subject of race. It was the same with Joseph, a good lad from Ghana he used to play football with in his early days on the sites. A fair enough bloke. Very friendly. But little by little he'd been forced – that's how he saw it now – to see these so-called immigrants as his enemies. "She's no mug," was all his father had to say about her, as if Richie was the catch of the century, as if she'd been deviously hatching some fiendish plot against them all.

He didn't take long to get himself together once he had decided to go up to Leicester and stay with Mumtaz. He felt her moving towards him, or maybe he was just thinking of her more often, as getting closer to him, swimming up out of the mists of the past, and then she'd called on his old mobile, the only number she had, weirdly enough just as he was about to throw it away in favour of a new smartphone. He had looked down at the buttons, worn transparent, flashing on and off, and he had known it was her calling. He recognized her number as it happened.

Everything that could be sold, everything he had hesitated over and couldn't bear to get rid of, it all went in a flash. Jags, Daimlers, loaded onto the back of a transporter and spirited away to Axminster. He knew they were worth something, worth more than he took, but there you are – he took it. He just phoned the bloke up, accepted his last offer and he came around pretty quickly. All his old junk, some kept, some dispersed for cash. Bikes got rid of, most of them, not all. A load of boxes of bike bits belonging to the Kilfoyles, they could have them back for a start. The caravan was soon towed away. He got something for everything, loaded what he could onto the back of a trailer and made a couple of trips up there to store in a lock-up he rented around the corner from where she lived.

Mumtaz was a care worker now. Chavs-R-Us, wasn't it? She did mega-hours in her place, a big home with all sorts in it. Sixteen-hour shifts, nights. Did alright out of it so far as he could tell. He scouted around, realized he could get plenty of work up there, so off he went. He'd be a fool not to give it a go, but you never knew how things were going to turn out until you tried. Bill went outside and watched him leave, one last time, towing the very last bits and pieces of his previous life behind him on the little trailer, never to be seen again. "Good luck, Richie," he called. "We hope to see you again sometime."

"You will, Bill, you will." Richie drove away from the crumpled old man and hunched down in concentration over the wheel of his small blue Fiesta.

Mumtaz didn't half get into some horrible moods sometimes, and when her moody tendency began to manifest itself, Richie usually found it favourite to do what he had always done with female ire, his mother's for example, and tried to stay out of her way. It wasn't easy, it was never easy with her, but he thought he had done good with everything he thought she wanted him for. He was big. She'd always found that reassuring, she thought it meant he was a person she could rely on, who could automatically and easily do anything she might want from him. That was obviously his role and fair dos he had really gone for it. But it wasn't easy though, it definitely wasn't easy.

Like the first thing was when her father came over to see her because he was dying and blow me down if he didn't spark out there and then in her front room, near enough like, and the medics came round and brought him back, and then he insisted he had to die at home, muggins Richie had to phone around every airline to book him on a flight where they could take care of him, all hooked up, and no carrier would take him, no carrier – until there was one said they would do it, Air France, they could just get him in there, Mumtaz and Rich had to go down there with him in the ambulance, and he'd helped slide him in flat on his back into a narrow shelf in the cargo hold, like a crate of meat, clearance just above his nose, and took him that way. They got the old man home alright and like he wanted he managed to peg out in his own bed. A lot of it had been down to him, Richie. Mumtaz never could have done it alone.

"Richie, can you please be taking your work clothes out of my washing machine now please?"

Her washing-machine? OK, so it was hers, but he paid half the bills, didn't he? He'd helped plumb it in when the old one went kaput. But he bent down and opened the door, pulled out four enormous shirts, a handful of work socks and pants, and a couple of pairs of his enormous jeans caked in mud.

"There! You will clog the filters again. Can you please wash mud off before you put them, under the cold tap in the yard? That is what it is for, please!" She was a small woman, frail as a butterfly, and ten years older than him. "And then," she laughed gaily, "I will be able to put my own things in first!" Which she did, closing the door in triumph, twisting the programme knob so that the machine immediately began squirting inside and rumbling through a warm cycle.

Richie stomped outside with his two massive pairs of jeans – it was freezing cold and dark out there – and directed a steady dribble of water at them. Impatiently he dropped them underneath the sozzling tap and went back indoors to watch EastEnders if that was allowed. Of course, it wasn't, not tonight it wasn't. Normally though, he reminded himself, they got on fine.

He tried to keep track of the doings on Albert Square for a few minutes. Mumtaz was bustling around in here now, plumping cushions, generally obstructing the big flat screen just as much as ever she could. Finally, she picked up the controller and turned it right down. "Richie, sorry, I have to work at the table. I have some forms to fill in. Very well you know I'm only in my own house for five of your earth minutes."

Forms! It was time to get out of her way. Not much he hated more than filling out of a form. He was more than happy to let her be a great expert on that side of things. She spent her whole life on it. She was naturally more gifted and all round cleverer, like most women seemed, but she really was though, all the same, he wasn't too happy to have to creep up to his little box room and turn on the computer. When did he ever see her? He himself would be out the back door at seven in the morning.

First off, he looked at one of the truthing sites, the one mentioned by Barbs, which he generally enjoyed, but there weren't nothing new breaking on the Princess Di assassin story, although thinking about it there wouldn't be now the last witness was dead. Nothing much there on the middle east, he noticed. Nah. He switched into the old Wolverine site Dave and him used to look at but it had been taken down, vanished without a trace, CIA had obviously clamped on that one, but it had taken a fair amount of time to cotton on to it. Maybe they had wanted it there. Maybe they stuck it up themselves. Bait. He had a look at *People of Walmart*. Quite funny pics of thick black fatties. Chav Towns. Nowhere he wanted to move – and the neo-Nazi podcasts were just no longer credible any more, not to Richie. He followed a link through from somewhere to White Lives Matter, under construction.

Worth checking back. A lot of the old truthing sites seemed to have gone or been moved, maybe into the dark web.

Even perfectly reliable conspiracy sites weren't what they used to be. It seemed the more they came true it was the more everyone accepted it, and then it was no longer such a mystery. Just a policy they had which everyone had known about for a long time. If truth be told it was probably only him and one or two others really cared what was going on in the world. Bored, he decided to have a look at Grand Theft Auto V, which one of Mumtaz's cousin's kids had mentioned to him. He'd remembered looking at it before but then it had just been matchboxes with red flares squirting out the sides of them, shuttling around a crossword-like grid. It was developed in Scotland but set in America and he wasn't surprised.

But that had been more than fifteen years back. Now it was the most successful video game of all time. There were three main characters, Franklin, Michael and Trevor, and in the game, you could play as all three of them if you wanted because they all got their own introduction. Franklin was the first character introduced to you, an African-American repo guy and part-time gangbanger. He lived at home with his auntie and wanted to get out of the Hood. Michael was a retired bank robber and a married man. He had two kids who were both grown up but still lived with him. He was also having relationship issues with his wife because he was going broke. After ten years of enjoying 20 million dollars he only had 900,000 dollars left. So he desperately wanted to hit one more big score before he retired for good.

They looked a lot more like real people now and you played along with them like an actor in their world. Trevor was a lunatic psychopath; this guy was a little bit crazy. He used to be best friends with Michael until he supposedly died after a score went wrong. Michael got shot and he had had to leave him behind. But when Trevor heard of a robbery in Los Santos and the person who did it was using Michael's old quotes, he had to go and find the guy and connect with him.

Richie made a few clumsy moves with a lumbering photo-avatar with a deep American voice, gestured with the muzzle of his Uzi for some sweating captured guards to fill up the empty back of a truck with crates of millions and millions of dollars. In the two decades since GTA came into existence, they'd made fifteen editions of the game, he read. Chinatown, Vice City, San Andreas, Liberty City, London 1969, Gay Tony ... who was counting? For GTA V they had gone all out. Some people couldn't tell if it was game or a movie, so Rusal had enthused to him, the graphics were that good and improving more every year.

Richie had been chatting with Rusal in the lounge while Mumtaz and her cousin made chapatis in the kitchen. Some people said it was too violent and sexual for children, he'd opined. Yes, it was an 18 rated game, but everyone knew a lot of kids played it. He didn't think it did any harm because it was just a video game and isn't real. The boy, about fourteen, had been babbling and nodding his head from side to side, delighted to find an adult who was so interested in his opinions. This game was so clever in the same way they planned it. It had something for everybody, which was why he saw his future in computer science.

His favourite character, he said with a laugh, was Gay Tony, because he liked his style. He wore female earrings like an auntie's and used his nightclub to push narcotics. Until he got killed by Nicko.

So, they killed the woofter, Richie thought. "It's all heists, is it?" he asked Rusal.

"It is all heists, yes," said the boy. "There are two people who are retired bank robbers and a new bank robber from the Los Santos ghetto. They are building now to take one last massive score before they all retire for good and each character takes home around $48, 000, 000 for their services."

A bit like life wasn't it. After you finished the final heist you had 48 million to enjoy on Ferraris, Lamborghinis, and other nice cars. You could buy apartments, mansions, planes, jets, helicopters, boats, yachts, motorbikes quads, dirt bikes, clothes, businesses. Rusal's eyes were glittering, as though he already owned all these things. You could also start illegal operations such as weapon trafficking. In other words, there was a whole world to live in. You could swim with the sharks but they would eat you. Rusal ended seriously: "This game is not suitable for people under the age of fourteen."

Richie hadn't managed to find any unsuitable content, but he powered down anyway and sat there looking past the dead screen to the lit-up windows of the row of houses opposite, a few hours well-wasted. He'd given up on games himself, he was never any good at them anyway. The others always had faster fingers and laughed at him. Therefore, he preferred to live in reality, because he had no choice. It was better in the end. After a while, Mumtaz came upstairs and went into her bedroom. He followed her in there, got undressed and snuggled in beside her.

"Did you finish your forms?" he asked.

"Yes," she said. "I have finished the everything forms for everyone and I have put your clothes in the washer to wash."

The good thing about Leicester was that they were always building something new up there now, so plenty of work going for somebody like him. Perched up in the air, when he got a few minutes to hang on his controls, he could see right over the town, the old parts, preserved rubble with lawns around about., well what else, and he couldn't see why they should have to pay for its upkeep. He would be more than happy if they sent the bulldozers in on rubbish like that, it served no useful purpose and he would have leapt at the chance to grapple with the ancient stones and help take them where they could be used, ground up or used for some granny's garden walls.

The Good Thing about India, and he'd been over there what three times now, was everything was fantastically dirt cheap over there. His teeth, for example, would have cost him two thousand pound easy over here, but in Mumbai, he could walk into a shack around the corner from Mumtaz's family home, with all the best modern equipment in it, and get the whole lot done for seventy quid, same day service. What did make him angry was when people thought he was the opposite of what he was, because when he was down that end he was in the Indian restaurant every weekend, usually with Mikey, talking to the blokes in there, because he was that used to them. He liked talking to them about anything really.

At work he kept his business mostly to himself, you had to like, anyways the days of sitting around on site in some tea hut were long gone for him, he didn't do that now, nor did anyone far as he could see, now it was get in there, do it and go home. He knew better than to expect any interest and you never knew who you were talking to really. Friendly people though, it had to be said. Leicester was a friendly enough place, which he supposed was why so many of Mumtaz's people had come up here. Was he wrong on that? He could generally be proved wrong, he knew it was so, but surely the general friendliness of the people and therefore of the place had to have something to do with the explanation of why Leicester had become an immigrant town. The Poles, the whole lot of them, they were all in cahoots. This was the main reason after all why he was up here. People were friendly alright. Once upon a time, in the seventies, the council had put a notice in the newspaper in Uganda saying Leicester couldn't take anymore, but instead they'd taken it as an advert and thousands more poured in and set up their shops.

Richie talked to anyone normally. It was how he was like, but whatever way you looked at it he was living a funny old life. Three times he'd been over there now. Once to bury her old dad, once to a wedding of her sister who was there still, and once to get his own teeth fixed. But it wasn't only to get his choppers done; there was also some shopping Mumtaz wanted to do, and Diwali.

The Golden Mile they called it, curries and saris and gold jewellery as far as the eye could stretch, Belgrave Road and Melton Road. India itself was obviously bigger and hotter. White people from Leicester were called 'chisits', from 'am a chisit', which meant 'How much is it?' in local lingo. Far as he could make out they didn't have much of an accent up here, not like Brummie, but they made up for it by calling everyone me old ducks and things of that sort. They said 'tabs' instead of 'lug-holes', 'prang' instead of 'scared'. Again, it was Rusal, born and bred, who told him these things. Mainly it was how kids talked at his school. Rusal gave him a long quiz on it one day. Cotty was when girls had their hair tied in knots, piff was when they were a looker, juicing was flirting, and a new girl at school was 'bouki' – strange, mysterious. The little alleyways around the market were called jittys, and in the olden days, poor kids used to hang around the stalls hoping to get given a bit of bread dipped in sausage fat. Crisps, pork pies, that's what they used to be famous for in Leicester, now it was curries.

Richie used to keep his tabs open to see if he could hear some of these words on sites, but he hadn't heard a single one of them. Now he kept his ear protectors on at all times unless someone was actually talking directly at him. Trading, that's what he liked, and Indians obviously liked it too, but there was no room at Mumtaz's for anything he might buy. She had told him right at the start that if he started bringing a load of junk home, he would be going out the door along with it.

There was this place he liked which he had found, and he would look in the window at lunchtimes, or sometimes he'd go in there and get the bloke to show him things, and dicker with him a bit about what he might pay. But he never bought anything, and the bloke knew by now he wasn't going to buy and ignored him by and large. But Richie asked him questions, really tried to convince him, until the bloke had to get whatever it was out of the window and let him turn it over, carefully considering whether he was going to purchase the item for his collection. The shop sold old military memorabilia mainly, really old proper English stuff. German as well, from the war. Some of it looked so new he wouldn't have been surprised if there was little workshop around the corner churning out Nazi daggers, Iron Crosses, and grey uniforms.

You wouldn't believe what he had in there! Medals, ribbons, knives and bayonets, grenades. He loved the place, it drew him in every time. Dad would have loved it for a start. He loved impersonating a Nazi officer. Even now it made Richie laugh, remembering how he'd made the kids laugh with that when they were watching some old film, like *Von Ryan's Express*, squinting his eyes cruelly and saying: 'Jawohl, Herr Kommandant!'

He always came away empty-handed. But always feeling better. For hours after he would be walking around with his head held high, like he knew who he was, just because he'd handled an actual Boer war rifle, you could laugh at it or find it scary but at the end of the day it's who they were, something that had to carry on, so that when he walked through the door back to Mumtaz he could enjoy being with her and her lot a bit more like. In their environment, say when half her relatives came down from Brum for a big visit and cookout, sleeping ten to a room (it was nostalgic for them!) he could take a certain amount of pleasure in being the odd one out, the English one, the only one on their street anyway to be shacked up with a real Indian who couldn't be understood without practice, and even his own family expected him to be different, wearing a red eye on his forehead or something, instead of being the same old Rich as he always had been, always would be, tucking into a homemade onion bhaji.

The Leicester buses were light blue, blue and white. That on its own was enough to make it seem like a foreign country to him, it was like being on holiday, although soon you got used to it and there was no real difference, not that he ever went on them. He was a car bloke, it was a point of pride not to travel on public transport with people who didn't have cars. What was a person without a car? In his eyes they were nothing much. Just nothing people, old dears carrying their shopping bags around on the bus. No thanks!

Richie tried to maintain a steady focus on what he was doing himself as he strode back to the blue Fiesta at five o'clock, shagged out, weary of heart and limb, dog-tired and ready to bark at a pint of Old Peculiar. He decided to scamper in with the rest of the skiving Chisits to the Seamstress, one of the few remaining old bloke pubs around the market and see what the craic was in there. Richie entered the low door, ducking under its lintel, and went through to the dingy bar where a few market traders were supping their pints, alongside of a few more who'd been there all day.

"Alright, ducks?" asked the barmaid.

"Alright, yeah," he replied. "Mine's a pint of mild and bitter."

"Blends together, does it?" The woman wasn't young, maybe ten years younger than Richie, her hair in a fluffy multiple blonde-streak style with rat's tails hanging down. He'd previously found her friendly and was glad she was working.

"They do seem to go together well," he said.

"We've got no mild on tap," she said. "But we've got some craft pale ales. I suppose you're gonna tell me that's not the same thing at all?"

"Right you are lovey, I'll have a Heineken." He handed over a twenty and waited for his change. "And one for yourself ... " he gestured as though expecting her name to appear at his fingertips.

"... Julie," she said. "Mine's a half, cheers."

She pulled his pint and disappeared towards the till, distracted at the last moment by a hail from the other end like. When she made it back she said sorry and handed him the change from a tenner, not including he noticed the price of the half, which she hadn't taken but had pocketed as a tip.

"Sorry, Julie," he said. "Wasn't that a twenty I gave you?"

"I thought it was a ten."

"It was a twenty," he said. "I know it was like."

Fair enough, she apologized for the mistake, corrected it from the till, and pulled herself a half, which she raised to him and sipped half an inch from. Another customer called her then and she turned away, to serve an old bloke who looked like a chiselled red brick wall which many names had been scratched upon. Richie turned away from the bar to find a seat at a long table near the door, knowing she'd tried to gyp him out of a ten-pound note, fuming but unable to do anything like.

"Alright mate?" he called at a bloke on the other side of the table. "Busy day?"

"Fairly," said his new if unwilling acquaintance. "Fairly quiet then a bit busier. Then when it died off completely, I shut up early."

Richie wanted to know what he had been selling, something he supposed. Fishheads? Bowls of veg? Cassettes? But he didn't volunteer anything and Richie didn't ask.

"What about you?" the bloke asked. "Knocked off early?"

"Not really."

"Building?"

Richie made driving and lever pulling movements. "Up on the ring road."

"Oh, I know. Used to be Bradley's. What's that to become then?"

"Office blocks," Richie said. "Dunno who for though."

The man turned his mouth down, like he'd given the wrong answer, and looked away indifferently as if he was talking to a real idiot. Richie picked up his pint glass and put it down at slow regular intervals. He did this until his glass was empty, simply focusing on a spot in the air ahead of him until he was done. He hesitated as to whether to have another pint, then stood up and left the bar.

Mumtaz was still at work when he got home; the house was empty. Richie let himself in through the backdoor and pottered around until she got in. He took his clothes out of the washing machine and transferred them to the drier. Then he got the remains of a curry and some rice out of the fridge and put it in the microwave to heat up. He ate it from a bowl watching the six o'clock news. It was the big vote coming up, a couple of days until the country decided on whether to leave the EU in the referendum, so the BBC was hot on the trail of discovering the mood around Britain. He could have told them what it was easy enough. His own mood wasn't the best he'd ever been in, but happy or sad he knew which way he would be voting – out, out, out. Let's get shot of them once and for all. This is the only chance we'll be given. A lot of Mumtaz's people agreed with him. They were workers, they and their parents put everything they had into this country, whereas the so-called European migrants, most of them, were just taking the piss out of the benefits system.

Richie could give you a thousand reasons why we should leave fucking Europe. Mumtaz herself wasn't so sure. She thought it would strengthen the hand of the worst elements and lead to economic disaster. He couldn't really argue with her except by examples, but she said they didn't really matter. She also said that it wasn't important if they disagreed. It was just a different opinion they had and would make not a bit of difference to what other people did. He heard her key going into the lock just after seven. She was bustling around as usual, but Richie got up and made her a cup of tea and put her half of the curry in the microwave. For once she settled down on the settee beside him and ate it; put her head on his shoulder and they sat like that and watched TV together until it was time to go upstairs to bed.

But although she said all that it was still true she got into horrible moods, and if he had to give a reason it would be that they seemed to come on badly whenever he tried to get her to something she didn't want to do, and then she stopped being the strong, capable woman who decided everything and turned into a stubborn little girl. And when it got really bad she would lie down on the floor, or even refuse to get out of bed altogether, and you couldn't make her do anything.

The Mudies always had thought well of themselves. The Mudies never stopped telling you how brilliant they were, and if you stood up to them they wouldn't let it go, they had to prove you wrong: it was a different but same story. That's what this mum always said, but in reality, they were ignorant pigs as it went. His grandfather: Let's have a few more ball-bearings on the plate, if you please, Mary. Her family was considered to be a cut above Dad's lot, by her. Her brother had been a printer and his grandparents had done something or other, he couldn't remember what, scuffling around here and there in Camberley. Anyway, his uncle Martin was thought to be the bright spark of her family. Richie and their lot used to visit his shop sometimes, that's how he remembered him best, in there, his business still ticking along.

He remembered the thick coating of dust on the shop window, so you couldn't see through it, the place looked deserted as you opened the door and walked across a disgusting carpet thick with mould, the dust was growing mould in there, carpeted in turn by shiny stuff that had come through the letterbox. Martin was at the back of the shop, working under an angled lamp.

Business cards, wedding invitations, menus, school sports' days, lists of cricket fixtures, and once a year the flower show schedule of events and prizes. Martin did a plain job with his boxes of old type and a treadle machine. He never stopped, was never at rest. It paid for his house. No, Richie corrected himself. He inherited his house. Paid for the upkeep, shall we say. He'd decided to hang onto it, so eventually, it went to his sister. That was Martin's achievement: he passed on the value of his house. He never married, no. He just wasn't cut out for it.

He was a thinnish bloke with a mop of greasy brown hair, then he was fattish with thin hair, which got greyer, then thinnish again, always incredibly scruffy. Thick peering glasses. When his eyes were no longer all that he started to get a few complaints; he lost the school and the flower show and sold the shop, all his equipment, the whole lot. Never showed any interest again. That was Martin. Martin Gibson.

The Mudies were of an entirely different species. They worshipped the past, collecting bits and pieces reminding them of olden times, which they would get out and stroke on a regular basis to marvel at and to repair, and to make money sprout like leaves. That was their version. Fixated, superstitious. Backward when it came to women. Look at the way your granny had to lay out her lord and master's razor every morning at the sink! She should've cut his throat with it! Where's my this, where's my that, always laughing at her behind her back. They were disgusting, Richie, men of that generation. I never put up with anything like that from your father. That's why Dad always bought her a bunch of flowers, a trinket. The men in that family thought they were something special.

Now in Mumtaz's family, you would of thought it'd be just the same, but it wasn't, not exactly. Lucknow, they were from originally, a place halfway up a mountain, a resort for the British officers in the days of the Raj. Her father worked for the railways, a clerk of some kind, but sort of in charge of the small office. Quite a good job. Anyways, he fed them all on it, his wife at home, taking in washing sometimes from the remaining hotels, bringing up a family of six children in a house half the size of the one she lived in now, let alone the place they'd had in Camberley.

Mumtaz's father was an old-fashioned man in some ways, she said, but he had believed in education. Education for his boys – and for his girls too. That is how they had all first managed to move from Lucknow to Mumbai, and it was why she was adapting so easily to life in England. But Richie knew this was only half-true. Her education was something she was proud of having – she knew a lot more than him about most subjects – but her father wasn't responsible, not really,

It was Mumtaz herself who'd learned everything about the contents of her first husband's chemist's shop, she who had taken every care training course going, she who had the intelligence to work out everyone's shifts so they didn't clash. She was a right little brain box. Compared to his mum, for example. One of her jobs – apart from cashier in the Co-op and office cleaner – had been freelance proofreading. She always liked reading, mum, and Martin had encouraged her to try proofreading. All sorts of people did it. She thought if he could do it, it must be easy. But soon got bored with the stuff she had to read, all the crappy novels, and she made a lot of mistakes and they'd stopped using her, just as dad told her they would. "It's not for you, girl," he said. "You want to do something less finicky." The old man had been right as it happened.

One day, playing GTA up in the box room, Richie broke off in mid-heist and typed: 'What makes red Leicester red?' into his search engine and read the explanation. Red Leicester, formerly known as Leicester or Leicestershire cheese, was a traditional hard English cheese made from unpasteurised cow's milk. Apparently, it dated back to the 17th century when farmers wanted to make their cheeses stand apart from cheese made in other parts of the country. They decided that the colour of the cheese should show its richness and creaminess. To set it apart from cheddar and highlight the quality, Leicester began to be coloured with a vegetable dye called annatto. The rind was described as reddish-orange with a powdery mould on it. But only a couple of farms in Leicestershire still made it using traditional methods and raw milk.

He'd always wondered about that, and he'd always forgot his interest a second later; now, at last, the impulse to know and the bored opportunity had come together at the precise same moment. Now he knew. In other words, it was dying out like everything English. It was interesting in a way. Down below it told you what wines it went with. They'd always had it on a cob roll with pickle, with a quick cup of tea if they were passing near the house at lunchtime. He would've called it orange rather than red, more the colour of a lot of Indian grub, but apparently, they hadn't adopted it into their cooking. Funny how the red, or orange, was just a colour, something to make it look different to cheddar; it had no flavour of its own as such, which could be said of Leicester itself. The city was always trying to sound different, unique, but it was just average, like a lot of other places.

It was weird to think they'd always been like that, even back in the seventeenth century. He'd been hoping the colouring would turn out to be sheep's blood or something, and that it symbolized the royal blood of King Charles, or maybe the end of royalty when they chopped his head off. But face facts, and here's where it got weird: they wouldn't admit it even if it was true. You had to admit though, Leicester had changed muchly in a shortish time. Leicester was a peak place now, or so Mumtaz thought, in Rusal's words. She thought with her heart, like women do.

He went downstairs to find Mumtaz and tell her about the cheese. He found her in front of the flat screen. She was watching Poldark on the sofa, hugging a cushion, looking over it fearfully.

"I don't like this programme, Richie," she said. "It is too violent. It is violent towards women."

He glanced at the screen where a big-chested bloke in a ripped shirt was strutting around with a whip. "Why are you watching it then?"

Mumtaz smiled up at him bleakly. "I lost one of my patients today. One of the real old dears."

"Oh."

"Mrs. Danvers, I told you about her. She didn't know."

"Best way," Richie said. "I'm making a cup of tea – want one?"

It was his answer to anything, a cup of tea. A good habit. Something he'd got into as a way of pleasing his mother. "OK, I will have one," said Mumtaz.

Another day, coming down the same stairs at around the same time, he had picked up the *Leicester Mercury* from the coffee table, unfolded it and blow me down if it didn't have a photograph of Rusal on the front page. He was wearing a sharp cut suit like they like and a fancy dyed carrot haircut and standing in front of a brand-new Porsche with personalized plates. Richie scanned the article quickly. He'd become some amazing local success story, a multi-millionaire at twenty-one years old.

He could hardly believe his eyes. "Look, didn't you see this?" he asked Mumtaz. "Rusal's in the paper."

Mumtaz was watching the box. He tossed the *Mercury* into her lap, and she picked it up. "You idiot," she said. "That's not Rusal. Rusal is sixteen years old. He's just doing his GCSEs." She threw the paper aside in anger. "Sometimes I think there must be something wrong with you," she said.

Richie picked up the *Mercury* and looked more closely at the article. It wasn't Rusal after all, just some young bloke who looked exactly, uncannily like her nephew. Something to do with computers as usual. What a complete plonker he was – he felt it sharply, suddenly, felt like he should crawl away and die. "Oh yeah," he said feebly.

Mumtaz didn't even look at him, she just kept watching the screen, some kind of thing about rogue builders overcharging people, not doing the work right etc. There was a lot of it about. He looked down at her briefly, trying to think of something to say, watching the light slide over her small brown concentrating features. "These people are criminals," she said. "This sort of thing would never happen back home."

Sometimes after they'd had one of their arguments – like when she told him she never wanted to get married again – he went out and drove round and round the ring road. The golden ring road, the beauty of it leading you round to a better way of thinking. It was daft really to think about, a bloke was a fool when he could just live with a woman. She'd brought up her kids, they were both grown and flown, Amrit and Nada, they lived in another world to chemist shops and Camberley, and she wanted to please herself, no ties, no responsibilities you couldn't unbind. And then he just forgot it. Fuck patriarchal institutions, Richie. Fuck everything.

But it was these everythings of hers which led to his longer practice circuits, and he hung on in the little blue Fiesta, hurtling around the centre of Leicester, a giant in a dodgem a wasp buzzing in a milk bottle. It was scenic though. Cavities you didn't miss once they were filled, but there were enough old factory buildings to remind you of what the town had been, and the stacks of new offices dealt out like cards weren't a problem to him, and the ring road itself was a relic of the woven concrete era, crafted by bygone Chisits from bars of two-tone grey plasticine.

Everything was curling up underneath something, like the dining table, for example, and refusing to speak or come out, just curling up in a ball, right into the corner of the wall. Who would believe a grown woman did that? A woman who brought up two children, nursed people who were dying, hosted brilliant parties for cousins and aunties and kids from the four corners of everywhere, who told him incredulous at herself that she had once cooked two months of curries for her husband, left them stacked and labelled in the freezer for her husband when she had taken her children to Bangalore to visit their dying grandmother. Most of the time she was in constant motion. This was the other side of Mumtaz, the part of her that couldn't cope at all with her memories, her life, her job. This was the woman who refused to speak to him, who pushed him away.

And this is where Richie sometimes fell down. He wouldn't leave her be to simmer down, he had to have it out with her and argue with her, as though she was just a something that didn't make proper sense, who might be made to talk reasonably by shouting and insisting. It wasn't easy, it was always never easy with Mumtaz when she got in one of her moods, not moods exactly, her states.

There were exits all around the inner ring road, exits to here and there, suburban Leicester, some places he'd never even been, Birmingham, Coventry, Wolverhampton, adjacent towns that weren't much, when you got to them, and he'd wonder what exit to take as they peeled by one after another. There were no good exits, nowhere for him to go, which she knew like. One time she had lain in the back of the car for two hundred miles, first on the seat, then on the floor. She wouldn't get up while he drove two hundred miles to Honiton, all the way down there first thing in the morning to uncle Peter's funeral.

Richie parked in the forecourt of the crematorium, got out to chat to Mikey and his brother, looked around at Pete's friends milling to go in, or maybe they'd just come out, and all this time Mumtaz was lying flat out on the floor in the back of his car – and would she get out? No, she wouldn't. She stayed there in hiding. Until eventually he just had to say goodbye to them and drive back to Leicester. No way was he going to take her across to see Barbara.

It all broke down, broke off into some craziness, a contest of wills. Until – and this is how it usually happened, he noticed, as it did now: he was running low on juice and pulled into a garage to fill her up – and when he went to pay he bought her a bunch of flowers to take back or nosed around the petrol station shop for a while in search of some splendid trinket, an amulet that would bind them closely together.

Richie got a job at Mount Sorrell, one of the deepest granite quarries in Europe. The hole in the ground was like a great countersunk pyramid, way below sea-level, the roadways cut out, wound up it in stages, driving the big trucks loaded with 100 tonnes of material blasted out of the ground, and trundled up to one of the processing plants. The slowly lumbering trucks were covered in granite dust but the caged-in cabs were air-conditioned, soundproofed, quite cozy really. Richie never stopped quoting statistics about the enormous quarry, and Mumtaz was impressed by his achievement.

He ate more of her curries and grew even larger, as though it was necessary to grow himself up into the giant trucks, to be that big, the size of a bloke who could handle that size of a machine, which would otherwise be like trying to wear boots five sizes too big. Not all the drivers were as big as Richie, mind you, but it didn't do him any harm to be a mountain of a man. Mumtaz was proud of him. She thought his work was vital – there was something beautiful about it for her, that he was a person who trawled up the hard material that buildings and roads and railway culverts were made from, out of the bowels of the earth; he was a demi-god of primary or secondary construction.

When he landed the job at the quarry, he felt he'd come home; it was the ultimate, the actual thing he'd been thinking of when he first got into heavy plant driving. His ship had come in, and all at once he saw his way. What did it for him was seeing the whole process. They set off a huge blast every day around lunchtime, laid the charges in deep holes which were drilled down into the rock with a massive bit, then *ka-boom*, and they were scurrying around it like ants, carrying off the scattered chunks of stone, some for buildings, others to be ground up smaller and smaller, some into a fine powder that got everywhere. It made you think, it made you think alright.

If something so hard that had lain under the earth for hundreds of thousands of years, which was the earth, could be budged so easily and made into so many things, what was the point of being a stick-in-the-mud? Even mud was temporary and would soon be washed away. Out of these enormous holes in the ground – which were upside-down temples, bigger than any cathedral – city after city had been built. The earth felt rock solid to him. To Richie it definitely didn't feel like it was moving. If the earth really moved at all that speed, as Mikey thought, how come you didn't fall over when you jumped up in the air and landed somewhere else? Some scientists agreed with him, he knew. Mumtaz thought exactly the same. He didn't see why Mikey couldn't be more open-minded about these things.

Mumtaz was of the Ba'hai faith, so she held what we all did for a living to be important. Her work, for example, involved practical caring for people, and therefore, in Ba'hai, was seen as having a highly spiritual dimension. But – and here she was a free-thinker – she also felt that Richie was a spiritual being, possessed of a rational soul because he was always asking how the world linked up, and what was the underlying order of things. Nobody could say that what he did for a living wasn't useful to humanity. There weren't many Ba'hais in Leicester, but at least they weren't persecuted. A lot of Indians, of course, both Hindu and Muslim, so her appearance fitted in okay, but she was still an outsider, apart from her cousins. Anyway, she felt – as had her beloved father – she was a cut above the ordinary Muslim or Hindu, for whilst she recognized their spiritual paths, they didn't recognize hers. She believed that Ba'hai represented a further step along God's highway, which led eventually to a unified world government and a great peace for all the peoples of the Earth.

Nothing was going to make her step back from this or persuade her to leave it behind. This is what she had been taught from early childhood: That God had gifted man with a rational soul, and despite his breaking up of the covenant, this human soul would eventually triumph over superstition and fear. Ba'hai believed in the education of women and girls, which was important to her, and she had always been encouraged to exercise her own judgement under the guidance of good authority. On her kitchen wall she had put up a photograph of Abdu'l-Bahá, who was the saddest, wisest old man she had ever seen, and in the sitting room a print of an enormous blue nightingale perched in a bare sprouting tree, which symbolized Bahá'u'lláh, his father, and the founder of their faith.

At the end of the day Richie respected her religion. He could at least see that it was good for her, and what she told him of their beliefs started to make sense to him, not a lot, but a little. If the divine being hadn't brought them together, what had? It was beyond his understanding. How random was the world? He had never thought it was random at all, then he thought it was, and now he could see how easily everything could be blasted away. Although he would never be a religious person the way Mumtaz was, they had got to know one another fairly well, and when she broached the subject of getting married he thought this idea of conversion to Ba'hai was a step he might be prepared to take for the sake of a quiet life. You're a sly one, his mother had always said. Because it would make her happy. Because, let's face it – if Mumtaz was happy, Richie was happy.

Late Driver

Pauline didn't learn to drive until relatively late in life. She must've been at least forty-five years old, and the reason for it was her need to drive between the various branches of Antoinette's. Her job there was to organize and supervise the staff, make sure their new lines were being presented properly, were actually selling, and old stock duly palmed off on the matrons. There had been various earlier attempts to motorize her, but neither the early red scooter nor sporadic tuition from Bill behind the wheels of various small cars that had come his way over the years had resulted in anything except a lot of frustration. Either he couldn't teach her or she couldn't learn, not from him. There had been a lot of blow-ups, which always ended in rows and tight-lipped silence or open anger. Bill said she would not be told; she said he couldn't explain himself or let her do anything properly. The only iron she would ever be able to handle was a steam iron.

Bill had taught several other people to drive quite easily, and they had commented on his relaxed, confidence-inspiring manner; but with her, he seemed to lack patience. Once she had even had a few lessons from somebody else; that too had come to nothing – at least not what the offerer of those lessons had wanted – and, finally, when it was really needed, she had learned at a driving school and passed her test without difficulty. It was as though she'd always known how to drive, which is what Bill had always been telling her, so he said, but she wouldn't believe him. All the same, she was reluctant to let him go out with her, except once or twice at the very last minute, to practice before the test.

Her first car had been a mini, her second a VW beetle like Bill's father's, in which she'd felt a bit safer up against the big lorries, and finally an Opel Kadett that had happened to come along. She was driving it right this minute over Marlow bridge, following the morning traffic past the naked lady statue, seated demurely on her plinth and dabbling her teenager's feet in the Thames, turning right through the old pleasure centre of this ancient riverside town towards Antoinette's, which should have been open for an hour by now. She parked on The Causeway, checked her make-up in the rear-view mirror, a touch up on the lipstick, and treated herself to a cigarette: a picture of mature and well-dressed elegance, a model of a customer, in fact, her handbag over her forearm; she pushed in through the dark wooden door and a bell jangled on its bouncy bracket.

The women were huddled in the back of the shop – Mrs. Finch, dowdy, moody Jacqueline, and Ursula, a bony-looking girl of about thirty-five whom Pauline had never really liked. As she approached she noticed that Jacqueline had been crying, dabbing at her eyes with a crumpled handkerchief. It was often this way when she arrived. They seemed to need her to mollify them, set their lives straight. They struck her as naughty schoolgirls, people who couldn't get on with things on their own and were always waiting for her to sort out their problems: minor things which she thought Mrs. Finch should've been able to cope with herself. After all, she was being employed as manageress of the branch.

The trouble was, they didn't like one another very much either. Instead of co-operating and working things out between them, they were always trying to get the best of one another, do one another down. In this case it was a simple matter of arranging the shifts so that Jacqueline, who was having severe problems with her husband and her daughter – it sounded to Pauline like he was a real bully, always throwing his weight around, just the sort of thing she hated – could take Friday afternoon off to go to an event at her daughter's school. She was worried about how she was getting on there and she wanted a chance to speak to her teachers properly about some problems she was having. It seemed she'd been accused of something, although the details of exactly what had never come out, and although Pauline could see why the other women got fed up with her moaning, she failed to see why Mrs. Finch couldn't just say yes on this occasion and they would manage somehow, just the two of them. Finally, she said she would come over herself, to which Mrs. Finch said, "Oh, there's really no need."

The clothes, the new lines – dresses, skirts, and tops – were all on their racks. Pauline walked up and down them, straightening the odd ruffled item, smoothing them here and there, while the other women stood back watching her inspection. When she was satisfied that everything was immaculate she quickly chose two items – a pair of wide black silk trousers and a blouse printed with large orange flowers and dark, twisting stems – and asked Ursula to put them on the mannikin nearest the window, replacing the pale green tweed suit it wore currently, or rather, she changed her mind, just move the suited dummy further back to the suit display, and bring out and dress another mannikin from the storeroom. Once she had done that, Pauline herself would accessorise it.

Ursula lifted the dressed mannikin to the back of the shop and parked it in front of the suits rack. She went through to the back and reappeared with another dummy, naked, and older. Its breasts were more prominent, lipstick painted on in fifties style, pursed lips, moulded perm, and thinly plucked eyebrows. Pauline thought of telling her to take it back and get one of the slimmer, blank-faced dummies, but decided that this one would look alright, a change, something a little bit old fashioned, brought back, so said nothing for the time being.

Ursula obviously knew what she was doing. She lifted the mannikin from its base, upended it expertly and slid on the trousers, which she pinned to prevent them from falling down. She fitted an ample bra and the blouse was soon on over it. Ursula then got to work with a mouthful of pins to try and give some shape to the model and the baggy, flowing garments. She concentrated intensely, absorbed in her work, and by the time Pauline returned with a pair of knee-length stockingettes and a pair of elegant, casual shoes in beige, she was ready to stand back and look at her work. Pauline moved in, and before long the mannikin was looking good, and the presence of two serious women seen through the window had drawn in a few passing customers to look around the shop.

Pauline broke off from her work on the mannikin to ask if she could be of any help to the customers. They were mostly women in their thirties and forties, with a few older ladies. Mrs. Finch and Jacqueline were alert but low key at their stations. It was with the older women that Pauline felt she came into her own. Women in their thirties, she felt, generally knew what they wanted to look like; they had their own sense of style worked out, whereas older women tended to feel they were lagging behind, which they generally were, and needed the advice of somebody closer to their own age, deferential although more glamorous.

Somebody like Pauline, resplendent in her fine ruby red sweater-dress, flaring away from the waist in fine pleats, her volumised chestnut perm, her gold accessories, and her colouring and her delicate, aquiline nose. Pauline knew how to talk to them, how to light a flame in their hearts: she genuinely had the power to make them look better than they ever had before, not to speak of a magical ability to compel self-belief through not so subtle flattery which played on their sense of superiority to others.

Before midday they had between them sold several versions of the ensemble displayed on the mannikin, which was now completely accessorised but in danger of losing her clothes again as the blouses ran low. Even the lime green tweed suit had found a buyer, located beside the rack of suits ably womaned by Mrs. Finch, Jacqueline helping customers in and out of the fitting rooms, Ursula primly but competently handling summer frocks, convinced that it was her pinning which had triggered this particular burst of trade. The spate ebbed at 11.45 am when their class of customer became too frazzled to do anything other than a stop for coffee or lunch, and the women took an opportunity to make a cup of tea and take the weight off their feet on the four old bentwood chairs beside the small storeroom.

Pauline and Ursula smoked. Jacqueline and Mrs. Finch were far happier and more relaxed than they had been earlier, and after a chat and a glance at her slim watch, Pauline said it was time for her to head over to the Walton-on-Thames branch to see how they were getting on with everything. After a few words of advice about the new and old stock (Pauline thought one or two of the summer coats could be brought out and displayed since the weather was so unsettled) she put her own coat on and headed towards her car for the thirty-mile drive to Walton-on-Thames. She bought a cheese salad sandwich on the way and ate it at the wheel, checked her make-up again and carefully inched out into the steady stream of lunchtime traffic where one thing was more or less similar to another.

Bill said this. But then again, he would, wouldn't he? Still, she found that the sense of concentration, of rhythm she had achieved in the shop left her with enough power of self-extension to carry her easily as far as Staines. The familiar if tricky journey unfurled under her wheels through villages and intersections. It was nothing really, as, concentrating intently on the road, she let he mind replay some of the conversations she'd had in the shop that morning. Ursula worked well if she was watched, but that was true of all of them, wasn't it? Mrs. Finch and Jacqueline had resolved their conflict, for now. She felt as though she had bodily lifted them through the morning, and was tired by the effort of filling them with her light; however, she could push this feeling away by moving out into the passing scene, anticipating Walton until the voices of customers and the words she had spoken to them to clinch sales faded out in the wisps of trues and trees and landmark white houses strewn along her route, their roofs glittering with the new solar energy panels: the turnings she'd have liked to live in.

Pauline had been miles away. It wasn't until she was taking the third exit from the Staines roundabout on the A244 that she noticed that the car she drove was no longer an Opel Kadett, it was a navy-blue Volkswagen beetle. Suddenly it was lighter at the front, wider and longer than the Opel, the bonnet sloping downwards, engine droning away behind her, and yet she felt she'd been driving it all along. She had, hadn't she? She glanced in the rear-view mirror, reached, and felt behind her. The summer raincoats she had brought from Cobham that morning to take to Walton were still there in their polythene wrappers. The ashtray was pulled out from the dash and a half-smoked cigarette she remembered lighting was crammed in there, extinguished with her lipstick around the filter.

Somewhat reassured that nothing was amiss, that she was driving along in the perfectly familiar car she normally drove, she turned right. Bill had got rid of the Opel, she remembered, bought her this newer automatic, which she had become so used to that she thought for a moment it was the old green metallic Opel Kadett, a stylish little car she had been able to handle quite comfortably. There was a wide avenue of remembrance leading into the centre of Walton. She found herself on it, looking out for the second roundabout which would take her straight into the shopping centre – so modern and different from Marlow – where she would have to park in the multi-storey and walk down to the shop, which wasn't in the precinct itself but in a road facing it, alongside some other posher premises.

Pauline parked and walked down to the shop, with the coats over her arm. This year's summer stock had been particularly hard to come by, in a way, and the strange event of a couple of months ago had thrown her off balance, but it had also brought out a determination in her, in a way it had confirmed her new power. She had attended a fashion show of one of the big houses in Oxford Street. That day she had been done up to the nines so she could stand up to the other buyers, the women from the big London shops and chain stores. At first, she had thought she would be overwhelmed by it all, but she wasn't, and now she usually looked forward to her buying trips. And it was always very interesting for her to see what they bought, and of course, the reps from the fashion wholesalers were all over you to buy certain things. Pauline knew what she wanted; she just knew what would go with her customers: tasteful, with a bit of dash. She knew the type of colours they liked – russet, with a slash of brightness; and the patterns – bold but not too gaudy. She enjoyed talking to the other buyers, most of them middle-aged women like herself, and the catwalk show itself – well, it was fantastic! Pauline took note of things she liked, marked them in the catalogue, and later placed her orders with one of the assistants.

It had been afterwards on the escalators, down and then up, at Oxford Circus, that she had been in a world of her own, tired, quite hot and a bit stressed, just standing there. Her mind had been elsewhere as she was jostled, as usual, and people had pushed behind her, and looking back on it she felt a shadow, a man she supposed, moving behind her, flickering, the shadow of a man, and thought nothing more about it, this shadow, until she was coming up on another escalator at Waterloo station, and felt a soft breeze on her skin rushing up from the tunnels. She thought of the trains pushing hot air around and it was a pleasant feeling, but then she suddenly thought she shouldn't be feeling it through her clothes.

Emerging onto the busy concourse, she realized that her clothes, including her light summer coat and the dress beneath it, had been cut from behind with a sharp blade, and were loosely flapping apart and away from her body. Her underwear was showing right through. She was indecent. She stood there in the middle of the passing crowds, feeling naked, exposed, but nobody seemed to notice her. She turned right and descended into the Ladies' loos, where she turned her back to the mirror above the sinks and looked over her shoulder. At the back of her clothes was cut to ribbons, hanging off in layers, cut right through to the skin. The knife, or razor, or whatever it was had been pulled right down, so that her backside showed, even the back of her stockings and suspenders, obviously used with considerable force, although her skin itself had not been touched. Everything was completely ruined. She thought of the shadow she had felt moving behind her, that jostle on the Oxford Circus escalator. She had thought nothing at the time., Now she found she was shaking like a leaf, but it only lasted for a few moments. Until she managed to gain possession of herself.

One or two women coming in from upstairs or letting themselves out of the cubicles glanced in her direction, but none of them spoke to her, just passed by, and climbed up to catch their trains. Pauline locked herself in one of the cubicles and took the coat and dress off. She sorted through her handbag and found a few safety pins in the bottom, with which she pinned together the back of her dress and her coat as best she could. It still looked terrible, but there was nothing else for it but to get home somehow, catch her train and get out of this hell hole. On the way, she passed a pair of policemen but she didn't approach them – what could they have done? – and they didn't look at her either. Perhaps they could arrest her for indecency, she didn't know. She looked up at the clacking boards which showed the trains. Fortunately, hers was waiting for her. She got into a smoking carriage and sat in a corner, her bag on her knees, and lit a cigarette with her gold lighter, noticing that her hands were, in fact, still trembling. She managed to get it alight and inhaled deeply. Then she felt a little bit better. She didn't normally smoke on trains. It was unladylike, the sort of thing Joan would have done.

She found her car reassuringly where she had left it in the station carpark, the metallic green Opel Kadett, and drove home, feeling numb inside. Bill was sitting there in the living room with Mikey, waiting for her to get home and cook their dinner. Pauline had gone straight upstairs to change, and it was only when she'd failed to come down after fifteen minutes that Bill came up to see what was wrong. She showed him the clothes and explained what had happened. But Bill had become angry with her, as though it was her fault that she'd been attacked by this maniac, this shadow creature. He asked her to go through it again as if he didn't understand, which she did, and then she started shouting at him. She realized that he didn't believe her.

Pauline pushed in through the door of the Walton-on-Thames branch with the summer coats over her arm, into a situation that was even worse than that she had found in Marlow that morning. The women were just standing around, the place looked chaotic and they hadn't had a single customer. As if they didn't have problems enough, Paul had been in with Nicole and had started shouting at them. Taking her cue from her husband, Nicole, a petite, sharp-featured Frenchwoman, had been sneery and spiteful to Mrs Cassell, the branch manageress, telling her she was an idiot in an all-too-comprehensible accent, and commenting to one of the girls that she looked scruffy and should go home and change into something more appropriate. The girl, Roberta, had left immediately; and was unlikely to return, so said Mrs. Cassell.

In spite of being in an old building the shop was wider and shallower than the other branches, with more window frontage, which might have made for some attractive displays but now only revealed chaos within. Paul's business plan had been to take over existing dress shops that were struggling and turn them around. Walton was an exception to this – it used to be a record shop. Nicole was to have managed them but had little aptitude or patience for the job. She had no idea, really, what this type of English woman wanted to wear, so despite her own stylishness had turned out to be something of a liability. Pauline had been a Godsend to her boss. He asked her advice on everything, paid her well but expected a lot in return.

She was supposed to oversee the refit of the shop, but honestly, the task had been beyond her. Paul had drawn-up plans in the end, and the shopfitters had moved in and spruced up a quick job over one weekend, and the result was that nothing looked right, and the floor space always had a half-unpacked look. It was obvious now that Paul's design had split the shop in half with a till in the middle from which whoever was on it gazed vacantly out at the street beyond. Accessories and tops were on one side and skirts and dresses on the other, which made it awkward to move back and forth, to compare things. The changing rooms were poky and inadequate, storage space poor, and the full-length mirror wouldn't swivel properly and seemed to cut most people off at the neck. It was difficult for customers and staff alike not to feel like spare parts on view to all and sundry, a sideshow for scores of passers-by on a busy corner.

Nevertheless, she had to admire Paul. He was clever. He had good ideas. He did really well with them – he just seemed to know how things worked, more or less. And he did brilliantly, considering he had that Nicole hanging around his neck. She was never satisfied with anything. She made his life a misery. A few weeks ago he'd been considering suicide, walking over Marlow bridge and thinking of throwing himself in the Thames – Nicole had been tormenting him so much, how she was going to leave him and go back to France – but he knew he wouldn't drown and Pauline made him laugh about that on the phone when he called her to share his anguish, and it had been that laughter which had finally got him to hang up and go to bed. Pauline didn't see how long it could go on though, not very long she wouldn't have thought before everything fell apart. He relied on her too much – and didn't seem to understand she had her own life to live, her own problems and difficulties; although while she was talking to him they seemed distant and she would have been hard put to say what they were – if he'd ever shown the faintest interest.

Paul seemed to think she was marvellous: a woman of limitless resources and energy, and often spoke of how much he admired her resilience, thanking her, thanking her again for everything and for listening in detail and for so long to his stories of unhappiness and his difficult relationship with Nicole. Now he had left her to sort out his mess again – offering her only the advice that he had the greatest confidence in her and that she had carte blanche to do whatever she wished with the staff, the shops: everything was in her hands.

Everybody seemed to think a great deal of Pauline. This was something she always had in her favour. Her first action was to ask Mrs. Cassell for Roberta's phone number and to call her up in front of them. "This is Pauline speaking," she said. "You can come back now, she's gone."

And so, Roberta came back and Pauline worked with Mrs. Cassell and her and Florence for the rest of the afternoon. They tidied the shop up a bit, tried out some of the wheeled chrome racks in different positions and dressed a dummy in an outfit from the new stock, with one of the summer coats thrown over its shoulder, a loosely-tied scarf at the neck. All this activity resulted in nothing like the flood of customers in Marlow, but one or two women did come in and look through the racks, and although Pauline knew by instinct about how to leave well alone, when to offer help, this afternoon none of them bought anything. If this went on the shop would have to close and they would all lose their jobs. But why didn't it work in Walton? What was so different about Marlow and Cobham? Pauline didn't know, and she knew from experience that it wasn't going to be worth asking any of this particular bunch of women, who had applied, had been taken on by Paul and Nicole, and had seemed alright at the time. They had no idea at all about anything. Unless it was the shape of the shop itself, the awkward dog-leg of it right on the corner. They were useless really, far worse than the Marlow women, especially Mrs. Cassell and Florence. Pauline had got to know them; she didn't have the heart to tell Paul to get rid of any of them.

Just after four o'clock, a solitary woman of about forty-five came into the shop. She was quite short, a little plump. Something about her bearing, and especially her voice, revealed her as county, and, Pauline thought, a bit stupid. She was the customer from hell but nothing was going to deter her from making sure she bought a complete outfit. The funny thing was it came true again. Somehow – she didn't really know how she did it – she hefted the woman upwards, caught and held her in her eye-beams and by means of her curving mouth, her flaring aquiline nostrils (somebody had once noticed that they always looked as if they had blood in them) and the nuances of her clever, detached voice, soothing, stroking, made her customer laugh with her. She was going to her daughter's wedding or something. After forty minutes the woman left the shop with more bags than she could comfortably carry.

After that ordeal, Pauline needed a cup of tea and a cigarette. She drank it with the others, offering Roberta (the only other smoker) one hanging like a loose tooth from her packet to celebrate their unique sale of the day. It was nearly twenty past five when she left the shop. She was feeling exhausted, her calves ached from so much standing around and she had pain across her back from the anticipated stress of more driving. She would never enjoy it the way men did – for her, it was simply a necessity. On her way back to the multi-storey she popped into a supermarket and bought some things for tonight's dinner. A packet of chicken kievs, a bag of frozen chips, frozen peas (she couldn't remember whether there were enough left in the packet she had used yesterday), and as an afterthought a couple of jars of bloater paste for Bill's future sandwiches, a loaf of bread and a box of Mr Kipling apple pies.

She climbed up to the third floor of the multi-storey – she couldn't be bothered to wait for the stinking lift – and put her shopping in the passenger seat of her little red mini, the car that had served her so well on her many zig-zag journeys back and forth across Berkshire and Surrey, slid into her seat with relief, fastened her seat belt and turned the key. She handed her ticket in to the man at the barrier and the pole swung up and she rolled out into the rush hour traffic of Walton-on-Thames. Although only six miles from home she knew it was going to be a tortuous journey, just when everyone else had been struck by the same idea of getting home quickly. She was already feeling claustrophobic as she thought of edging slowly bumper to bumper back down the Avenue of Remembrance turned into reality. She was, to tell the truth, beginning to find the car cramped and wondered if Bill might be able to find her something a bit roomier. She didn't feel completely safe in the Mini. She never had done. She always felt she might be crushed by a lorry.

Brought to a halt, she reached forward and took the half-smoked cigarette from her ashtray and lit it with the slim Ronson in her hand. This last part of her journey home always wound her up tight. Bill said she should get away earlier, before the rush hour, but she never could.

She was always exhausted, her thoughts darting homeward with darker focus, closed down to that end, and all the things she might have said to the women or to Paul or anyone else were directed towards the men at the end of her journey. Sitting there. Waiting for her. These thoughts swarmed up like wasps in her brain, as if a great cloud of the things had got into the car, were attacking her, stinging her as she inched forward in the tiny sweatbox, filling up the space with their dark furry bodies and crawling all over her. It would have been so clever if somebody had known how to kill them all.

But she found her gap and broke right through it in a wave, moving along now in reasonable traffic past the densely-planted woods at the edge of St George's Hill, and felt every summit and plummet on the Seven Hills Road pushing her heart up high as the car hopped over the bumps, and by the time she'd pulled up in front of the house in Lockhart Road, picked up her shopping and walked in through the kitchen door, the wasps were feasting on her body, covering her like a black electrical shroud, so that she was pushing a charged cone of anger sharp end first into the room where they sat waiting for her, innocently watching a VHS cassette of motorcycle racing.

"Are you quite comfortable in there?" Pauline called in a harsh, metallic tone. "Are you feeling quite comfortable?" As she spoke the first of the wasp-squadrons lifted from her shoulders and swarmed in through the gap of the half-open door. The two men sat there murmuring patiently as they waited to be stung, untroubled to be the cause of her nightly blow-up, targets of her controlling rage.

After dinner Bill washed the plates up and made her another cup of tea. Pauline went upstairs to change out of her work clothes, but she found herself too tired to run a bath. Instead, she put her nightdress on and a dressing gown over it, and sat with Bill in front of the television, her feet in a bowl of hot water with a towel under it into which she had sprinkled some red Radox crystals. Mikey had gone upstairs to listen to some music. Only the table lamp beside her chair was on, and a standard lamp beside the big old broken-down radiogram, a Grundig that had once belonged to Bill's father. Finally, after all that, she subsided into a truce for the sake of what she really wanted: the peaceful rest of her own inward thoughts. Once this job came to an end, she knew she would never drive again. There was a film or a documentary or something on, but she couldn't concentrate on what it was about. Bill watched intently in the shadow-light as the world sped before his eyes.

Pauline lay back on her recliner with her cat. Mr. Jinx, a large, lazy tortoiseshell, was fast asleep on her lap. She was being soothed by the continuous circling vibrations of his flopped out body, heavy and inert, his weight on her abdomen holding her in place, firmly on the ground, her eyes hooded in semi-disgruntled torpor. And not long after he had decided to climb up to bed for the night, Bill hobbled out to the kitchen and pulled down the single grey blind. For a few moments he looked blankly out into the road, where at the kerb, beside the grass verge, stood the pale, gleaming vehicle. The gold-plated Opel. Metallic blue. Metallic light green, or whatever colour it had been originally.